Praise for Vicki Hinze:

"An edgy romantic thriller [by] a
very creative author. *Body Double*
becomes a book that must be read."
—The Romance Readers Connection

"Vicki Hinze has a brisk, engaging writing style,
and her heroine is a powerhouse."
—*Romantic Times*

* * *

*Adrift in the cave, Kate finished weighing
the challenges of rescuing the hostages
and then turned to making plans.*

Every way she looked at it, she was left with only
one viable solution: to return to the outpost and
enlist the aid of the missing soldiers' commander.

What was his name? Forester. Nathan Forester.

Conditions wouldn't improve substantially with his
tactical help, but Kate would have slightly better
odds of rescuing any hostages and surviving with—

Something slammed into her back, hammering her
into the cave wall.

Pulling on reserves, she harnessed her energy and
reacted on pure instinct. Choking the handle of her
knife, she turned and swiped.

The fight of her life had begun.

Dear Reader,

June marks the end of the first full year of Silhouette Bombshell, and we're proud to tell you our lineup is strong, suspenseful and hotter than ever! As the summer takes hold, grab your gear and some Bombshell books and head out for some R & R. Let us entertain you! ·

Meet Captain Katherine Kane. When she uncovers a weapons cache and a dangerous criminal thought to be behind bars, this intrepid heroine gets the help she needs from an unlikely source, in beloved military-thriller author Vicki Hinze's riveting new novel in the WAR GAMES miniseries, *Double Vision*.

Don't miss the incredible finale to our popular ATHENA FORCE continuity series. A legal attaché is trapped when insurgents take over a foreign capitol building—and she'll go head to head with the canny rebel leader to rescue hostages, stop the rebel troops and avert disaster, in *Checkmate* by Doranna Durgin.

Silhouette Intimate Moments author Maggie Price brings her exciting miniseries LINE OF DUTY to Bombshell with *Trigger Effect,* in which a forensic statement analyst brings criminals down by their words alone—much to the dismay of one know-it-all homicide detective.

And you'll love author Peggy Nicholson's feisty heroine, Raine Ashaway, in *An Angel in Stone*, the first in THE BONE HUNTERS miniseries. Raine's after a priceless opal dinosaur fossil—and to get it, she'll have to outwit and outrun not just her sexy competition but a cunning killer!

Enjoy all four fabulous reads and when you're done, please send your comments to my attention, c/o Silhouette Books, 233 Broadway, Ste. 1001, New York, NY 10279.

Best wishes

Natashya Wilson
Associate Senior Editor, Silhouette Bombshell

Please address questions and book requests to:
Silhouette Reader Service
U.S.: 3010 Walden Ave., P.O. Box 1325, Buffalo, NY 14269
Canadian: P.O. Box 609, Fort Erie, Ont. L2A 5X3

VICKI HINZE
DOUBLE VISION

Published by Silhouette Books
America's Publisher of Contemporary Romance

SILHOUETTE BOOKS

ISBN 0-373-51359-3

DOUBLE VISION

Copyright © 2005 by Vicki Hinze

Books by Vicki Hinze

Silhouette Bombshell

Body Double #12
Double Vision #45

Silhouette Books

Smokescreen
"Total Recall"

*War Games

VICKI HINZE

is the author of fourteen novels, one nonfiction book and hundreds of articles published in more than forty countries. Her books have received many prestigious awards and nominations, including her selection for *Who's Who in America* (as a writer and educator) and a multiple nominee for Career Achievement Awards from *Romantic Times* magazine. She's credited with having cocreated the first open-ended continuity series of single-title romance novels and with being among the first writers to create and establish subgenres in military women's fiction (suspense and intrigue) and military romantic-thriller novels.

To Kristen Leigh Hinze Early

You are a miracle, a precious gift mightily treasured.
I am so grateful for the privilege of being your mother.
Thank you, Krissie, for all you've taught me.
When I grow up, I want to be just like you.
Love,
Mom

Chapter 1

"Okay, Home Base." Staring through her diving mask, Captain Katherine Kane swam toward the rocks above the newly discovered underwater cave. Cold water swirled around her. "I'm almost there."

"Roger that, Bluefish." Considering the distance between Kate and Home Base, Captain Maggie Holt's voice sounded surprisingly clear through Kane's earpiece. "I don't like the idea of you diving alone. The boss would have a fit."

The boss, Colonel Sally Drake, would understand completely. "Sorry, no choice." Captain Douglas and his tactical team had been diverted. "If we want to find GRID's weapons cache, then I've got to do this now—before they have time to move it."

Douglas and his men had assisted Kate on a former mission, intercepting GRID—Group Resources for Individual Development—assets, and when he'd summoned Kate to the Persian Gulf, she'd known he suspected a GRID presence and needed help. All the key players in the Black World community knew that pursuing GRID, the largest black-market sellers of U.S. intelligence and weapons in the world, was Kate's organization's top priority. And it had been designated such by presidential order.

"I still think we should follow the usual chain of command," Maggie said. "If the boss were here, you know she would agree with me."

If Colonel Drake was there and not at the intelligence community summit meeting coordinating on the war on terror, Kate and Maggie wouldn't be having this conversation and there would be no debate. Kate resisted a sigh.

Maggie was new to this level of covert operations and still adjusting to tossing out standard operating procedure and assuming command in critical circumstances. But she had all the right stuff; she'd grow into the job eventually. Nothing taught operatives better than experience, and she'd get plenty in their unit. Still, for everyone's sake, including her own, Kate hoped Maggie adjusted and grew into it soon.

"Look," Kate said, speeding the process along. "Ordinarily, Douglas would have worked up the chain. This time, he came straight to us." Secret Assignment Security Specialists—S.A.S.S.—were the last resort, and Douglas respected that. "I know this man and he knows us. He's got a fix on GRID." Kate couldn't resist an impatient huff. "No offense intended, Home Base, but you've got to learn to trust your allies." That included Douglas, his team and Kate.

"Yeah, well. I'm gun-shy. You have to prove you deserve it."

That response surprised Kate. "How?"

"Don't get yourself killed today. Do you realize how much paperwork I'd have to do?"

Kate smiled. Okay, she'd cut Maggie a little slack. The woman was trying. "Waking up dead isn't my idea of a fun way to start the day, either, Base." She reached the finger of rocky land jutting out into the gulf and, treading water, removed the black box from her tool bag.

Stiff-fingered from the cold chill, she flipped the switch to activate the C-273 communications device and affixed it to the rock just below the waterline. If this leading-edge technology worked as promised, she would still be able to communicate with Maggie at Home Base via satellite. Supposedly, the water would conduct Kate's signal from inside the cave to this box and then transmit via satellite to Home Base, completing the link to Maggie. Kate hoped to spit it worked. "Okay, C-273 is seated. We're good to go."

Looking up, she again checked the face of the rock above the waterline. Worn smooth *and* scarred by deep gouges. *Definite signs of traffic.*

That oddity had caught her eye initially and led her to dive here for a closer look. Otherwise even with Douglas's coordinates, she never would have found this particular cave—and she seriously doubted anyone short of an oceanographer charting the gulf floor would have, either.

"Bluefish?" Worry filled Maggie's voice. "The guys at the lab swear this device will work, but if it doesn't and we lose contact, I want you out of there pronto. I mean it."

"Here we go again. Trust a little. Remember, no guts, no glory." Kate adjusted her diving headgear, checked to make sure her knife was secure in the sheath strapped to her thigh, pulled her flashlight from her tool belt, turned it on, then dove.

"Glory?" Maggie's sigh crackled static through Kate's earpiece. "What glory? You're a phantom. Less than three hundred people know you exist."

S.A.S.S. were a highly skilled, special-detail unit of covert operatives assigned to the Office of Special Investigations and buried in the Office of Personnel Management for the United States Air Force. The unit didn't exist on paper, its missions didn't exist on paper—the unit's name even changed every six months for security purposes, which is why those who knew of S.A.S.S. operatives referred to them by what they did and not by their official organizational name.

"Personal power, Home Base." Kate had learned from the cradle to expect no other kind. "Doesn't matter a damn who else knows it as long as I do."

At the mouth of the cave, she paused to scan the rock. More of the same worn smoothness and deep gouges. Even considering tidal fluxes, too many deep gouges rimmed the actual opening. Water action alone couldn't explain it. She swam forward, entering the cave.

"Are you inside?"

"Yes," Kate whispered, keeping her voice as quiet as possible. Snake-curved, the inner cave was about three feet wide. She swam close to the ceiling. Suddenly the width expanded to nearly ten feet. "The cave's opened up." She lifted her head above water, cranked her neck back and shone the light above her. "This is bizarre."

"What?"

"I dove a solid twenty feet to get to the mouth, then swam a couple football fields to get to this point. The water rode the cave ceiling the whole way. Now I'm seeing a stretch of wall that's exposed a good nine feet above the waterline." She stopped treading water and tested for bottom. Her fin swiped the sand and she stood. "Water level's dropped. It's chest deep."

"I'm plotting your GPS," Maggie said.

"Good, because even considering an umbrella effect, this shouldn't be possible." Kate kept her diving mask on in case she was standing on a shelf or sand bar. False bottoms had proven common in her explorations. She then looked down the throat of the cave. Diffused light emanated from somewhere far ahead, creating a haze. The rocks jutting out from the cave walls cast deep shadows. Reflections shining through the water or cracks in the rock? Neither seemed possible, but the alternative... "Oh, man."

"What is it?" Anxiety etched Maggie's voice.

"This is more than we bargained for." Kate's heart beat hard and fast. "A whole lot more."

Rushing water poured in with the tide, nearly knocking her off her feet. Kate braced against it, hunkering down until the water swirled around her chin, her wet suit and oxygen tank. Once it was calm, she removed her mask. "The salt in here smells strong—too strong. Saline content has to be off the charts."

"If so, it should be strong enough to burn your nose," Maggie responded.

"It does." Kate's nostrils stung like fire. "But it's still *too* strong. Note that and my position on the plotter." After putting her mask back on to block the smell, Kate depressed a sensor embedded under the skin at the base of her neck to pulse a signal the operatives had dubbed "Big Brother." Only Home Base could activate it, but Kate could transmit her location at a given time with a pulse signal.

"Roger. Home Base is now plotting." A pause, then, "Do you see any reason for the olfactory oddity?"

Looking through the water droplets spotting her wide-angle vision screen, Kate scanned the cave but saw nothing to account for the intense smell. One hundred percent saline content couldn't take it to this level, and there was no way the cave water could be a hundred percent. It would show in the rocks.

"No, not a thing," Kate admitted, expelling an impatient breath through pursed lips. "Maybe it's just me." Diving alone wasn't unusual for S.A.S.S. operatives, but the increased risks and dangers definitely heightened awareness. Maybe she was hyperalert *and* extra-hypersensitive.

She rounded a bend. The dim haze shone brighter. A chill crept up Kate's back and tingled the roof of her mouth. "There's light in here, Base. I'd hoped it was a crack in the rock or some weird reflection caused by my flashlight, but it's not."

"You're under water. It should be dark—all the other caves were dark. Briefing reports have been consistent on that."

"Yeah, well, this cave didn't read them. There's always that ten percent that doesn't get the word, you know?"

"But why would this one be different?"

"Don't know. Do know it's not dark." Kate moved slowly down the tunnel, hugging the rough cave wall, the swift water pushing her along faster than she wanted to go. She turned off her flashlight. Double-checked. "Definitely not a reflection. It's light, Base."

"Wait," Maggie said. "I'm running the topography on your coordinates." A few moments later she added, "Your cave is located under a finger of land that juts out into the gulf. It's hilly in your immediate area, and the hills are full of man-made caves. Maybe one of them leads to your location and the light is filtering through from above ground."

"Maybe." The eerie light was actually a series of dim rays; glowing beams that hindered her sight despite her gear being night-vision equipped. Kate's mouth went desert-dry. "On second thought, that's unlikely." To be certain, Kate lifted off her headgear and checked again.

She could see no better. That was the worst news yet. Rattled, her nerves tingled, prickling her skin, and her voice shook. "Visual observation is distorted with the night-vision goggles *and* the naked eye."

"What are you telling me?" Maggie asked.

"Getting this perfect balance to blind you with both the naked eye and your NVG isn't a natural occurrence. I'm telling you that the spectrum's too narrow for this light to be natural. It's not achieved by accident, Base." U.S. scientists had spent years and millions of dollars identifying the perimeters of that spectrum.

"So your determination is that it's man-made and deliberate, correct?"

"Affirmative. At this point, that's my take on it." Only a few groups outside the U.S. government had access to spectrum technology—but only one had a reason to corrupt it. S.A.S.S.'s nemesis. GRID.

So far, Kate had been involved in taking down three GRID compounds. But with Thomas Kunz, the sadistic German and anti-American at GRID's helm, there would always be another compound.

Kunz blamed America for Germany's troubled economy and, in a twisted quest for revenge, acquired members for GRID from all nationalities and devoted himself and his massive resources to using the organization to drag down America's economy by selling classified intelligence on U.S. assets, technology and personnel. Unfortunately, Kunz had proved to be expert, cunning and creative. He was more devious and deadly than anyone Kate had ever known. There was nothing he wouldn't do to achieve his goals.

Edgy, she tensed and immediately rolled her shoulders to release it. "You'd better notify the program honchos that they've got a security breach," she told Maggie. The light-spectrum technology had been developed under a top-secret classification. That the security had been violated meant bad news for the program.

"Um, just a second." Maggie hesitated and, when she returned, her voice sounded like tin. She was obviously very uneasy. "You do know where you are, right?"

"On the border between Iraq and Iran?" Purely speculation. But wasn't she? "You're looking at the GPS coordinates, you tell me."

"You don't want to know," Maggie assured her. "I'm calling the boss."

Damn it. Kate had crossed a freaking national boundary line. She should tell Maggie not to bother Colonel Drake; she knew the drill. *Get in and out. Avoid detection by any means necessary.* But she was just edgy enough and eager enough to stay quiet. She hadn't seen any evidence of detection and the idea of maybe exposing another Kunz operative carried many positives in her book, and no negatives. Obviously the operative, who had infiltrated a top-secret program and successfully occupied a classified position by impersonating a legitimate U.S. government employee, would be the nature of a security breach required to get such technology out of the lab and into GRID's greedy, grimy hands.

Three minutes passed, then Maggie returned. "The boss feels breaching security, stealing and using this light-spectrum technology in this manner is right up Big Fish's alley.

Intel says he's the only current prospect capable of that deep a penetration into our programs."

Kate agreed with Intel, aka Captain Darcy Clark. Darcy had total recall, thanks to a head injury that had taken her out of the field as an active operative. She now worked solely on intelligence assimilation for the S.A.S.S. unit. The recall challenge that kept her isolated to avoid sensory overload had repeatedly proved to be a lifesaver for the other S.A.S.S. operatives still in the field.

"The boss is notifying the honchos in the need-to-know loop," Maggie said. "She wants you to pull out, return to the outpost and wait for backup to go in with you."

Before Kate could think of a way to sidestep the order, something alerted her honed instincts. Some sound or sense of movement. Some…something. Whatever it was had her attention. The hair on her neck prickled. "Stand by, Base."

An internal alarm flashed *Danger!* Kate's heart kicked into overdrive, thumping hard against her ribs. With her thumb, she unsnapped the loop on her knife's sheath and slowly scanned the rock walls, then the water's shimmering surface. Shadows. Dull beams. No odd ripples or breaks in the water. "Okay," she said, calming. "Okay, we're fine."

Kate sucked in a steadying breath. Strange for her instincts to be wrong; they rarely veered off target. Yet logic insisted that the odds of anyone else finding this uncharted cave were slim to none. The water blasting the rocks could have sanded them smooth, but it hadn't caused the gouges. Those could only have come from fast-moving water sending something heavy crashing against the rocks.

That anomaly warranted investigation. But this perfect spectrum of light added another complex layer to the reasons she must keep investigating.

"Bluefish?" Maggie asked. "Did you hear what I said?"

Great. A classic catch-22. If she acknowledged, she'd have to disobey a direct order. If she didn't acknowledge, the lab would be informed that its new C-273 communications device had failed its field test. Kate decided to ignore the question and the order, and turned the topic. "This perfect illumination proves Captain Douglas was on the money."

"Oh, no. You're not pulling this on me. Acknowledge the order, Bluefish," Maggie insisted, her tone short and sharp. "Get out of there, go the outpost and wait for Douglas and Tactical. Then return with them and investigate."

Kate frowned. Damn it. Any other S.A.S.S. operative—Amanda, Darcy, Julia—*any* of them would have let that slide.

But then, they all had more experience than Maggie. Just Kate's dumb luck that Amanda was out on a mission for the next few days and Maggie was manning the watch. "I won't say I can't hear you. The C-273 device is working great and I don't want it reported that it's not. But I can't acknowledge that order."

"Damn it, Kate."

Now Maggie was transmitting her name! "Hey, don't let your temper put a target on my back. Just calm down, okay?"

"Sorry."

Jeez! Kate licked at her lips. *Make her think. Make her think.* "Listen, you know the enemy," she reminded Maggie, who had read the dossiers on Thomas Kunz and GRID. "He could shut down this operation in a matter of minutes—he's done it before with others. If we wait, and that happens, then all we'll find down here is an empty hole."

"But we've got—"

She might be hearing, but she damn well wasn't listening. "What *we've* got doesn't matter. It's what *he's* got that counts." Kate swallowed a lump in her throat. "He's holding at least thirty Americans permanent hostage. They're stashed for life in one of his hellholes unless we get them out. What if they're stashed here?"

S.A.S.S. knew for fact he had at least that many American government employees under wraps at his various compounds.

They also knew those employees' GRID operative counterparts remained inserted and undetected in classified positions within the CIA, FBI, NAS, INS and U.S. military. Those agencies had been identified and were being watched. Yet there were other GRID operatives who remained unknown, and had not yet been identified by S.A.S.S.

Exactly how many? Only God and Thomas Kunz knew for sure. But they were active inside the U.S. government in classified positions, which is why the president had designated GRID as S.A.S.S.'s top priority.

The hostages had to be rescued to determine their doubles' identities, their specific program affiliations and to determine their access level to classified information. And hopefully this would be accomplished before those GRID operative counterparts managed to do irreparable harm to the U.S.

"What if the hostages aren't there and you're walking into a trap?"

"Highly unlikely, Base. The coordinates weren't fixed and there weren't any guideposts, leading me here. No one meant for me to find this particular cave. I literally stumbled into it." True, thanks to high tide, swift water currents and a curiosity about defaced rocks.

It seemed vulgar in a way, to have so much technology and sophisticated detection systems available, yet if the hostages were here and rescued, or if the GRID weapons cache were found, it would be as a direct result of simple unsophisticated things and blind luck.

"Which is exactly why you need to wait for Tactical. You could be walking into anything."

It was walking into the unknown that troubled Maggie. Kate rolled her gaze ceilingward, edgy and annoyed now. Maggie's lack of experience was weighing Kate down. The woman really shouldn't be cutting her teeth on this mission.

But she had to cut them somewhere, and since the president had changed the unit's priorities, there'd been no latitude or choice in the matter. Hell, Maggie probably wasn't crazy about the situation, either.

Realizing the truth in that, Kate calmed down and dredged the depths of her soul for another helping of patience. In short supply, she grabbed the meager bits she could pull together and then explained. "No, Base. That's exactly why I can't wait. I've got to check this out now—before the enemy discovers I'm here."

"He could already know it," Maggie said. "The whole damn cave could be wired with surveillance equipment. He could be intercepting our communications. I know the lab says we're secure, but this is the C-273's maiden voyage. They can't know it for fact. Any communications device can be intercepted—you don't need Intel to verify that. All the experts agree. What if the guys at the lab are wrong, Bluefish? What if he's waiting for you?"

The idea chilled Kate's blood. Kunz looked like a sunny kind of guy. Forty, blond and blue-eyed, casual and elegant, he appeared to be totally benevolent and good-natured. But he wasn't. He was a sick, sadistic bastard who got off on torture and stealing other people's lives. Amanda's confrontation with him on a previous mission had made all of that clear, and Kate definitely would prefer to avoid him on this mission—if given a choice.

"Listen," she told Maggie. "Some risks you've got to take. If any of the hostages are here, I have to take the shot at getting them out."

"And if they're not?"

"Then we've still got the weapons cache to worry about. There's been a lot of chatter lately about the enemy trying to move bio weapons systems. You've heard the reports. Douglas suspects they're hidden somewhere in the area." Darcy did, too, and Kate had a healthy respect for her deductions. She was an ace at them. "We can't risk bio weapons getting loose on the black market. Odds are they'll be used against us, Base. I'm not willing to risk that." She sure as hell didn't need to add responsibility for that to her personal, emotional baggage.

"Okay, okay. But just do reconnaissance. Don't approach, and don't reveal yourself. I understand your motives, Bluefish, but you can't prevent any crisis if you're dead. If you find anything, get Douglas and Tactical to go in with you. I'll put his commander on alert."

"Who is his CO?"

Maggie answered in code.

Kate translated. Major Nathan Forester. She let his name meander through her mind. They'd never met, but his name seemed familiar to Kate. She couldn't recall why. "Ask Intel to get me a dossier on him."

"Stand by." A lengthy few minutes later Maggie returned and relayed the encrypted information.

Kate automatically decoded it in her head.

Nathan G. Forester. Thirty-one, black hair, blue eyes, solid build. No remarkable scars or identifying marks. Graduated from the Academy top of his class. Awarded a Purple Heart in Afghanistan, another in Iraq. Bio field-specialist. Expert marksman. Worked under Secretary Reynolds at the Pentagon on analysis of bio intelligence. Currently commanding the 123rd Tactical Force.

Intriguing. "Put him on notice," Kate said. Her heart hammering, she looked down the cave. Pale light glinted on the water's surface as far as she could see. This compound— every instinct in her body screamed this cave was a GRID compound—appeared to be as unique as the others discovered by the S.A.S.S. units—and as problematic to breach. Underwater entrance: one means of ingress and egress. If Kate ran into trouble, escaping would be significantly challenging, which was probably why Kunz had chosen this one.

"Okay, the commander has been notified," Maggie said. Then her tone dropped a notch. "He also delivered some bad news, Bluefish."

"What now?" Kate snapped, unable to keep her irritation out of her voice.

"Douglas and his team are unavailable. The commander is trying to make contact but the team's been locked down and radio silent for almost twenty-four hours."

"Do they need backup?"

"No. They're functional, just out of pocket."

Not pinned down by someone else, just locked down observing someone else, Kate supposed.

"There's more." Even the terminally cheerful Maggie sighed. "The commander informed me that the CIA and Special Forces have scoured the hills above you from land. Apparently there's a maze of caves. But an intense exploration netted only dead ends."

Kate chewed at her inner lip, fully understanding why the compound had been nearly impossible to locate. Her mind raced ahead as she crept through the bowels of the cave, her left shoulder scraping against the jagged rock wall, her fins scouring the sandy bottom. Launching a successful attack on this place wouldn't be a picnic. Actually, it'd be damn near impossible. Alone, her odds of success were astronomically small. And that, too, no doubt had been Kunz's intention.

"I updated the boss," Maggie said. "She's ordered me to remind you that you're under direct order to pull out now and to wait for tactical assistance before reentering."

Kate considered it. The odds for her survival, and for the survival of the American detainees Kunz was holding hostage—if in fact any of them were here—ranked a one on the colonel's infamous one-to-ten scale: zero probability of success. The mission difficulty ranked ten. Translated and simply put, succeeding required a miracle.

And who dies if you fail, Kate?

The fears and old feelings of not being good enough to do what needed doing shot up out of a dark, secret niche inside her. She'd buried all that unworthiness baggage years ago, but the memory of it persisted, as ingrained things do, and on occasion it surfaced. Naturally, because the timing couldn't be worse, it had chosen to surface now.

Resentment slid through her and, steeped in it, she stiffened, clenched her jaw and strengthened her resolve. *Knock it off. Now, Kate. You can't afford any doubts. Bio weapons, classified information on only God knows what programs… Millions of potential victims are depending on you, and they definitely can't afford any doubts.*

Summoning her will, which had always proven stronger than her fears, she shoved her doubts back down, burying the emotional baggage that just wouldn't die, then turned her thoughts back to the challenge at hand.

As well as that one means of ingress and egress through an underwater cave, and the compound being inside a hill of rock, other challenges lay ahead.

Significant challenges.

Aided by former Soviet plastic surgeons and psychiatrists with expertise in psychological warfare and mind manipulation, Kunz had created doubles. Very well-trained, well-motivated clones. She would have to determine which people were GRID operative clones and which were true U.S. government employees.

As if that wasn't enough of a challenge to make sane woman nuts, Kunz would more than likely spice up things to amuse himself by adding his own cloned surrogate into the mix. It would be just like him to mimic Saddam Hussein, pose his double to GRID members and have him run operations in the compound while Kunz remained removed from the fray.

This man-made clone, without a doubt, would be surrounded by seasoned GRID operatives who existed for the sole purpose of protecting him from any enemy, including Kate.

The real Thomas Kunz—thank heaven and Amanda and Kate—had had been arrested during the last GRID compound raid. He currently sat stashed behind bars in Leavenworth. Whether he remained in command of GRID, running operations from his prison cell or had handed over power to some subordinate GRID member remained undetermined.

If betting, Kate would put her money on his empowering a double. It'd be more effective—especially if the GRID members didn't know he was a double.

That was possible. S.A.S.S. had encountered one Kunz double already and unfortunately had no idea how many others existed. Hopefully he hadn't copied Saddam Hussein, in that, too. He had at least eight known doubles. Yet with Thomas Kunz, experience proved it wise to pray for the best but to expect the worst.

The sorry bastard probably had a dozen.

Under these circumstances, would even a single miracle do the job?

Unsure, Kate tightened her grip on her knife, dragged in a steadying breath and admitted the truth. Her odds sucked. She'd need at least a fistful of miracles to pull this off.

The back of her neck prickled. She removed her mask and opened her senses, then slowly turned in a circle and studied everything in sight. Nothing seemed out of the ordinary. Calm. Silent. Just her and the moving water and eerie light. *Definitely hyperalert.*

Giving herself a mental shake, she finished weighing her challenges and then turned to plans. How should she proceed? What moves gave her the highest probability of success?

Water splashed and hit her full in the face. The strong salt stank and had her eyes tearing. She wiped at them with her free hand and mentally worked through potential plans of action. She couldn't just blow the compound to hell and back as she had the first one she'd found in the Middle East. Thomas Kunz's surrogate and the GRID operatives would die, but so would the hostages—if any of them were here—and detonating biological-laced weaponry wasn't something she would willingly do. Not in this lifetime.

She thought on it some more, certain she could find something to better her odds... Even if the explosives were strategically positioned and fitted out with remote detonators, they could cause a collapse in the cave. Percussion alone could kill anyone inside. Water was a hell of a conductor, it would amplify the effects.

Every way she looked at it, a person attempting to escape would face insurmountable odds, including her. And she'd have to be in the cave to relay the remote or the signal wouldn't penetrate. There were alternative devices that could be used, but she couldn't get them down here to use them. Not without help.

She played with a few more possibilities, but none were feasible much less wise, which left her with only one viable solution: to return to the outpost and draft a plan enlisting the aid of Douglas's commander.

What was his name? Forest? Framer?

Forester. That was it. Forester. Nathan Forester.

Conditions wouldn't improve substantially with his tactical help, but Kate would have slightly better odds of rescuing any hostages and surviving with—

Something slammed into her back.

Hard and huge, it knocked her off her feet, hammering her into the cave wall.

Her head collided with the saw-toothed surface. Her breath gushed out. The jagged rocks dug into her face and shoulder, slicing through her wet suit and skin, tearing her flesh. Salt water invaded the wounds, burning like fire. Seeing spots, her head swimming, she gasped for air. *Focus or die, Kate. Focus or die!*

Warm blood washed down her face and arm, and she forced herself to stay conscious.

Focus or die!

Pulling on reserves, she harnessed her energy and fought until the spots started to subside and the truth dawned.

The wise move was no longer an option.

Blocking out the pain searing her face, arm, chest and thigh, she regained her footing and reacted on pure instinct. Choking the handle of her knife, she turned and swiped the air.

The fight had begun.

Chapter 2

The knife slit a man's neck, laying it wide open.

His thin lips pulled back in raw pain, revealing an extreme overbite. Definitely GRID. When held captive, Amanda had tangled with him. Though she'd had no name to attach to the man with the overbite—GRID had been very circumspect about identities—her description fit him perfectly.

A gurgle started in his throat. He palmed the wound as if pressure would help.

It wouldn't; his jugular had been severed.

Pulsing blood spurted through his fingers to stream over the sleeve of his yellow wet suit and splash into the water.

His eyes widened in surprise. He reached for her and his knees collapsed. Bleeding out, he sank into the water and submerged.

"Hold it." Another man shouted, more distant, from behind her. He leveled a .45-caliber pistol on Kate.

Seeing him in her peripheral vision, she stopped dead in her tracks, tucked the knife into its sheath below the waterline, then raised her hands just above her waist. This man, too, had been previously identified as a GRID operative, right down to his crew cut, thick neck and large ears.

Looking satisfied, the man Amanda had dubbed "Beefy" adjusted a mike and spoke into it. "Intruder at the gate. Repeat, intruder at the gate. Female." He spotted her gear bag. "She looks American."

Kate rolled her eyes, making sure he saw it. With luck, she'd instill a little doubt about that.

"Professional or recreational?" A man's disembodied voice rippled through the cave, proving Maggie had been right. The damn thing was wired with surveillance gear. But apparently GRID only had audio capability. Otherwise the man wouldn't have had to ask about her.

"I'd say professional, sir. She moves like she's military." Beefy nicked his lip with his teeth. "That's an unverified assumption. No specific branch is evident or identified."

The disembodied voice sounded again, its echo vibrating in her bones. "Is it Amanda West, Moss?"

Moss. Kate rocked against the tug of the water. So Beefy's real name was Moss. And that he'd revealed it signaled, in his mind, Kate wouldn't be leaving alive and able to repeat it.

"No, sir, she's not. This one is a blonde. Tall and skinny." Moss raised the nose of the .45 and pointed it at Kate's face. "She killed Parton, sir."

Amanda had been the primary operative on the original mission, investigating GRID. She'd been inserted undercover and had exposed GRID's black market weapon sales and Kunz's doubles. And she'd broken Moss's nose. He wouldn't likely ever forget her.

"How?"

"With a knife, sir," Moss said. "She cut his throat."

So he knew she had a knife. Why hadn't he taken her weapons? Moss, Kunz, or any of his doubles, would love to kill any S.A.S.S. operative, especially Amanda—and Kunz damn near had. But she had narrowly escaped death and had won that battle, and Kunz had landed in prison for life. So this disembodied voice conversing with Moss couldn't belong to Thomas Kunz. Yet it certainly sounded like him and, knowing his penchant for torture, that sent chills racing up and down Kate's back. Soon she'd be added to his "kill on sight" list.

"Who is she?"

Moss glared at her, stepped closer. "Who are you?"

She dragged her lips back from her teeth, praying Maggie was picking up this conversation and had summoned backup from the outpost. But if Tactical was locked down and she'd crossed a national boundary line, odds for help were slim. She almost certainly would be stuck on her own.

"I asked you a question," Moss shouted, and backhanded her across the face. "Who are you?"

Kate reeled on her feet. Her lip split and the entire side of her face stung. Tasting her own blood, she got her balance and glared at Moss. "Your worst nightmare."

Moss involuntarily pulled back his hand to hit her again.

"Do it and you'll die."

He started, caught himself and stilled his arm midair. The gun wobbled, but he didn't seem to notice; he kept staring into her eyes. Whatever he saw there convinced him. He lowered his hand and reclaimed his lost ground with a grunt. "She's a little smart-ass, sir. Definitely a professional, judging by her mouth and her gear."

"Well, bring the professional little smart-ass in," the Kunz sound-alike said, clearly impatient. "Try not to kill her, unless of course she gives you no choice."

"Yes, sir." Moss shoved the throat mike out of his way and then nodded at Kate. "You heard the man. You've got two choices. I don't care which you pick. You can head down the cave and live, or refuse. If you refuse, I'll shoot you now and spare myself some aggravation."

If she went deeper into the cave, she'd never come out alive, and only an idiot wouldn't know it. If she didn't go, he'd shoot her here. Buying time, she agreed. "I'll go, Moss."

"Good." He straightened and rolled his shoulder. "Move."

Kate turned and began walking through the water, taking small steps. She needed time to think—and an opening when he was vulnerable to overtake him. But, hanging back, he wasn't making it easy. She shortened her stride even more, convinced the moving water would conceal her tiny steps. Fortunately the current was swift. That should help give her cover.

Finally he came alongside her, his gun still raised and aimed at her chest. She inched her fingers down her body and curled them tightly around the handle of her knife. Firming her grip, she eased the blade up and out of its sheath.

Moss caught a hint of motion from the arrhythmic ripple in the water. Snarling, he snagged the rubber-tube casing looped around her neck and jerked it tight. Her dog tags jangled. "Don't even think about it."

Was this the opening she'd awaited? So close she could

smell the sweat on his skin, Kate looked him right in the eye and nodded.

He relaxed and loosened his hold.

In a flash, she laid out a flurry of moves: knocked his hand with the gun, delivered a debilitating blow to his neck, slashed through his mike, severing his communications with the Kunz sound-alike, and then drove the knife into his stomach up to its hilt.

A direct hit.

Moss howled, deep and loud. The sound reverberated, echoing through the cave in waves. Kate spun out of his grip, turned and fled.

"Home Base? Home Base, do you copy?" Tugging on her headgear, Kate dove and swam hard and fast. "Home Base?"

No response from Maggie.

Terrific. Finally, Kate reached the mouth of the cave. She followed the markings she'd put down on entering, swam until she'd cleared the rocky protrusions, then surfaced.

Water streamed down her face. "Home Base?" She tried again, scanned the rocks for the C-273 black box.

It was gone.

Damn it. Moss? Another GRID member? The water action? It was high tide, totally possible. Pulling a fast visual, she saw no one. "Base?" Kate tried Maggie again.

Still no answer.

The last thing they needed was the C-273 communications device in GRID hands. Kunz would sell it to every hostile on the planet.

Her boat rocked on gentle waves about twenty yards to her left. Safer under water, she dove and swam toward it; the salt water burning her scrapes and cuts. Seeing the bottom of the hull above her, she stroked to the boat's far side, again surfaced, then climbed aboard.

An engine's roar split the silence. She darted her gaze toward the sound as she started her own engine. A boat rounded the tip of the finger of land and headed in her direction. She slapped the throttle in gear and hauled out.

Kate glanced back to see the other boat cutting across the whitecaps, spraying a wide arc and leaving a huge wake. Its sudden appearance hadn't been a coincidence; it was clearly following her. From the size of its wake, that boat was a hell of a lot faster than hers. But who manned it? Iranian authorities or GRID?

She couldn't tell, but either was equally bad. Her orders were to remain undetected, and she'd failed to do so. She sped up, opening the throttle until the engines screamed, and targeted the shore, determined not to end up captured and held prisoner. If the authorities took her into custody, it would create an international incident, she'd be tried for treason against Iran, and executed. If GRID caught her, she'd be tortured and killed or just killed. Either way, she'd end up dead.

The little boat shuddered with effort, but it was just too small. There was no way she could outrun the larger boat all the way to port. She'd have to create a diversion and hope like hell they fell for it.

Kate darted a quick look behind her. The boat was gaining. Two men—no, three—rode in it. They were wearing black wet suits, not uniforms. Did that mean anything?

Wishing she knew, she scanned the shoreline for a safe place and spotted a clump of trees and sandy beach. A couple of large rocks littered the water. It wasn't a great place to hide out, but it was her best shot.

Cutting off her dog tags, she looped half the tubing between the throttle and a hitch on the dash to keep the engine running wide-open. Stuffing the other half of the tubing and her dog tags into her pocket, she twisted the steering wheel to take a swing behind the rocks. GRID would think she'd hidden near them. For that reason, she would not.

Behind the cover of the rocks, her boat's bow hit an angle that would track to the open gulf. She jammed the steering wheel with the emergency paddle, then dove off and swam under water toward the shore, praying the men chasing her would continue to follow the boat until she'd had time to disappear.

The water shallowed to waist-deep. She risked surfacing and spotted the boats. GRID had taken the bait and continued the chase.

Grateful for even a spare respite, she seized it. They wouldn't be fooled long, but with luck, long enough for her to evade them.

Kate ditched her fins and tank in the water and hurried ashore, scanning the terrain for somewhere to hide. She'd love to just run for the caves—openings dotted the hills—but experience warned her she was too short of time to make it and the consequences of not making it carried costs too high to pay.

At the water's edge, she snaked low to the ground, took cover in the clump of trees and then sank deeper into the brush. Still searching, she forced herself to pause and think. These trees were the logical dry-ground hiding place; they'd find her here. She had to find an *illogical* place to hide.

She ran on and reached an oblong clearing about three hundred yards across. A single large boulder sat on the far edge of it. It had to be at least eight feet wide. On three sides of it, a person could see forever. And that's where she'd hide—in plain sight.

Well, almost.

Near the base of the boulder, under a natural ledge, she dropped to her knees and scooped out a shallow grave, dumped in her diving mask and then crawled inside. She smoothed the sand over her lower body. It would be hotter than hell itself in the wet suit, but she didn't dare risk removing it. She needed the added protection against scorpions and snakes, which happened to love the crevices of the rocks. Cool places to wait out the hot sun.

Buried to her chest, she pulled the remaining half of the tubing from her pocket. Putting one end in her mouth, she clamped down with her teeth and put the other end into an open notch under the edge of the boulder. She could take air in, but the tube wouldn't be easily spotted. Then she finished burying herself, punching outward from the inside, forcing the sand under the ledge to collapse over her hand.

The sand wasn't uncomfortably hot, but if she'd been dry, she'd already be sweating. She just wasn't deep enough to get to a stable, lower temperature. The grit against her eyes and nose irritated her, urged her to scratch, but she stayed put, didn't move, and willed herself to relax and breathe.

A good forty-five minutes later, the sand around her vibrated.

Footsteps.

Her heart rate jackhammered into high gear, her nerves stood on end, hyperalert. She'd had to stay shallow to keep the weight of the sand light enough to allow her rib cage to expand, to drag breath. If the bastards had a handheld thermal detector, she was dead. The sand covering her wasn't deep enough to block the signal.

The vibrations grew stronger and muffled voices joined them. "No tracks through here, Mr. Kunz."

"She didn't just disappear into thin air." Kunz sounded more than a little annoyed.

Shock ripped over Kate. She knew that voice too well to be fooled. She'd done an audio study from a S.A.S.S. intercept the CIA had verified to be Kunz. This man was not a Kunz double.

He *was* Kunz.

She couldn't believe it. Didn't want to believe it—or all it implied. Maybe her ears were playing tricks on her. The sand could be distorting more than expected. Maybe being hypersensitive, she was skewing things, manifesting her worst fears.

She told herself all that and more, but the fact of the matter was, she didn't believe any of it. He was Kunz. And that terrified her. Because if the real Thomas Kunz was here, then the Thomas Kunz in Leavenworth was a double....

The truth slithered over her, then seeped in. *Damn it!* He'd done it to them again. He'd passed off one of his doubles as himself.

"You're certain she wasn't Amanda West?" a second man asked.

"I'm sure. This was a tall, skinny blonde. Short, curly hair. Her face was pretty messed up from hitting the rocks, but the woman definitely was not Amanda West."

Disappointment lurched through Kate. That was Moss talking. Obviously his stab wound hadn't been fatal or even debilitating.

Venom filled his voice. "That bitch broke my nose. I'd know West anywhere."

"It sounds like Captain Katherine Kane," Kunz said,

"S.A.S.S.'s explosives expert. She bombed my former Iranian compound to hell and back, thinking I was in it. Cost me a fortune." He sneezed, then added, "Find this woman and bring her to me—alive, Moss. Let's see if it's Kane, and exactly what S.A.S.S. knows about us."

Kate shivered. Kunz was thinking torture, and he was a master at it. His reputation for gruesome violence was legendary. Amanda had reported a clinical accounting of what he'd done to her, but Kate had enough experience to fill in the gaps. The woman had suffered at his hands. Kunz did horrific things to people with information he wanted. Things like removing bones, performing amputations, hammering metal punches through eardrums. He *liked* inducing pain, the sadistic bastard. The more pain, the better.

Determined not to become one of his victims, Kate didn't move, scarcely took breath.

Finally the voices faded and the vibrations of their footsteps grew faint and then ceased. Uncertain they really were gone, she hesitated to leave her hiding spot. They could be waiting for her. Setting her up. She didn't think so. Instinctively she sensed their absence, but with Kunz waiting to torture her, she wasn't taking any chances.

The afternoon heat grew almost unbearable. Itching and miserable, her throat parched, her entire body drenched in sweat, Kate longed to get up and move, but long years of discipline and training kicked in and kept her in her grave.

When the air taken in through the tube cooled and the heat subsided, she knew night had fallen. Quietly she lifted her head and her arm nearest the rock. Brushing the sand from her eyes, she opened them and scoured the starlit landscape for odd or unusual shapes.

Seeing none, she reared up, reveling in the cool breeze brushing across her. Swearing it felt better than sex, she smoothed over her grave in case she needed to use the tactic again, then checked her coordinates on her GPS unit. With her location confirmed, she began the hike back to the outpost.

Even if she moved at a good clip, it would take her the better part of an hour on foot to get to the outpost. She hoped she could make it. Already she was feeling exhausted and nauseous. Naturally she hadn't carried her canteen with her on the dive, and she had developed several symptoms of dehydration. "Home Base?" She tried Maggie again through the face mask. Her throat raw and scratchy, she dusted caked sand off the mike and tried again. "Home Base?"

Still no response.

Either someone else had activated the C-273 communications device and Home Base knew any conversation would be monitored, or the damn satellite had been diverted.

Grimacing, totally drained, Kate moved, and kept moving, kept putting one foot in front of the other on the uneven ground. More than ever, she needed to contact Home Base and to warn Colonel Drake about what she'd found.

The woman was going to freak.

Comforted at knowing it, Kate walked on, her legs trembling, her stomach shaking. She'd hate to be the only one Kunz and his goon GRID operatives had given double vision.

A long and grueling hour later, Kate arrived at the small tent camp dubbed "the outpost." A perimeter guard let her through with a snappy salute and a worried look. "You okay, Captain Kane?"

Douglas had cued someone she was coming. Word traveled fast in an outpost. So much for anonymity. She couldn't muster even a throaty croak so she nodded—and stole the water bottle clipped to his belt. Taking in a long drag that cooled her parched throat, she screwed the cap back on and passed the bottle to him. "Thank you," she said, then heaved on his boots.

He started to radio for a medic, but Kate stopped him.

"Ma'am," he protested. "You need help. You're dehydrated and your head is bleeding."

"I'm fine. I can take care of myself." She sighed and dragged a hand through her sand-crusted hair. "I'm sorry about your boots."

"No problem. It's not the first time," he said, being really good-natured about it. "But I should get a medic to look at your head."

"No, just drop it."

"But, ma'am—"

"Drop it! That's an order, Private," she said, noting his rank sewn to his sleeve.

"Yes, ma'am."

Because he'd tried to do her a good turn and he looked genuinely concerned, she softened her voice. "But thank you."

His pinched lips spread into an easy grin, though worry still shone in his eyes. "You're welcome, ma'am."

She moved on through the row of tents to the mess hall, where she snagged two liters of water and then two more and a packet of salt. She added the salt to one of the bottles, wary of drinking too much too fast and depleting the salt from her body.

She'd seen that happen once on a field maneuver and the guy had suffered seizures. Wanting no part of that, she stepped around a sandbag barrier and headed to her tent, weary to the bone.

What country she was in, she didn't have a clue. Could be Iraq or Iran or any of several other Middle Eastern countries. The outpost's location was classified and she'd been flown in blindfolded, which wasn't an unusual event since the start of the war on terror, but it never failed to give her the willies. It gave everyone in the field attached to Black World operations the willies. But some of their allies didn't want it advertised that they were allies. So the U.S. accommodated them.

She downed another liter of water, snagged some clothes and crossed the post to the showers. Until she got cleaned up, she'd never revive.

Stepping into the drab-green fiberglass stall, she cranked the spigot and washed off the grit and salt. Reveling in the water sluicing over her body, she thought about the sheer joy of feeling clean. Only once before had she felt as joyful. The day she'd successfully stopped a chemical attack on the White House.

"Hey, you gonna be in there all night?"

Kate looked over and saw half a dozen men lined up, waiting to use the shower. The fiberglass shielded from their view a swath between her shoulders and thighs. "Give me a minute. I spent half the damn day buried in sand."

That they understood. And for the next ten minutes, until she finished her shower, not one of them said a word or showed the least sign of impatience.

Kate wrapped herself in a towel and departed. "Thanks," she said, walking past them.

"Any time, ma'am."

Amazingly, none leered. But then, for that small segment of time, they'd forgotten rivalry and seen the "Outsider" as one who endured. As one of them.

She returned to her tent, switched the towel for a T-shirt

and panties, then broke down her headgear. Pulling the throat mike into position, she collapsed onto her cot with yet another bottle of water. Her legs felt like limp noodles. Her arms weren't much better. If she didn't get hydrated quickly, she was in for a wicked night of muscle cramps and spasms that would have her bent double.

Staring at the dim, bare bulb hanging from the center of the tent, she tried Maggie again. "Home Base?" Kate said. "Home Base, do you copy?"

"Identify."

A voice. Not Maggie's. Male. "I need a satellite link to Colonel Drake at S.A.S.S. headquarters." Blood trickled down her face. The damn cut on her forehead was bleeding again.

She was going to have to get up. Not giving into a sigh was just more than she could manage, so she let one out with gusto and rolled off the cot, then stretched for her gear.

"Code and authorization number?" the guy asked.

She riffled through her stuff. No bandages handy. *Oh, to hell with it.* She snagged a pair of panties and shoved them against her head. "Bluefish One," she reported, applying firm pressure and falling back onto her cot. "Authorization code BF10210."

A click signaled verification of her identity and approval to transmit. Moments later Amanda answered the call. "Home Base secure. Go ahead."

Half relieved it wasn't Maggie, and ashamed for feeling that way, Kate swallowed a swig of water. "Hey, it's me."

"Thank God." The earpiece hissed; Amanda let out a held breath. "What happened to the C-273?"

"It's gone." Her stomach muscles clenched. The lab

would have their noses out of joint for months over this. "I don't know if it got washed out or if it was taken out, but it's gone." Kate took a breath. "Activate Big Brother right away."

Each S.A.S.S. operative had a chip embedded under the skin in their nape. That chip allowed satellite tracking to wherever the operative happened to be on the planet. "We've got a colossal mess here. I need major backup immediately."

"I can't activate Big Brother," Amanda said. "Wherever the hell you are, it's been designated a no-activation zone. Do *not*, I repeat, do *not* relay your GPS coordinates."

"I did already." In the cave, Maggie had plotted her.

"Then was fine. Now isn't."

Kate understood the unstated message. *Relay and you'll be dead in five minutes.* She was definitely in hostile territory. Letting out a frustrated sigh, she refolded the panties to expose a dry spot, then slapped them back against her forehead. If she couldn't activate Big Brother to watch over her, then what was she supposed to do for assistance? She hadn't been given a location and she'd arrived blindfolded. "Recommendation?"

"Tactical is on site. You're under orders and authorized to rely on them for assistance. The major is expecting you to request through him."

Maggie had asked Darcy to run a dossier on Major Forester, and Maggie had given Kate the bones. She needed a little flesh. "Skip the details and just give me the upshot."

"He's really quite interesting."

She frowned. "Upshot. Please."

"He's a highly decorated hard-ass."

So she figured. "Is he going to divert Douglas's tactical unit to me?" Her fingers wet, Kate frowned. She tossed the blood-soaked panties onto the dirt floor, grabbed a second pair and placed them against her forehead. Her legs tingled. She stretched out and elevated them on a bunched-up green blanket.

"Roger that."

Douglas had done well at mopping up on their last mission. But this one was active; it would be much tougher, and he was a brash young guy. Trained, but without much battle experience. She needed seasoned help. This was GRID, and all of Kunz's operatives were seriously seasoned. "You don't understand."

"What?"

Kate sat up straight and grabbed her water bottle from the dirt floor. She hated telling anyone this, but especially Amanda. Still, there was no easy way to do it, so she just blurted it out. "The Big Fish is not in the tank."

Amanda would decipher that she was being told Thomas Kunz was not in Leavenworth.

A long hesitation settled between them, then, "Would you…would you repeat that, please?" Amanda reacted as expected. Her voice deepened, etched with a tremor that proved she was shaken up by the news. "I—I couldn't have heard you correctly."

She'd heard fine. After going through what she had with Kunz, Amanda didn't *want* to hear Kate—not that she could blame her. Hearing demanded listening. Listening induced fear, and there was nothing Amanda West hated more than fear.

Not overly fond of it herself, Kate repeated, "The Big Fish is not in the tank." Kunz wasn't killed in the Texas explosion. He wasn't taken into custody in the Middle Eastern compound and incarcerated at Leavenworth. That was the message, and it had Kate feeling queasy, too. "He's here."

"Alive?"

Amanda had gotten it, all right, and Kate could tell that it had rattled her to her toenails. "Alive and well enough to put me in his crosshairs."

"Oh, God." Kate's friend, not her co-worker, reacted. The friend who had tangled with the sadistic monster and had been held prisoner by him for three months. She'd been tortured, and only God and Amanda knew what all that had entailed. "Are you sure?"

"Ninety-nine percent. Unobserved audio confirmation with verified intercept." Swinging from the technical to the nitty-gritty, Kate added, "A GRID operative called him by name."

"But this can't be. We've got his damn DNA."

The panic in Amanda's voice was all too clear. Kate couldn't blame her after her experience and then what Kunz had pulled after his arrest, during interrogation. He'd relentlessly taunted her, mostly with heavy sexual innuendos. It'd nearly driven Amanda nuts. "Take a couple deep breaths and clear your head, okay?" Kate stopped short of telling Amanda she wasn't thinking straight. "Joan warned us that substituting DNA isn't a problem for Big Fish. He did it on every GRID operative he inserted."

Dr. Joan Foster, an expert psychiatrist with extensive experience in psychological warfare tactics and specifically memory manipulation, had been taken hostage and forced to either cooperate and do all Kunz asked in programming GRID-doubled operatives to replace genuine U.S. government employees or watch her husband and child be mutilated and murdered. Kunz had already killed both her parents and in-laws.

"But that was with captives." Amanda was stretching, looking for any excuse to deny the truth.

Kate couldn't let her. "It was. His goons did plastic surgery, substituted medical and dental records, biometric iris scans, fingerprints—any and every thing that could give us a positive ID on all of them. He successfully substituted DNA in *our* systems. What makes it more difficult for him to substitute his own?"

A long silence played out. Kate waited, giving Amanda time to work through the emotions and to accept the truth.

"Damn it, you're right," she finally said, still not recovered from the shock; her voice was thinner than a 3 mm detonator wire. "But I do have a way to prove whether or not the man locked up in Leavenworth is the real Big Fish."

He had successfully fooled more than sixty known and separate employees and the circles of people around them, people who had been stationed in various U.S. installations around the world, the court—everyone. But Amanda had a way to tell? "How?"

"When I was in the compound, I bagged a coffee cup with his prints on it," Amanda said. "I have no doubt that man drinking from that cup was the real Big Fish."

Hope sparked in Kate and she sat straight up, swung her legs over the cot's edge and planted her feet firmly on the floor. "That's right, you did." This could be their break. "Well, for God's sake run it on the prisoner to see if we've got a match."

"I'm on it. Will get back to you on that ASAP. I need to prime the test."

The DNA test itself would take twenty-four to forty-eight hours to complete. But results came up in layers. If any layer didn't match, they'd know right away the creep wasn't Kunz. Actually, far sooner than they'd know if the DNA matched perfectly.

Kate tapped her fingers against her forehead. The blood flow must be slowing down; her panties were still dry against her fingertips. Priming the test would take a few minutes now. Amanda had to call up the honchos in the need-to-know loop and get them patched in on the secure call: their boss, Colonel Drake; her boss, General Shaw, the OSI Commander at the Pentagon; and likely his boss, Secretary of Defense Reynolds.

S.A.S.S. operatives were active-duty Air Force but the unit functioned outside it. Carrying presidential-endorsed autonomy, S.A.S.S. answered directly to the Secretary of Defense. Reynolds had assigned General Shaw as a liaison and point of immediate contact as a courtesy to Colonel Drake. Occasionally she wanted a sounding board that didn't carry the burden of a heavily scheduled, full-fledge secretary.

An intuitive sense of knowing crept through Kate and she swallowed hard. She couldn't explain it, but she innately knew it to be the ultimate truth.

The decision next made by her superior officers would, by mission's end, determine her fate.

Determine if she lived or died.

Chapter 3

Being the only woman at the small outpost had perks. Kate had a private tent. While waiting for Amanda to get back in touch, she lay stretched out on her cot, half dozing, half listening to the steady drone of wind and sand beating against the canvas. A storm had blown in, and it was a bad one.

"Captain Kane?"

Following the man's voice, Kate turned to look toward the tent opening. She didn't bother cursing, though she thought about it. Her backside was dragging. She needed rest. "Yes?"

"Could you step out here, please?" He'd elevated his voice to be heard over the racket Mother Nature had stirred up.

"We're in the middle of a sandstorm," she said, stating the obvious. *Step out?* The guy had to be joking.

Fearing he wasn't, which meant he had to be a lunatic, she snagged her fatigue pants from the floor beside the cot, shoved her legs into them and tugged them up over her hips. "I'm decent. Come on in." She tucked in the hem of her drab-green T-shirt and quickly fastened the button at her waist.

"Damn it!" He cranked up the volume and it had nothing to do with the noise outside; he was ticked. "Fall out, Captain."

Only an idiot would miss the authority sharpening his tone. It startled her as much as his insistence to come outside. Whoever this guy was, he damn well better outrank her, shouting at her like an idiot. If he didn't, by the time she got through ripping him a new backside for his lack of respect, he'd damn well wish he did.

She shoved back the tent flap. "What in hell is wrong with you?"

"Sir," he added. Flying sand beat at his short black hair and the side of his angular face. His eyebrows knit in a skin-creasing frown. "And absolutely nothing is wrong with me, Captain. I need to speak with you."

Oh, spit. "Out here?" Okay, so he was a major and she'd have to eat the ass-chewing clogging her throat. But why stand out in the sandstorm to hear what he had to say? Sand swirled all around them like a thick cloud of choking dust, niggling at her throat, torturing her eyes. It could only be worse for him. Her back was to the wind. She cupped her hand to protect her eyes.

"I don't go into women's tents," he said, blunt and unapologetic. "Personal policy."

Ah, self-preservation. Making himself invulnerable to claims he'd compromised any female subordinates. Definitely a cover-your-ass policy. Having mixed emotions about that, Kate stepped further outside, and stiffened against the pelting sand, her hands dangling at her sides. Finally able, she read the name tag sewn just above his left pocket. *Forester.* Douglas's highly decorated, hard-ass commander.

"Major Nathan G. Forester, Captain. Outpost commander."

"Katherine Kane, sir." She extended a hand, but he didn't shake it. She waited a moment, but when it became clear he had no intention of touching her, she withdrew it. "Feel free to call me Kate."

He stretched his lips in a semblance of a smile. "A couple things to discuss with you."

She waited.

"First, keep your damn clothes on."

"Excuse me?"

"Don't bother denying it." He looked more disappointed than ticked, and he was plenty ticked. "And don't ever again strut around my post in a towel."

"I do not strut, Commander, and I was being considerate." She sniffed. "There's only one shower and there was a line six-deep waiting to use it."

"I don't care what the circumstances were, Kane. Spend the fifteen seconds to throw on your clothes. Got it?"

She nodded. "Is that it?"

"Sir," he reminded her again. "I'll let you know when you're dismissed. Until then plant your ass right where you're standing."

She held her tongue and waited. It'd been far too long a day for this bullshit—and she'd address this rioting junkyard dog as *sir* the very moment hell froze over and C-4 stopped exploding.

"General Shaw's put me on alert and ordered me to assist you here."

Oh, great. Fabulous. He'd slow her down and have her going nuts within an hour. And that innate feeling she'd had about her fate? She might as well put a bullet in her head right now. "I guess I'd better brief you then."

"It isn't necessary." He shoved a hand into his pants pocket. It was fisted.

He clearly wasn't happy about this order to assist her, either. "I'm afraid it is necessary, Major."

"Your commander is Colonel Sally Drake, action officer and commander of S.A.S.S., correct?"

He'd already bitched about the shower strut to Colonel Drake. Even greater. More fabulous. Kate slumped. Maybe with a little luck, she'd get a chance to shoot him. "That is correct."

"Then we're covered, Captain Kane." He changed topics without so much as a pause. "My men are disciplined. They conduct themselves with integrity and their focus needs to stay right where it is—on their mission. Your parading through the post more naked than dressed doesn't do a…"

Kate tuned him out. After the day she'd had, she had one nerve left. It was raw and ragged, and Forester was strumming the damn thing. Worse, he was gorgeous, and looking at him—even when he stood ranting—stirred her in a way she didn't want to be stirred by any man. For the first time since her split with Alan DeVane, a very talented surgeon who'd have to be neutered to be faithful, her hormones were in overdrive. Alan had been her one and only serious relationship ever, and it had been a mistake. Maybe she just needed a few more mistakes to numb her to reacting to men like this one.

She gave him a slow second look. No, that wouldn't help. Forester had too much going for him: great build, midnight-black hair, gorgeous blue eyes and a hard face that had known a lot of laughter and sorrow. He intrigued the hell out of her. Serious shame that he shattered the package's appeal by having the temperament of a pig. Speaking strictly from a hormonal sense—a woman alone for more than a year couldn't help but often speak strictly from a hormonal sense—Kate could overlook his oinker attitude but she couldn't overlook the wedding band on his left finger. That kept rein on her hormones as nothing else could.

Gaining the appropriate distance, she turned her tone stiff and formal. "I appreciate your concern and your assistance."

He frowned at her, clearly pissed and wanting her to say something, anything, to give him just cause to unload more on her. He wiped at his eyes with a forefinger, then flicked the sand onto the ground. "Conditions here are also tough enough without having half the brass in Washington crawling up my ass and down my throat. Next time you want help from me, Kane, leave your clout at home and just ask."

"I didn't pull an end run around you, Major. I was satellite linked during the entire phase of my operation."

"In the future, link your ass to me. This is my operation and it's critical. You come in here and screw things up, and you're going to get a lot of good people killed. My people. If that happens, I'll shoot you myself."

With her pride pricked, Kate glared up at him, grains of sand stinging her ankles and knees through her pants. "I'm not a rookie, Major, and I'm damn good at my job."

"Glad to hear it." He shifted on his feet, turning his back to the brunt of the blowing sand. "Colonel Drake asked me to relay that the DNA on the prisoner didn't match. He's a double." A hand at his brow protecting his eyes, Forester scanned behind him, then looked back at her. "I take it you know what that means."

"Unfortunately." It meant Kunz was on the loose, which had to be sending shock waves throughout the system. Frustrated and frightened, Kate accepted that S.A.S.S. had already once believed they'd killed the man only to have him resurface. Then until today, they'd believed he was alive but neutralized, serving a life sentence in Leavenworth. Now, damn it, they discover the truth. Thomas Kunz was alive and well and running loose somewhere on the planet.

How many doubles did he have, anyway? And had it been one of them she'd encountered earlier while in the grave? Or was that Kunz the real McCoy? The voice seemed to match, but what if that, too, had been altered? It wouldn't have to be perfect to fool the human ear. With Kunz's surgical and medical teams, S.A.S.S. was learning the hard way that very little remained impossible for him.

And that news might just scare her most of all.

"Your operation has been upgraded to a Code Two," Forester said, certain he'd left her to her thoughts long enough.

Kate nodded. A Code Two was one step out of a full-scale attack. A Code Two mission authorized operatives to function outside normal Homeland Security perimeters and channels. Restrictions imposed were minimal, and the operatives gained a lot of procedural latitude.

"Why?"

"Excuse me?" She looked up at Forester.

"What happened to warrant the upgrade?" The heat had left his tone and his eyes no longer sparked anger. Worry had replaced it.

"Have they put you inside the need-to-know loop?"

He nodded. "Don't worry, Captain. My security clearance is higher than yours."

Kate doubted it, but Colonel Drake had brought him into their circle, so Kate could tell him as much as she thought he needed to know. "Can we talk inside? My ankles are pitted."

He looked down at swirl of sand. "No, but we will talk in my office at the command post. Grab a jacket and boots or the rest of you will be pitted, too. And what happened to your face? It looks like raw meat."

Surely he wasn't just now noticing the cuts, scrapes and bruises. Then again, it's hard to see what's in front of you when you're looking at everything through an angry red haze. "Kissing rocks."

His eyebrow crinkled, perplexed, then smoothed out again. "Never mind. You can explain later. Get your gear."

Kate ducked into the tent, snagged a jacket and quickly fitted up in her combat boots. Then she went back outside. Surprised to see Forester waiting for her, she smiled.

"I, um, thought you might not know the way to the command post."

He was embarrassed. How totally charming. "Thank you."

Standing straight as a blade despite the sand shower, he nodded and then took off at a brisk clip. She followed him past the rows of tents to a large one near the center of the outpost.

Inside it, Kate noted five desks—all unoccupied—a ton of electronics. In its center, a clear-walled booth that surely had been designated for use by the commander. There, Forester could see all…and be seen by all.

She let her gaze drift from it to him. "Major, may I ask a question?"

He entered the booth and sat, then motioned for her to sit in the visitor's chair opposite his desk. "Go ahead."

"Has someone filed harassment charges against you or something?" Kate took her seat. "I couldn't help but notice… The visibility…" She let her voice fade.

"Between that and my policy on not entering women's tents, this is your conclusion?"

"I haven't drawn a conclusion, Major," she said, hiking her chin. "Just asked a question about something that strikes me as odd."

"It is odd, isn't it?" He didn't smile, but amusement put a lilt in his voice.

Kate thought she might just love that. Add that twinkle in his eye and it was a combustible mix. "I think so."

"No, no one has filed harassment charges against me, Captain Kane."

"Kate. Please." It was friendlier, and they were to be allies on this mission.

He nodded, acknowledging her, but she didn't hold out hope that he'd actually call her by her given name, or explain his penchant for visibility.

"So why is a Code Two critical in this situation?" He poured a cup of coffee from a maker on a table beside his desk and slid it across the desktop to her. "The truth, please."

Kate started to smile. S.A.S.S. had no choice but to fabricate plausible scenarios all too often. And it appeared that all the commanders knew it. "Are you familiar with GRID?"

"Yes," he admitted, then elaborated. "Largest black market seller of U.S. intelligence and weapons in the world."

He was definitely in the loop.

"That's right," Kate confirmed. "But there's more to them."

"Disclosure is authorized, Captain," he said softly. "Colonel Drake informed me that you would brief me in detail."

"You said it wasn't necessary." She frowned at him.

"I've changed my mind."

Kate tilted her head, stared at him a moment. Amanda had relayed the authorization to rely on him. Kate couldn't very well do so if he was assisting her from the dark. "What do you know about GRID operatives?"

"Covert. Experienced. Very highly skilled, and they'll do anything to anyone for money."

"Anything is right," Kate said. "Some have undergone plastic surgery, mind-altering therapy sessions, and only God and Thomas Kunz knows what else, Major. They're doubles for real, live counterparts currently holding classified, intelligence-heavy positions throughout the government." She paused for a second to let that sink in. "Obviously we don't know who is genuine and who isn't."

"That explains how he's getting his intelligence." Forester sipped from his own steaming cup. "What happens to the real employees? Does he kill them?"

"We have reason to believe he holds them permanent prisoner so they're available to fill in any blanks that arise for the GRID doubles." Actually, S.A.S.S. knew that for fact.

Surprise flashed through his eyes. "Just how well has Kunz done at this?"

"Very." Kate frowned. "We know of thirty cases and we strongly suspect there are at least that many more. How many more is anyone's guess."

"He's been at this awhile, then."

Kate nodded. "The truth is, we don't know exactly how long."

"And these doubles are still functioning within our ranks?"

"Until we weed them out, yes," Kate replied.

Forester set down his cup. It clanked against the gritty desktop. Sand got into everything here. "How the hell does he duplicate our people? That takes time—"

"He preys on loners, Major. People making permanent changes of station, so their co-workers are new and their habits unknown. He's also been known to abduct them during remote tours where no one knows them, isolate them by feigned illness, and various other methods."

"Incredible." Forester shook his head, rubbed at his nape.

"He keeps them out of commission for three months, studying them. Only, thanks to a combination of drug-therapy and psych-warfare processes, the captives don't realize they've been away for three months, and they have no recollection of what happened to them during that time."

Kate realized how this sounded. If she hadn't seen evidence of it firsthand, she would have been skeptical of the process. But she'd seen it twice personally, and reviewed more than a dozen case studies of other victims S.A.S.S. had already discovered. "It's a complex process, but very effective." She paused to drink from her cup and motioned for a tissue.

Forester passed her one from the box on his desk.

She wiped at her eyes, still bleary from the trek to the command post. "Thomas Kunz runs GRID—"

"I'm familiar with Kunz, Captain." Venom laced Forester's voice; the kind of venom that came from firsthand experience. He leaned forward, lacing his hands atop his desk. "You were going to explain why this mission has been upgraded to a Code Two."

"Yes, Major." Before continuing, Kate inhaled slowly, collecting her thoughts. Apparently he had enough background now to feel comfortable. "The designation keeps the need-to-know loop small. That's important, particularly in this case, because the longer news stays suppressed, the greater our odds for revealing infiltrators and for capturing Kunz. Without him, GRID is no longer a significant force."

"Wait a minute." Again, surprise twisted Forester's face. "Thomas Kunz is serving a life sentence in Leavenworth."

"Yes, I know that." Kate lifted her cup toward the coffeepot, silently requesting a refill. "I arrested him."

Forester poured to the rim and then returned the pot to its metal seat in the coffeemaker. A drop of liquid hit the metal and hissed. "Did he escape?"

"No, Major. He did not."

"Then you'd better explain what you're talking about, because I'm not tracking."

Kate looked up from a file labeled "Douglas" on the desk and met Forester's gaze. "According to the message you gave me from Colonel Drake, the Thomas Kunz in Leavenworth isn't the real Thomas Kunz."

Shock lit Forester's eyes. "He's a double?"

Kate nodded. "We've gotten his doubles before, too. And the one I heard today could be another—or it could be him."

"The hits are rolling in for you today, aren't they?"

She shrugged. "Some days you're the windshield, some, you're the bug."

Forester grunted, watching a young private enter and

take a seat at his desk. "Colonel Drake also mentioned that when you return to the States you're to go to Providence Air Force Base down in Florida and not to D.C."

"Thank you," Kate said. Secretary Reynolds had moved the S.A.S.S. office out of Washington to put distance between it and Congress, hoping to give S.A.S.S. a little less well-intentioned interference, but Kate had her doubts. Colonel Gray, the Providence base commander, was in a full-fledge pissing contest with Colonel Drake. The entire S.A.S.S. would have to fight Gray tooth and nail for so much as a paperclip.

Leaning forward, Forester tapped his index fingertips together. "Colonel Drake also asked that you be reminded to trust no one."

Kate blinked hard, looked over and up at him. He didn't much like being included in that remark. It shone in his eyes.

"To keep the truth buried, Kunz will kill you, Kate. You, Douglas and anyone else in his way—even if he has to blow up one of his own compounds to do it."

"Yes, Major, he will," she agreed. "He did in Texas."

"Commander?" A young man wearing owl glasses and a sparse mustache walked to the door of the clear booth from his desk near the tent opening, carrying a clipboard.

"What is it, Riley?"

"Douglas, sir." Riley's eyes stretched wide and his thumb flicked at the metal clasp on the clipboard. "He disappeared during the diving training exercise early this morning, sir. Search and Rescue are on it, but they haven't spotted him. Tide's moving out. They say odds are that he's…" His Adam's apple bobbed hard. "Odds are that he's drowned, sir."

Kate's stomach dropped to her knees, curdled, then shot up to her throat, pouring acid all along the way.

"You'll have to excuse me, Captain," Forester announced.

Somehow Kate managed to get to her feet. "Of course, sir." She moved to the booth's door. "I'd like to be in on the search, Major."

He frowned. "Did you and Douglas have a thing?"

"Define 'thing,' Major."

"Are you involved?"

"We're professional associates. We both put our asses on the line for others."

Forester's face flushed. "Point taken."

Kate turned to Riley. "Was Douglas alone at the time he disappeared? Injured in any way? Did anyone see him go under?"

"No, ma'am. He was with a team, not injured, and no one saw him go under. One minute he was there with them, bringing up the rear, and the next minute he was gone. Just that fast."

She looked at Forester and saw the truth she felt burning in his eyes. Someone had snagged Douglas.

Considering the proximity, GRID was a strong possibility. Of course, Iranian authorities, any of a half dozen groups of Iraqi insurgents were strong possibilities, too. Unfortunately any one of them meant that the odds were better than even Douglas was already dead. A knot swelled in Kate's throat.

Forester softened his tone and compassion rose in him. "Go back to your tent, Captain. I'll let you know the minute I hear anything that requires action."

"I want to be in on the search," she repeated. She wanted firsthand proof of what happened to him. She wanted hard evidence.

When Forester nodded, she left the booth and then the

tent, certain that something sinister had happened to Douglas. His disappearance reeked of foul play. He had been far from isolated, under no hostile pressure, and he was trained. He knew what to do if caught by a riptide or other natural occurrence. Douglas hadn't just stopped swimming. He hadn't just disappeared without a trace in the presence of his training team.

Someone had definitely intercepted him.

Chapter 4

Kate tugged on a fresh set of fatigues, preparing to search for Douglas. The obvious answer to what happened to him was that GRID had snatched him, but was that the right answer?

It seemed logical that GRID would snatch the entire team—they were all present and within easy reach. And the stealth factor wouldn't have been as challenging since GRID would be removing the entire group, leaving behind no witnesses.

Standing in front of a cracked mirror attached to the tent's center post, she ruffled her fingers through her short, curly hair. Douglas had brought her here. He had risked ticking off his commander by skipping up the chain of command and exposing his knowledge of S.A.S.S. to help her get GRID. Now she feared the worst had happened to him because he had.

A sliver of guilt cut through her. She wiped a hand across her chest, told herself all the reasons she shouldn't feel guilty, but of course, she did anyway. And of course, she had to do what she could to help him.

She just had to get through Commander Nathan Forester to do it.

Giving her cheeks a final swipe, she turned toward the tent opening. Forester was going to either include her in the search or have the MPs arrest her. She headed out into the sandstorm toward Forester's command post. One way or another she was going to find out what happened to Douglas.

The command post tent hummed. Where desks had been empty, people sat and stood gathered around. Four men stood shoulder-to-shoulder crammed inside Forester's Plexiglas-walled cubicle, scribbling notes and cross reporting. Forester sat at his desk, a phone receiver cradled at one ear, his mouth pressed to a radio mike. In between transmissions on the radio, he barked orders to the four men, all of whom looked as worried and serious as Forester.

"I want divers down there now. Keep them down there until you find Douglas or his body."

Kate stood beside the door and observed, sure that if she interrupted at the moment, Forester would just send her back to her tent. If circumstances hadn't been what they were, she would have enjoyed watching him in action. His face was expressive, his focus intense. Did his left eye always flicker when he was under pressure?

He glanced over and saw her. The heat in his gaze could have melted her into the tent's canvas. What perceived slight would she have to apologize for now?

He issued a hasty dismissal to the men in his cubicle.

They didn't waste any time leaving and rushed out of the tent. Watching them go, Kate didn't sense the animosity coming from them that she had seen on Forester's face. Most people here ignored her. She was an outsider, and they didn't want her to forget it. That didn't bother Kate. Hell, it was normal. She'd been an outsider all her life. But a fresh-faced lieutenant surprised her. He actually smiled at her.

She smiled back. "Hi."

Forester noticed. "Captain Kane." His voice boomed through the tent. "In here. Now."

That shout had half the heads in the tent turning toward her and the other half checking out Forester to see what had riled him before turning to stare at her.

Irritated by his shout, she lifted her chin to a haughty angle and walked over to the clear-walled cubicle. She sure as hell wasn't going to hurry, not after being treated with such a lack of respect. "You bellowed, sir?"

"Watch it, Captain." He slammed down the phone. "Now is not a good time for you to be cute."

She stiffened. "I had no intentions of being cute. I had every intention of pointing out your obvious animosity. I can't imagine your reason for it. I certainly haven't earned it."

Surprise flickered through his eyes. "Haven't earned it?" Anger rippled off him in waves. "Come with me, Captain."

Following him to the tent opening, she frowned. "We're going back out into the sandstorm?"

"Yes." He clamped his jaw shut and tossed her a once-white muffler. A rack of them hung on a peg-stand by the tent door. "Move it."

In her three days here, she had wearied of having gritty

sand invade her every orifice. The sandstorm had only hit this evening about 9:00 p.m., but it had hit with a vengeance. By ten, when Kate walked over to the command post, the entire landscape had changed. Some of the tents on the south side had drifts halfway up the outer walls. She swung the muffler around her throat, quickly wrapped her head to shield her face, then followed him out of the tent, ignoring the people inside who pretended not to notice that a world war was about to erupt between their commander and the outsider.

Darkness surrounded them. Forester disappeared into a thick cloud of wind-whipped sand. The damn stuff stung like splinters. The wind had to be forty knots. Breathing as little as possible to keep grit out of her nose, Kate pulled up her shirt collar and scrunched her shoulders to hide more of her exposed skin. Following Forester's shadow, she wondered what had pissed him off and where the commander who never permitted himself to be alone with a female officer was taking her.

A wind gust slammed into her and, for a second, she lost sight of his shadow. He snaked out a hand and tugged her into a tent. "Here."

Brushing the grit from her face, she frowned at him. They were alone, inside a tent. A serious breach of typical Forester policy, which had her edgy and nervous. This wasn't going to be a typical ass-chewing. It was going to be major. "What's wrong?"

Surprised by her insight, he took a step back from her. "I wanted to speak to you privately."

"I see." She didn't really see at all, and looked around. Personal quarters. Definitely his tent. He was either really rattled or supremely perturbed. "About something specific?"

He stiffened. "When I give orders, I expect them to be obeyed, Captain. I don't know how things are run at S.A.S.S., but at this outpost, when I tell you to go to your tent, I expect you to do it."

"I did go to my tent." She nearly sighed, but caught herself. Unit commanders exerting their authority over S.A.S.S. operatives temporarily assigned to their unit for expediency's sake was unfortunately common. Kate shifted her weight, unwrapped her muffler and let it dangle like a scarf wrapped around her neck. She knew the drill. Play the game. Let him rant and rave and get it out. Then do the job, whether or not he agrees with what she's doing or the way she's doing it.

"You didn't stay there."

"I didn't realize I'd been placed on quarters." In this situation, that amounted to house arrest, which had an indignant squall fighting hard for its rightful place in her voice. "Is that what you did, Commander?" She narrowed her eyes, glared at him. "Placed me on quarters?"

He didn't answer, but his disdain and her guilt over Douglas mixed and mingled with her aggravation at tasting sand grit and suffering Forester's attitude. She snapped. "Why don't you skip the nonsense and just tell me what's really eating at you?"

"In my unit, disobeying a direct order isn't nonsense."

"First, I didn't disobey your order." She dipped her chin. "Second, *that* is not why you're looking at me as if you'd like to flay the skin off my bones."

"Douglas's disappearance wasn't an accident, Captain." Forester's voice was tight, his jaw tighter.

Damn. Now he was back to calling her captain. Tired, worried, annoyed to the point of mayhem, she felt like spitting nails. "Yes, I know."

"How?" His frown deepened and his eyes turned to furious laser points. "Exactly how did you know it?"

She didn't even have to work at it to pick up on the suspicions running rampant and banging off the walls of his mind. They were blatantly clear. Bristling, she told him. "Douglas was on an exercise mission with a team. He wouldn't just disappear without someone noticing. He had to have been lured away, isolated and then—"

Forester erupted. "If Douglas was alive, he'd be on the job! He isn't, so he has to be dead. And if he's dead—"

The man hesitated a tick too long. "What?" she interjected. "Then it's my fault? Is that right?"

"That's how I see it." He leaned back, folded his arms at his chest.

Her temper jacked up from a controlled simmer to a roiling boil. It took work, but she managed to tamp it down, drop her voice and chill her tone. "Are you thinking I had something to do with Douglas's disappearance?" She couldn't believe it.

Guilt rushed through his eyes. He lowered his gaze to mask it. That was exactly what he was thinking. "Did you?"

"No!" Realizing she'd shouted, she lowered the volume, replaced it with steel, and spoke through clenched teeth. Still not wise—he could have her arrested—but it was the best she could manage under the circumstances. When Forester reported her, Colonel Drake would just have to get over it. "You didn't order me to my tent because you were preparing an investigation. You didn't want me to overhear your plans or conversations with Search and Rescue." She couldn't help it, she gasped. "I can't believe—"

"Believe it." He glared at her without apology.

Belligerent, misguided, bastard. She crossed her chest

with her arms and matched his stance. Katherine Kane tolerated a lot. She had to. She was the guest. But damn it, there were limits, and he'd exceeded them.

"Looking at me like I'm a bastard that crawled out from under a rock doesn't change the facts. It's a logical deduction, considering your actions."

"What actions?"

"You never should've involved Douglas in a mission outside the scope of his orders. You divided his focus and put him in danger."

"I *what?*" She couldn't believe her ears.

"You increased the obstacles and raised his risks and you're oblivious?" He looked at her as if she were a raunchy maggot. "You're senior to him, Captain. Didn't you even once think about the consequences to him?"

"You're wrong, Commander." She lifted a hand in protest, intending to set him and the record straight. "I—"

"No, you're wrong." Forester was too angry to listen and plowed on. "Your actions undermined my mission. You had no right—"

"Now wait just a minute." She propped a hand on her hip.

He lifted a warning finger at her. "Do *not* interrupt me again."

She shoved it out of her face. "No, you listen. Damn it, I will not stand here and listen to you make false accusations. I didn't undermine a thing and I'm not going to be a whipping post for you to dump all your fears on because Douglas is missing. I've got worries of my own about that, thank you very much."

Stunned, Forester just stared at her.

Certain when the shock wore off, he'd have her ass thrown in the brig, she spoke quickly. "I interrupted to save you from having to eat even more of your words later. You're wrong coming out of the gate on this. *I* didn't involve Douglas. *He* involved me. I didn't ask for his help or do anything to divide his focus. I didn't ask anything of him. He sent for me. So, you can take all that righteous hyperbole you've been spewing and just stuff it—" Oh, hell. She'd lost her mind. Gnawing on a senior officer's ass? Her host? She'd clearly left her sanity in the grave! "—right into the garbage, sir." Small save. Probably nowhere near large enough to spare her hide.

Forester took in a deep breath and rubbed at his chin. His wedding band winked in the raw light glaring from the single bulb dangling from a black cord at the center of his tent. When he spoke, his voice came out soft. Soft and terribly still. "I'm going to pretend I didn't hear any of that, Kate. For your sake, I hope you aren't such a hot-headed fool that you repeat it."

Genuinely offended but substantially cooler, she checked a look meant to stop a clock and held her tongue.

He uncrossed his arms and let them dangle at his sides. "Douglas came to you on his own?"

"Not exactly."

"Aha."

"No, 'aha,'" she insisted, letting some of the tension ebb out of her shoulders. Forester was off his war footing; he'd visibly calmed down. "He summoned me. I didn't talk with him. He, um, contacted me in a way he knew I'd get the message."

Curiosity lightened in his eyes. "How's that?"

The man was going to love this. "He mailed me a bag of sand, sir." It sounded even more absurd than expected, but it was all she could tell him. To disclose the coordinates given would require a breach of protocol. Colonel Drake would court-martial her. "Through the courier pouch," she added, but that didn't sound a bit better.

"What?" Forester looked confused.

Kate well imagined he was confused. It looked pretty good on him, too. Damn shame he was married—and a pig. "I said he mailed me a bag of sand."

"And you took that as a summons?"

"Yes, I did."

"Why?"

Kate debated on whether or not to tell him, then figured if she didn't, he'd just call Colonel Drake, and then she'd call and crawl up Kate's ass for being uncooperative. "A few months ago, we took down a GRID compound in the Gulf region." No way was she mentioning it was in Iran, or that she strongly suspected she was within spitting distance of that same place now. Maggie's *you don't want to know* remark replayed in her mind. "Douglas and his tactical team assisted."

"I'm aware of that, Kate. I issued the order."

"Then why are you asking me about the significance of the sand?" Good grief. If he had the answers, then why ask her the questions?

"Because I don't get the correlation between that mission and a damn bag of sand."

That, she could explain. "Douglas knows GRID is a S.A.S.S. priority. That he'd mail me anything at all would automatically relate it to GRID. Why else would he contact me?" She shrugged. "It was a summons, clear and simple."

Just as clear and simple, Forester was trying to wrap his mind around her logic. "And in your mind, there's no other possible explanation?"

"None."

"Are you sure?"

"Positive."

That earned her an unqualified grunt. "Did it occur to you that you flirted like crazy with Douglas on that mission and that he might just want to get in touch?" Forester lifted a hand, palm up. "Hell, half my unit heard the radio transmissions between you two, and by any measure, you can't deny that they were… suggestive."

With Forester, at this point, Kate expected any response. Any response except that one. "What?" Kate replied, shaking her head in disbelief. "That never occurred to me. It was just preattack banter. A stress-breaker. Nothing more than that."

"Tell me, Captain." He gave her a haughty look she'd love to knock off his face. "Did Douglas know that?"

"Of course he knew it. For pity's sake, any normal male operative would know it. Douglas is Tactical. How could he not know it?"

"It isn't out of the realm that a man would take you seriously."

He was kidding, right? She looked into his solemn face. He wasn't. Great. Maybe being married had twisted his memories of being a single operative, or maybe he'd never been a single operative. Or maybe he was just twisted. "Do you honestly believe it was personal interest? Is that what you're saying, Major?"

He hiked his chin. "It's possible."

Amazing. Utterly amazing. She stroked her temple before putting syrup in her tone. "Fine. Then tell me, Major. When you want to get in touch with a woman—and it's personal—do you always mail her a bag of sand?"

"Actually, no, I don't. But this isn't about me. It's about

Douglas. And if you're speaking hypothetically, I'm not a good example, Captain."

"Why not? You're a male operative. That's all we're talking about here, since I'd never before laid eyes on Douglas at the time these events occurred."

The starch went out of Forester's shoulders and then his voice. "Because I don't get in touch with women for personal reasons, Captain."

Kate again looked at his wedding ring, thinking the woman wearing the mate to it was pretty lucky, even if Forester did have a prickly disposition and probably twisted memories. But she couldn't see herself praising him for not screwing around on his wife. Fidelity was part of the promise, after all. Still, plenty of men did it, and she was glad—more so than she should be, really—that Forester wasn't one of them.

She looked past the mortar scars on the tent canvas to his cot, and then to a crate beside the bed that served as a table. A photo of a pretty redhead with a gentle smile sat on top. Kate assumed it was of his wife. The intricate silver frame was dented. "I'm sure Mrs. Forester appreciates that. But in the land of singles, a bag of sand to express interest is an abnormal dating ritual."

"I doubt it," he said baldly.

That set Kate back on her heels. "In your circles, sand is common?"

"No. No, I meant my wife, Emily. She wouldn't appreciate it. The idea of me getting in touch with other women would never occur to her. That's just not something I would do."

Telling comment. The woman was secure in her marriage and certain Forester didn't play around. Kate liked that, though she did so grudgingly, not wanting to like anything about him. "So why is her photo frame dented?" she asked before catching herself. "Wait. Let me guess. You lost your sweet disposition and tossed it?"

"Never." He looked over at the photo with longing and something in his eyes so tender that it softened his entire expression.

It left Kate breathless, filling her with pure envy. Alan had never looked at her that way. Every remnant of bitterness that had been etched into Forester's face drained away, and what remained appealed, tugged at her.

Until that moment she hadn't noticed that he was gorgeous in a compelling way. Not traditionally: his nose was too broad, his chin too strong, his cheekbones too sharp for the traditional. But packaged together in his specific bundle, they made for a gorgeous man.

How could a woman consider a man compelling, sexy, gorgeous *and* a pig? It made no sense.

"A few days before you arrived, the outpost was attacked by a small cell of insurgents." He let his gaze rove the inside of the tent, over patches and small holes in through which sand slid inside. "As you can see, the mortar was pretty heavy. The photo frame deflected a bullet meant to kill me."

"Would it have?" Kate couldn't even think it. A world without Forester? Even a toothache would be missed. He was a pain, but he had a special mystique.

"Yes." He swiveled his gaze from the photo back to Kate and tapped his chest. "Instead, I caught a flesh wound. Different angle and it would have penetrated my heart."

Kate swallowed hard, her stomach turning flips. Why was she having such a strong reaction to him? The man was married, a senior officer, and for both reasons, totally off-limits.

"GRID?"

He shook his head. "Local insurgents that stumbled onto us." He walked over to a squat table that served as a desk. A tall bottle of amber liquid sat atop it. "I need a drink. Do you want one?"

She turned her attention from the photo of his wife to him. "Yes, please." God knew it'd been a long enough day. She'd like to just go for the bottle.

He poured a finger's worth into a drinking glass and then passed it to her. "It's rotgut, all the way. But it's the best we've got at the moment and, believe it or not, we're grateful for it."

The outpost definitely wasn't in Saudi, Kate thought, taking the glass. Not six months ago, her mouthwash and cough syrup had been confiscated on entering the country because they contained alcohol. She took a sip from her glass. It singed her tongue and burned all the way down her throat. *Definitely rotgut.* "Whoa, that'll get your attention." Her eyes were watering.

The corner of his mouth curved up, hinting at a smile. "You get used to it."

She cleared her throat. "Would that be before or after it burns out the lining of your throat and stomach?"

"Just before." He sat on the edge of his cot. "You have no idea why Douglas sent for you, do you?"

Recalling Colonel Drake's "trust no one" warning had Kate stalling, but then Drake herself had brought Forester into the loop on this, which signaled he had the needed clearance to be told whatever proved necessary. "Not a clue." She sat on a stool beside the cot. "Do you know?"

He rubbed at his nape—clearly a habit when mulling something over—and held her gaze for what seemed an eternity. "I think I might have most of it figured out."

Progress. Progress was good. "Well, would you care to enlighten me?" By the skin of her teeth, she stopped short of reminding him they were on the same side.

Another hesitation, though shorter this time. "I can't tell you where we are. That's classified."

"So is everything I've told you about GRID."

"Yes, but you have authorization to tell me those things." He drank from his glass, dabbed at his mouth with the back of his hand. "I don't have authorization to tell you."

"Fair enough." She leaned forward, bracing her fore-arms on her knees.

"This region is mountainous," he started, setting his glass down next to his wife's photo. "Beneath the surface is a Swiss cheese maze of caves that extend out into the knuckles and toes of the water for miles."

"I'm aware of that," she reminded him. "I've spent three days exploring."

"We've been here two months," he said. "Exploring the caves."

"What exactly are you looking for?" Kate felt confident she knew, at least in part, but she wasn't at all certain if he would tell her, and if they were going to work together, she needed to know his boundaries.

"Terrorists, weapon caches and all relative intelligence."

Pleased and more than a little surprised, she nodded.

"Douglas has been diving south of the outpost for two weeks."

"And this is significant because…"

"It's not," Forester admitted. "What is significant is that he noted an oddity in some ships heading to port," Forester said. He held up the whiskey bottle, silently asking if she wanted more. When she shook her head, he went on. "They were weighted down and for all intents and purposes appeared to be full of cargo. Douglas deduced that explained why they rode lower than usual in the water."

"The weapons arriving?"

"A three-mile stretch inland has been dredged for shallow watercraft. These ships were too heavy to make it through the channel."

Kate was confused. Why was this significant? "So they off-loaded at the main port and didn't move inland. What's the challenge there?"

"Oh," Forester's eyes gleamed. "But they did move inland."

"How? If the water was only deep enough for shallow craft, they couldn't use it."

"That's what Douglas wanted to know." Forester leaned forward, legs spread, hands laced between his knees. "He suspected the added weight was weapons, but he claimed his reasons for believing so were based on classified information he couldn't share." Forester straightened, stiffened, a knowing gleam in his eyes. "I'm guessing that classified information came from you."

Kate nearly frowned. "Forget speculating that I breached security. I didn't. All the tactical team on the ground during the compound raid in Iran knew GRID would sell weapons, technology and drugs for quick money."

"GRID's very successful. Why would it need quick money?"

"Because we'd taken out two compounds in short order. It takes a great deal of money to replace lost resources at that level."

"GRID knows you've arrived here," Forester speculated.

"Yes," she confessed. "I was nearly captured." And she'd lost the C-273 communications device. God, but she hoped it wasn't in Thomas Kunz's grubby, greedy hands. Hostiles would pay a fortune for it—and use it against them.

Forester's solemn expression sobered even more. "Does GRID know this outpost exists?"

"I have no way of knowing that."

"But you're sure you didn't compromise our position during your escape from them?"

"No, I'm sure." She explained how she'd hidden in the grave and stayed there until darkness fell and then made her way back to the outpost. "However, it's hard for me to believe that they're operating in such close proximity and haven't discovered you on their own."

"If they have, then why haven't they destroyed us?"

It was a reasonable question. Unfortunately it was one Kate lacked sufficient information to answer. *Damn it, she needed to talk with Douglas.* "Only GRID can answer that question."

He smoothed his fatigues over his thigh with his hand. "I requested intervention on the ships."

"You did?" Kate felt a crease form between her eyebrows. She'd have to report this to Home Base, and have Maggie relay it to Darcy. Nothing had come through from outside to intel sources—or if it had, Darcy hadn't considered it worthy of mention. Now, in context of GRID being in the immediate vicinity, it could be an important key to finding weapons, and if they were here, the hostages.

Forester nodded. "The Navy intercepted and ran a topical search on three vessels, but they didn't find any contraband. Nothing illegal."

"Then there has to be another explanation." The ships

couldn't be carrying weapons. If they hadn't put into port, and the Navy hadn't observed the vessels off-loading cargo onto another ship, where the hell could it have gone?

"I'm not ready to consider that this isn't the explanation. Neither is Douglas," Forester said. "The vessels the Navy searched rode low in the water, obviously weighted down. Nothing illegal was found on the topical. Yet when they reached port and underwent a thorough search, all three of the ships were riding high, not low, in the water."

"How did the captain explain the difference?"

"He couldn't."

"Played dumb?" That, unfortunately, often worked. Can't get blood out of a stone.

"The naval inspectors weren't sure he was playing."

"Someone had to have a hypothesis."

"They had no idea." Forester shrugged. "The Navy didn't have a 360-degree visual on the ships, but if anything was dumped off, divers didn't spot it. What we know is that no cargo washed up on the shore." He rubbed at his nape, pondering again, and his left eye started to flicker. "Douglas felt certain the crews were dumping and later retrieving weapons, anyway. Though he had no idea how they were doing it."

Kate rolled this all over in her mind, waiting for the puzzle pieces to find their proper slots and fall into place. When they had, huge gaps still riddled the puzzle. "Did any proof surface later? Anything that could explain the oddity?"

"No." Forester stood and began to pace. He'd apparently thought about this a great deal and that he couldn't figure out what was happening frustrated him. "No hard evidence of anything we could attribute to any of the ships was located."

"Then whatever they dumped had to be liquid." Which raised some pretty scary possibilities. Some chemicals never break down. The water would be contaminated, killing anything in it and they could get into the saline conversion systems that refined the water to make it potable. Drinking water would be a thing of the past; they'd have to import it.

"I thought of that, too," Forester said. "But we ran water samples and they came back normal."

Kate breathed a sigh of relief. "Then Douglas had to be right—unless they released air." Which could also be laced with deadly contaminants.

"Air samples were clean, too." Forester paused near the center tent pole and looked back at her over his shoulder. "Douglas was monitoring another low-riding boat when he disappeared, Kate. I authorized it and signed the order."

"Oh, boy." She could've condemned him, but from the look in the major's eyes, he was slamming himself more than enough for both of them. "Why?"

"Because of this classified information he had, Douglas considered it essential to the security of our troops. We have 150,000 men and women in theater, Kate. How could I refuse to authorize it?"

She stared at him, long and hard. "You couldn't."

He swallowed hard. "What if GRID does have him? After all you've told me about what they do, this doubling business…" He stopped and shook, before stuffing a tightly clenched fist into his pants pocket. "What have I done to him?"

Kate searched for the right words, but concluded there weren't any. It was the burden of every senior officer who sends those under his command into harm's way. Responsibility. Fear for their safety. Guilt. More guilt. And still more.

Such a bitch of an emotion, guilt. It doesn't care where it hangs its hat. It'll settle on anyone's head that isn't covered.

"Commander, look—"

"Nathan," he said softly. "Call me Nathan."

"Okay, Nathan." She walked over, clasped a reassuring hand to his biceps. "You did your job. Douglas is in a dangerous profession by choice. He isn't a lamb you led blindly to slaughter. You need to remember that—and to believe that we'll find him."

"But when we do, will it be him or one of GRID's doubles?" Forester's frustration escalated. "Hell, Kunz was in Leavenworth. Arrested, tried and convicted, and it wasn't even him. How will we know Douglas is Douglas?"

Kate scanned for a way. "We'll use the bag of sand. Only Douglas would know he sent me the bag of sand."

"Unless he tells them."

Drug and mind manipulation therapy. He could tell them. "Remember the flirting?"

Forester frowned.

"We can use that. We can act as if Douglas and I have a thing. If he goes along with it, we know he's not Douglas. If he doesn't, then we'll know he's himself."

"Seems rather simplistic."

"Who cares?" she said with a huff. "Will it be effective? That's all that matters."

Forester looked at her hard, as if he'd only now noticed she wasn't just a woman some man—Douglas—might desire but also a soldier. "It might."

She wasn't sure if she should be flattered or insulted, so she settled for neither. "Okay, then."

Forester nodded. "Kate," he started, looking as if the words he was about to say choked him. "I haven't been easy on you. But I want you to know I appreciate your help."

The words had cost him. Nathan Forester was a proud man. But he was also realistic, and Kate was grateful for it. "You're welcome, Nathan. We'll visit the site—"

Gunfire erupted, spraying the tent.

Chapter 5

Nathan shoved Kate down to the sandy floor, shielding her with his body.

With adrenaline gushing through her veins, Kate struggled against his weight, her hip grinding into the gritty dirt, stretching to grab the edge of the cot. A partial sheet of plywood was wedged behind it, blocking a hole blown it in from the previous attack. If she could snag it, it would give them a little more protection…

Gunfire erupted constantly: sand sprayed, fragments exploded. Dangerously close. Automatic weapon. Submachine gun.

"Soviet?" Nathan rendered his opinion on the make.

"No." She involuntarily jerked. "German." The timing was a dead giveaway.

The gunman swept a line of fire two feet in front of them. Sand scattered, stinging her wounded face, her arms, even her legs through her clothes. Nathan took the brunt of it and the sting had every muscle in his body tight, his face contorting.

Stretching, trying again, she let out a deep groan and her fingers locked on to the green Army blanket. She jerked with all her might.

The blanket went lax.

The cot tumbled over them.

The plywood fell, slapping Nathan across the back. His breath swooshed out; Kate felt it in her chest.

Bullets continued to rip through the width of the tent, loud and piercing, showering sand, bursting everything in site. The center pole took a direct hit. Wooden splinters flew like targeted arrows and the top of the pole collapsed.

The tent caved in.

"We've got to get out of here." Nathan rolled off her and motioned to the hole in the canvas the plywood had been blocking. "This way."

She hand-signaled Nathan to crawl on his belly. Even on his haunches he was too tall for the collapsed tent; he'd be an easy target. Down on her haunches, using the plywood as a shield to protect them both, she inched toward the hole. The gunfire continued to storm from behind them.

At the tent's edge, Kate snagged Nathan's gun, darted a quick glance outside into the darkness. Convinced by the shots a single gunman was launching this attack, she squinted, strained, but trying to see through the wind-driven sand was an exercise in futility. Her stomach flipped, and so did her attitude. Visuals sucked, and that was bad—and good. It would be equally hard for the gunman to spot them. She signaled for Nathan to trail her.

He inched to a duffel bag, pulled out a second gun and followed her lead.

The firing suddenly stopped.

"Gone?" Nathan whispered.

Kate shook her head. The jerk's gun had jammed or he was reloading.

She seized the opportunity and scanned the immediate vicinity. She dipped the nose of her gun, signaling Nathan to go left. When he nodded, she headed to the right. Her blood thrummed in her temples as sweat poured down her face, between her breasts, soaking the back of her shirt. The bullet's spray pattern had been right to left. The gun-man had to be to her right.

Another *rat-a-tat* spray of bullets fired.

So much for the jam theory. The jerk was active again, continuing to drop a deluge of bullets on the tent. Who-ever this was, he wanted to make damn sure she and Forester were dead.

The rapid-fire bullets sounded like a series of taps. It couldn't compete with the howl of the wind or the noise of the sand beating against everything in sight. That howl had her ears ringing so loudly that if Nathan was calling her, she wouldn't hear him.

Kate blew out three puffed breaths to steady herself, hugged the canvas to her back and stretched tall, then she moved. The gunman was aiming low, assuming they'd be belly-crawling in the dirt. Upright, at worse, she'd end up with a blown-out ankle or shin wound. At best, he'd miss.

She turned a corner and nearly bumped noses with Nathan. The barrel of a gun shoved deep into her stomach. "Don't shoot!"

Nathan jumped, swerved the nose of the gun away from her. "Jesus, Kate."

Realizing how close she'd come to getting killed, she started to shake and tried hard to refocus. "See anything?"

"Sand."

"Same here." She grimaced, turning her attention to the gunfire. "Timing's changed."

"He's shooting shorter."

"Out in front of the tent," she stated. Now why would he deliberately drop good ordnance into the sand?

The gunfire abruptly stopped.

Kate caught a glimpse of something red and charged after it. It moved through the blinding sand haphazardly, but she kept a fix on it from one end of the outpost to the other, never losing sight of it.

It's a trap. It's a trap. He's leading you out into it, Kate. Stop!

She pulled to a halt near the showers, taking cover more from the sand than the gunman. Sliding behind the drab-green stall wall, she dropped to her haunches. The rippled fiberglass had been worn nearly smooth by the sandstorm. Letting her forehead rest against it, she caught her breath. The blowing sand had made it almost impossible to breathe during the run, and her lungs were in full protest.

Forester caught up to her and dropped beside her, his chest heaving, his face raw and red from the grating sand. "Did you lose him?"

"It was a trap." Still trying to regain her breath, she looked over at him. "He was leading me out of the outpost."

"What warned you it was a trap?"

She took in a gulp of air, let it out and felt their breaths mingle. "How many times have you seen anyone wearing red here?"

He thought about it, then blinked hard. "It was a trap."

She nodded. "GRID members are a mixed bag of nationalities. Kunz doesn't want patriotism or religion interfering. He wants loyalty only to him and money. The shooter couldn't be local." Locals wore only black or white. That had clued Kate to her general location the first day here. "He didn't know red would flag him as an outsider."

"Could've been a deliberate ploy," Forester said as he stepped over her, turned on a shower, and rinsed off the sand caked on his face. The red in his skin deepened, hot and wind-burned and sand-scrubbed. "Possibly a local insurgent who wanted us to think he was an outsider."

"Who knew which was your tent? Attacked only it?" Kate shook her head at him. "That's not working for me."

He turned grim, slapped the shower tap and shut off the water. "GRID."

"I'm afraid so," she replied. "But something's still weird about it, Nathan."

He hiked up his eyebrows, asking without words.

"Remember when he shortened his aim?" Nathan nodded and she went on. "He laid down at least fifty rounds in the sand in front of the tent. Why would he do that? Just waste bullets?"

Nathan's left eye twitched. "I don't know."

"Me, either." She stood. "But I think it's important."

He stood beside her. "I believe you're right."

"But why?"

Nathan tilted his head. "Maybe he didn't want us dead? Maybe he wanted someone else to think we were?"

That possibility shed an entirely different light on the event. And opened doors on new possibilities that definitely needed to be explored.

"Let's go back, see if we can find anything to help us figure out the details on this."

"Okay." Kate turned to follow him.

They walked back toward the tent. About halfway, Kate felt the distinct shift in the wind. The weather was finally calming down.

The tent was totaled. What hadn't been shot up was sand torn. Taking a look around, Kate verified the spray pattern.

"Where was he firing from?" Whispering, Nathan looked left and then right.

So did Kate. "He was in motion the entire time. The bullet pattern was consistent, but the trajectory constantly altered." She treated the area as a crime scene and walked the grid anyway, but she wasn't so foolish as to think she'd find a solid lead to the gunman. Whipped for hours by violent, unrelenting winds, the entire outpost was sheathed in a heavy cloud no vision gear known to man could penetrate. Any leads were as gone as he was, swallowed by the sand.

The hair on her arms ruffled and something important nudged at her. Niggling. Niggling.

Then it hit her full-force. "Nathan?" She stopped and faced him, her head tilted to keep her face out of the wind. While no longer violent, it still pinged sand that stung through her clothes like thousands of tiny needles. "Where the hell are your people?"

Not one soul had responded to the gunfire.

Chapter 6

The sixty men in the outpost under Nathan's command were safe.

In the mess tent, they ate. In the recreation tent, they read, teamed up and played cards, waiting for the sandstorm to end so they could resume their search of the caves for the weapons cache. In the command post, they rushed about, conversing via satellite link, radio and field phones with Search and Rescue, trying to get more information on Douglas.

There wasn't any.

So far, there'd been no sign of him anywhere, Riley reported. "Search and Rescue is fighting the storm, too, sir."

"But they're flying over water," Nathan rumbled.

"Yes, sir," Riley said, thumbing his clipboard. "The sand isn't a problem so long as they're away from the shoreline, but the wind is kicking their backsides."

Nathan seemed more, not less, irritated by Riley's re-mark, so Kate interceded to take the heat off the owl-eyed clerk. "By regulation standards, the choppers should be grounded until the weather clears."

"Yes, ma'am. That's true, sir." Riley nodded at Nathan. "The pilots were ordered to return to base. The choppers were grounded. But the pilots all claimed they had com-munications malfunctions. The orders didn't get to them."

Appreciation funneled through Kate. She'd done the same thing herself, more than once. "They don't want to abandon one of their own."

Nathan swung a level gaze on her. "They don't want to discover later that he was under their noses and had died because they'd given up on him."

"That, too," Kate agreed. She certainly understood the complex emotions that went into making the call to quit. Too many times, she'd dealt with that demon in similar sit-uations. Regret, like guilt, was a merciless bitch.

Riley frowned at Nathan. "Sir, do you think they have a chance of finding him?"

Nathan hesitated. "I'm sure they'll do everything they can."

Innately, Kate knew that Search and Rescue didn't have a prayer of finding Douglas. Not until Thomas Kunz de-cided he wanted Douglas found and he had his GRID min-ions release him. But Riley looked so worried. She couldn't violate security to share her near certainty on what had happened to Douglas, which meant she couldn't reveal her honest opinion on this. Yet she didn't want to lie to Riley.

"They might get lucky," Nathan said, sparing her.

She shot him a grateful look. "Riley, did you hear gun-fire a few minutes ago?"

Surprise widened his eyes. "There was gunfire in the outpost a few minutes ago?"

"Never mind." Kate looked to Nathan, who silently shared her concern.

That was it then. No one at the outpost had heard the gunfire or seen anyone wearing a red scarf in the outpost.

Nathan turned for his cubicle. "Captain Kane." He nodded toward his office. "Please."

Kate followed him.

He sat behind his desk and motioned for her to take the visitor's chair. When she sat, he leaned forward and dropped his voice. "I can't believe that in a group of sixty men not one heard a submachine gun fire off a couple clips."

"I believe them, Nathan." Kate leaned toward him, held her voice just above a whisper. "We've been inside, out of the storm, a full fifteen minutes, and my ears are still roaring. Out there, I couldn't see a foot in front of my face. Even inside the tent and looking out, vision was impaired just beyond the edge of the tent. The gunfire sounded like light hammer taps."

"But a perimeter guard, someone, should have seen something."

"They're inside, out of the storm."

"So you don't think it was an inside job?"

"No, I don't. Your men would know better than to wear red."

"Okay." Nathan weighed all they'd been told and a strange look crossed his face. "Riley," he shouted loud enough for Riley to hear him from his desk.

"Yes, sir, Commander." He grabbed his clipboard and rushed over, poising his pen, ready to write.

"Set up a guard detail. Full circle around the outpost."

He spoke to Kate. "If someone can infiltrate the camp and pick any one of us off at will, we need an early warning system." He darted his gaze back to Riley. "Tell Kramer to trip-wire the damn perimeter—and make sure every man here knows it's wired."

"Yes, sir." Riley scribbled fast and looked up. "Is that all, sir?"

"Yeah, thank you."

When Riley left, Nathan looked at Kate. She sipped at a steaming cup of coffee more because it was wet than because she needed something hot to drink. Her throat felt raw and irritated, coated from the blowing sand. "What?"

"GRID didn't know until now the outpost existed. You were right. No one followed you back here."

"You're assuming they didn't know the outpost existed." She dipped her chin. "You have no evidence of that."

"I have circumstantial evidence," he countered, clearing his throat and then filling a cup with piping hot coffee. "If they'd known it, they would've sent in a team to take us all out, Kate. They wouldn't have messed around with a lone gunman."

Kate blew into her cup and thought about it. "On that, I happen to agree." She set down her cup. "The thing about him firing into the sand is really nagging at me."

"Me, too." He stood. "Maybe the bastard didn't want to kill us, after all?"

"What if it was someone who wanted to make GRID think we were dead?"

"Who?"

She shrugged. "Douglas?"

"What?"

"Bear with me." She stood beside Nathan. "What if

they did snatch Douglas. Habitually, GRID tries to convert abductees. What if Douglas played along? What if he deliberately missed us? What if he wore red so we'd see him and know what he was doing?"

Nathan stared at her, long and hard. His left eye twitched like crazy and the skin between his eyebrows creased deeply. "It's possible."

"It is," she said, unsure how her next revelation would be received. "Especially if Douglas has decided to insert himself undercover."

"Oh, man. He could." Nathan let his head loll back on his shoulders. "Surely he wouldn't do that, Kate. Surely he'd leave that to you. You're the professional at that type of thing."

"He might," she admitted, guilt stealing over her. "I didn't let him know I was coming. He could've thought he was on his own."

"Why didn't you tell him?"

"Honestly?" She swallowed hard. "I assumed he'd know. It didn't occur to me that he wouldn't know." She lowered her gaze, unable to bear to see condemnation in Nathan's eyes. "But I didn't think. He isn't S.A.S.S. He wouldn't automatically know that any summons is answered."

"We still don't have irrefutable proof it was him. It could've been, but it might've been GRID." He chewed at his inner lip, mulling, then checked his watch. "It's getting late. I need to see if there's anything I can salvage from my tent."

When he turned to walk out of his office, she called after him. "Can I help?"

He paused, stared into her eyes, then nodded. "Thanks."

Riley was sitting at his desk on the horn with someone.

Nathan didn't slow his stride when walking past, but Riley anticipated something; he grabbed his clipboard.

"Get me a tent, will you, Riley?"

He wrote furiously. "Yes, sir. Fifteen minutes, sir." Satisfied with himself, he set the clipboard back down.

Kate smiled and shot him a thumbs-up as she passed. He was an excellent clerk.

He smiled back at her and dipped his chin to his chest, embarrassed.

At the tent, Kate pulled a T-shirt from the rubble, shook it out and wrapped around her head to protect her face from the blowing sand. Bent double, she helped Nathan dig through the fallen tent for what was left of his possessions. Shoving aside a splintered piece of wood, she unearthed the zippered edge of his duffel bag, and looked over to Nathan to tell him, but the expression twisting his face stopped her dead in her tracks.

He stood, shoulders slumped, hands trembling, jaw clenched and blinking rapidly, holding the shattered photo of his wife.

Caught unaware in the clutches of raw pain, the arrogant, cold man who blamed her for Douglas's disappearance, who, she suspected, kept her nearby only so he knew exactly where she was and what she was doing, and who lacked more than a little faith in her expertise, appeared close to tears.

Something alien gushed through Kate's chest. Something not as simple as compassion, or as complex as sympathy. Something far more nebulous and subtle and yet so powerful it had her knees weak. Her eyes, too, burned—and the wind or gritty sand had nothing to do with the cause. The cause lay in what for Kate had been an age-old wound.

How did it feel to have someone—anyone—love you the way Nathan Forester clearly loved his wife? To know that to that one person you were vitally important? To know that you were in his heart and mind even when you were thousands of miles apart?

Kate had no idea. And only on the rare occasion did she indulge and allow herself to hope that one day she would know.

When he seemed over the worse of the shock—why it was a shock to find the photo he knew would be there, Kate had no idea, but it clearly was—she cleared her throat to remind him she was here. He didn't respond. Then she saw that the photograph had been destroyed. Her heart hitched, in pain for him. "I'm sorry about your photo, Nathan."

He looked over at her, but he didn't really see her. "Me, too."

His reaction surprised her. Why did he sound so forlorn? It was a photo. Sentimental, because it was of his wife and had once saved his life, but surely his wife would send him another one.

He didn't move, just stared at her, hopeless and help-less, and…devastated.

Confused and upset, Kate straightened. It hurt to see him this way. She'd rather face the arrogant pig he could be than this man so clearly suffering any day. That side of him didn't inspire a desire to reach out and comfort. This one did. This one shoved in her face all she was missing by not having a man in her life who loved her. A man like Nathan Forester.

And again a shaft of envy, hot and swift, stabbed at her, slicing into her heart, and stunned by it, she sat right where she stood. For some reason, here in the twilight, sitting among the half-collapsed tent, among the rubble and his destroyed possessions, she felt an overwhelming need, and began to talk. "My parents were workaholics," she said softly. "They ignored me most of my life."

Something glinted. A spare watch. She picked it up and rubbed its cracked crystal between her forefinger and thumb. "Actually, it was more like they forgot I existed than they ignored me," she corrected herself. "Until they wanted to pull me out of cold storage to parade around in front of people they wanted to impress."

Nathan walked over, sat across from her, and held the photo with both hands between them.

Kate pursed her lips and looked right into his eyes. Why she felt compelled to tell him this, she had no idea. But she did. "I never gave them a reason to regret it."

"You loved them," he said, his voice deep. "You wanted them to be proud of you."

She pursed her lips and gave him a little negative shake of her head, her expression reflecting the sadness tightening her chest. "I knew better than to hope for their love. But I thought if I could be perfect, then they would at least include me in their lives. I could stay off the shelf, waiting for the next parade."

His serious face grew more so. "Did they?"

"No, they didn't." Even now, all these years later, it hurt to admit that to herself, much less to anyone else. She sucked in a sharp breath. "I learned to live without it, without them, really. I relied only on myself. From kindergarten on, I packed my own lunches, cooked my own meals, and did my own laundry. I did everything I could do to avoid the mistake of bothering them." She let out a humorless laugh. "My parents didn't react well to being bothered, Nathan."

He frowned and rested the photo on one knee. "Did they punish you?"

"If razor-sharp tongues and brutal verbal skills qualify as punishment, yes." She grunted. "But I didn't let that stop me. I was determined to win them over. I worked really hard to trick them into liking me."

He stared at her with honed insight. "But you feel you failed."

"Oh, yes. I don't just feel it. I know it. Indeed, I failed. Unequivocally. Huge." She dusted at her knee though there was no lint, not even sand, clinging to it. "I kept trying, though. My freshman year in high school, I caught a lucky break." She smiled. It was a weepy smile, but she'd take whatever she could get that wasn't a railing protest. A kid—any kid—should feel loved by her parents. Even Kate.

"This lucky break got their attention and they saw the light?"

"Not exactly. They never saw the light, but I certainly got their attention."

"How?"

She grinned and, surprisingly, it was sincere. "I blew up the science lab at school."

He laughed out loud. "I'll bet that impressed the hell out of them."

"You know, it really did." She shrugged. "They had no idea I had enough smarts to actually cause something to deliberately combust."

"Fancy way of saying that you blew up the lab."

"They were fancy-talking people." She looked away, feeling a little wistful.

"And you've been blowing things up ever since, trying to impress them again."

Surprised and not totally comfortable with his insight, she jerked her gaze back to him. But she didn't see the censure in his eyes she expected. She saw understanding. And at that moment, Katherine Kane did the most stupid thing a woman can do.

She fell in love with a married man, and decided she absolutely hated his wife for being his wife.

Of course, he would never know it, and that was the only saving grace and salve for her wound.

She gave herself a mental shake. Love? Here? With a compelling, married pig?

Apparently.

Her conscience weighed in. Who in their right mind would ever imagine it? Who would be that stupid? Not her. That's for sure. It had to be delusions.

Try, fact.

Absurd. Delusions. No more, no less. Just delusions.

Possible? Yes. Probable? No.

Then evidently it was lust. Or better yet, indigestion from eating too much sand.

Perhaps.

That possibility made her feel better. Lust she could accept—would accept and cling to with the tenacity Nathan held on to his wife's photo—because that possibility didn't leave her with her heart exposed and her feelings hanging out on a line just waiting for tension to snap it and leave her in pieces.

Nathan was looking down at the photo again, and the sadness in him returned.

She had been self-sustained out of necessity, and she should never forget its lesson. Still, to have a man look at a photo of her that way, with such depth and tenderness, she might just risk loving. Someone. Someday.

Yet the need to comfort him arose as naturally as her breaths. "I'm sure she'll send you another photo, Nathan."

He looked up at Kate, agony burning in his eyes. "She can't."

"Sure she can. They'll pass it to you in a secure pouch."

"From heaven?"

Kate went stone still. "What?"

He dragged in a sharp breath, as if the words he was about to speak were heavy blows and he needed to brace to sustain himself against them. "My wife died five years ago, Kate." He licked at his lower lip. "This photo is all I have left of her."

Stunned, Kate couldn't pull her thoughts together long enough to grasp them or to find something decent to say. Finally she managed. "I'm sorry for your loss, Nathan." And she was grateful for saying it.

He nodded that he'd heard her, but kept his gaze fixed on the dirt, hiding from her the pain he clearly felt so intensely he knew it would reveal itself in his face even now.

Five years? Kate couldn't believe it. He still acted so…well, married. Still wore his wedding band, still slept with her photo beside his cot, still thought of himself as married.

Five years was a long time for a man to be a widower and still think and act and feel so married.

And that might just make Kate most envious of all.

"It's nearly 2:00 a.m.," Nathan said, then stood. "Let's call it a night, Kate. The storm's broken. In the morning, let's take a look at where Douglas went missing."

Kate stood, dragged the duffel bag out of the debris through an opening and left it in the sand with the other possessions pulled from the rubble. "Okay. I need to go back down where I dove today, as well."

"No," he insisted. "Not without a backup team."

She stiffened and looked him right in the eye. "I have

no choice." The C-273 had to be located. The sooner, the better.

His aversion to her objecting to his orders surfaced. "Why?"

He wouldn't like her answer any better. She resisted an urge to sigh. "I can't tell you that."

"Can't?" A speculative gleam lit in his eye. "Or won't?"

Not the anger she had expected, but why did the man always have to push? She wasn't sure she wanted to look that deeply herself. "I could," she clarified, and then decided to be totally honest. "But if I did, I'd have to kill you."

He gave her a strange glance, one she couldn't fully interpret, then drove it home with a snort. "I'm surprised you're not jumping at the chance."

Feeling just enough pressure not to resist the urge, she teased him. "Mosquitoes are annoying, Nathan, but you don't kill them with a cannon."

He laughed.

Even exhausted, standing in the middle of a half-collapsed tent with ringing ears, sand scratching every inch of her body, and worries flooding her mind and fighting for her attention, the sound of Nathan Forester laughing made her smile. She hated that.

"Sir?" Riley appeared just beyond the edge of the tent. "Kramer just radioed in. He's out at the perimeter, finishing the setup on the trip wire. He reported that someone just left the outpost, sir."

"Who?" Nathan asked, fully alert.

"He couldn't tell, sir. But it was a man and he had a red scarf on. And he was carrying a black box in his hand."

Kate's heart thud hard and fast against her ribs. "How big was it—the box, I mean?"

"Kramer said about six by six, ma'am."

"Inches, millimeters—what?" Kate knew she was shouting but, damn it, this information was vital and his description told her absolutely nothing.

Forester sensed something significant was going on with this black box. Kate saw it in his face, and while he shot her an unspoken question, and that importance resonated in Riley's expression, Kate ignored them both, waiting for an answer.

"Inches, ma'am," Riley said. "The box was six-by-six inches."

Knots cinched down in Kate's stomach. God help them. It could be the C-273 communications device.

Chapter 7

By dawn, the storm had passed and the dry, still heat had returned with a vengeance.

Kate suited up in her wet gear, and met Forester at the mess tent. They wolfed down a lousy breakfast of reconstituted powdered eggs, instant coffee and some kind of fried bread that the cook referred to as a whole cake.

Between bites, Forester issued Riley orders. "Get my tent moved. Being right next door to where I was, just makes it easier for the insurgents to hit me again."

Kate didn't miss his putting the attack off on insurgents, and she was glad to hear it. Informing the entire outpost about GRID wouldn't be a wise move at this point. Actually, if it could be avoided, it should be. Knowing GRID existed increased their odds of becoming targets.

Nathan wiped at his wide mouth with a paper napkin. "Get an update on Douglas from Search and Rescue, too."

He paused a second, then added, "Guess you'd better notify headquarters that we've had a perimeter breach, as well. Get authorization to move the outpost ASAP."

Riley scribbled the orders down on his habitual clipboard. "Sir, should I have Captain James start breaking down the camp to prepare for the move?"

"Yeah, James is fine."

Riley nodded, adding the note. "The boat you requested is ready and waiting for you and Captain Kane at the dock, sir."

"Thanks."

"Is that it, sir?"

"Yes."

Riley passed Kate a new loop of rubber tubing. "For your tags, ma'am." He shrugged. "I noticed yours was missing."

Very observant. A valuable asset in a unit clerk. "Thanks, Riley."

He gave her a shy grin. "Sure thing, ma'am."

Within minutes, Nathan and Kate loaded their gear into the jeep, and made their way to the dock. The going was slow due to the storm. Sand covered the road, so the entire trip was a four-wheel succession of bumps and jarred teeth.

Finally, Kate spotted the shore, then the dock. Nathan parked and they hauled their gear to the boat. Before boarding, Kate ran a check for explosive devices and bugs.

Nathan likely considered it unnecessary, but if he did, he kept any objections to himself. Kate appreciated that, because in her job, checking was as automatic as dreaming.

It took about thirty minutes to do the job right. Nathan stood on the dock, watching her every move, but never said a word. When she was done, she looked up at him from on the boat. "Let's roll."

He got in and they made ready. Nathan removed the ropes mooring the boat to the rocks and coiled them inside the boat. When he was finished, Kate slipped behind the wheel and took off for the site where Douglas had disappeared.

While she steered the boat, Nathan monitored their position on a handheld GPS that he was careful not to let Kate glimpse. She knew they were in the Middle East somewhere. Judging strictly by the landscape, they were either in Iraq or Iran.

Iran would certainly warrant the no-activation order on her Big Brother positioning system, and explain Nathan's lacking authorization to disclose their location to her.

Iraq could also warrant the security measure. The political climate there had changed substantially in the past three years, but relations were dicey at best. The newly elected leaders required a lot of "quiet" help in getting the new democracy off and running on stable ground, especially considering the level of opposition to democracy in surrounding countries, yet Darcy hadn't advised S.A.S.S. of any reports that supported making the entire country a deactivation zone.

A different thought ushered in a different perspective.

Maybe the reason had nothing to do with her and everything to do with Nathan and his mission. It could be that his unit was functioning on a stealth footing for security reasons. But that would mean his mission wasn't to check out caves.

Maybe Iran's nuclear program?

Maybe the weapons of mass destruction everyone in the know felt certain Saddam had buried somewhere in the sand?

Nathan tapped her on the shoulder. When she looked over, he motioned for her to veer west thirty degrees.

She turned the wheel, and then made a forward rolling motion with her finger, asking how much further. The rugged hills in the distance, the knuckles of land extending into the water, were familiar to her already. She was very close to the cave where she had found the GRID compound.

Uncomfortably close.

Douglas must have either found the compound, or come close to finding it on his own. That increased the odds GRID had him by at least fifty percent. And that had her flesh crawling.

She slowed the boat to a stop, throttled the engine to idle. "Nathan, this isn't good."

"You know something you want to share?" In his seat beside her, he flicked a thumb on the edge of the GPS. The screen went blank.

"Want to? No." It'd put him at greater risk. "But I need to," she said. "If this is where Douglas disappeared, he was within spitting distance of a suspected GRID compound."

"Oh, Christ." Nathan's left eye flickered like crazy. "You found an active compound? Here? Right under our noses?"

The salt spray settled a fine mist on her face. Kate licked her dry lips. "I haven't been in the compound, Nathan. But I'm just about positive that it's here. I was in the cave leading to it, when two men intercepted me. I know for fact that they were GRID operatives, and I know for fact the cave was audiocommunications wired to the rafters."

"Oh, great." He dragged a worried hand through his hair. The wind had it spiked.

"Not so great." She frowned. "Kunz, or one of his freaking clones, was talking to the guy holding a gun on me."

Nathan's face paled. "Damn it, Kate. Then they almost certainly have Douglas. Why didn't you tell me this last night?"

"I didn't know then Douglas had been diving here, and you couldn't have done anything last night anyway. We were in the middle of a sandstorm." She threw a level look his way. "Besides, I reported it to S.A.S.S. headquarters. At that point, I didn't have the appropriate authorization to report anything to you."

Nathan's jaw tightened and he slid her a sidelong look laced with steely resolve. "I know Colonel Drake told you to trust no one, Kate. Hell, I relayed the message. But from here on out, you damn well better trust me. They've got one of my men—now, I'm convinced of it—and I will do anything to anyone to get him back. Don't hold out on me again. For all of us, the stakes are too damn high."

"Okay, Nathan," she agreed, but not unconditionally. "We work together. From here on out, what I know, you know." She raised a finger into the air. "But that also means that anything you know, you damn well better tell me."

She shifted on her seat and chose her words carefully, tasting the slight salty tang in the gentle breeze. "There's more going on here than you realize, things that don't pertain in any way to Douglas that I can't tell you. So anything you know or learn might be exactly what I need to take care of this other business." She lifted a hand and hiked up her shoulder. "Understood?"

He gave her a brisk nod. "Last night, you told me that you could tell me, but then you'd have to kill me, remember?"

"I remember."

"Well, what I can share without killing you, I will." He held her gaze. "That's the best I can do."

"That's good enough. We consider ourselves agreed." Kate put her hand on the throttle. "Okay, where to?"

"Two minutes straight ahead, to that third knuckle." He pointed to the exact spot where she had lost the C-273 communications device.

Her stomach soured, but she headed the boat in that direction. GRID knew she had located the cave that tunneled into the compound. There was no telling what new obstacles Thomas Kunz had put in place to keep them from breaching the actual compound.

The sadistic bastard had no conscience, no morality, no humanity and no restrictions. With Kunz, every possibility was fair game, and that made him the most dangerous kind of enemy. He would initiate barriers, and they could be of any nature or type. Biological, chemical, nuclear. One of them *or* all of them. He couldn't care less about fallout or collateral damage.

Though it was hard to believe such a man could exist, he had proven himself to S.A.S.S. repeatedly. His defense would be deadly and could be in the form of anything.

Which meant Kate had better be ready for everything.

Two hours later Kate and Nathan had searched the area for Douglas, but had nearly tripped over Search and Rescue divers already searching.

Nathan received a quick report from a water-wrinkled member of Douglas's tactical team who he'd assigned to Search and Rescue. "No sign of him, sir."

They returned to the boat and moved even closer to the cave Kate had pegged as GRID's, then dived again. But another hour later, they again came up empty-handed.

Swimming back to the boat, Kate climbed the ladder and got inside, then pulled off her headgear and shook her hair loose.

When Nathan had gotten in and set his headgear aside, she looked over at him. "We've got to check the original place I went down."

"With a team, Kate."

Stubborn cuss. "No, Nathan. Now." She sent him her most genuine look. "I need to show you what I saw. I can't be the only one to physically see it. You said it yourself. GRID knows I'm here. They fear what I know. They will try to kill me, Nathan. Someone else has to have seen this firsthand."

" 'This' being the cave?"

" 'This' being the gouges in the rocks that led me to find the cave," she corrected him and then goosed the engine. "Catch that anchor, will you?"

He tugged the anchor up out of the water and set it on deck. "Why are you moving the boat?"

"It's a flashing beacon that we're here. I'd rather not advertise it."

He nodded and took his seat.

Kate shoved the stick forward. The engine whined and the boat nearly stood on end, then shot off across the water. On an angle with the large boulder, she backed off and again went to idle. "Here's good."

Nathan dropped the anchor.

They readied and then slipped over the side into the water.

By late afternoon they had been in the water for hours. Kate had pointed out the weathering on the rocks, the deep gouges just above the waterline—all the oddities that had led to her dive. They had explored, deliberately skirting the mouth of the GRID cave. Behind a large rock on the bottom, Kate pulled her binoculars out of her fanny pack, adjusted the setting, then looked through the lenses. The cave's mouth was clear. She passed them to Nathan and hand signaled.

He took the binoculars and looked, then scanned a bit back and forth. Looking at her, he shrugged.

Not surprised he didn't recognize it, she stood closer, backing against his chest, then set her sights on the cave's mouth again. Then she dipped her chin to her chest, holding the binoculars steady.

Nathan came closer, clasped his arms around her to hold himself in place, and again looked.

Kate's face felt like fire. How could a man snuggling up to her in a freaking wet suit turn her on? Every nerve in her body was on hyperalert.

He moved away and gave her a thumbs-up.

She frowned at him. He seemed so unaffected? How could being close to him rattle her to the bone and he be totally unaffected?

He motioned for them to move on.

A bit off and out of sorts, she swam on.

While Nathan hoped to find some sign of Douglas, Kate hoped to find some sign of him *and* the C-273 communications device. So far, they had failed to meet either objective. An hour later their luck hadn't improved.

But since the day wasn't over, she held on to hope.

Something odd snagged her attention and Kate paused outside the mouth of yet another cave opening for a better look. She closely examined the face rocks around the mouth, letting her fingertips drift over the rugged surface.

The tide and current shoved water against them, and

here too, there were gouges that cut into the rock far too deep to be attributed to water action alone.

These gouges were also manmade. Her stomach curled.

She kicked off to go inside, but felt Nathan tap her shoulder. This last time, they had dived with a mask rather than headgear to give them greater visibility. The tradeoff was their limited communication. She raised a questioning hand.

He pointed to her oxygen tank and then to his watch.

It was time to surface. Kate nodded that she understood and kicked upward.

The sun was sinking, casting a glare on the water. Taking off her mask, she squinted against it, smelled the fresh air and waited, but Nathan didn't surface immediately.

Kate was just about to go back down to check on him when he finally broke the surface near her. "I was getting worried," she told him. A swell rolled over her and a whitecap splashed in her face. "What took you so long?"

"I found something." Nathan raised his arm out of the water. In his hand, he held a six-by-six black box.

And wrapped around it was a red ribbon tied in a bow.

"Oh, God." GRID had found the C-273. "Let's go. I've got a report this to Home Base immediately."

"What is this thing?" Nathan held it up. "Are the contents lethal?"

Kate went to take the box from him, but he held on, staring at her, waiting for answers to his questions. "No, it's not lethal in the way you think. There's nothing in the actual box that will hurt you."

"Then why do you look is if someone's jumping on your grave?" He nodded to the C-273 device. "Kate, what is this thing?"

How the hell did she answer that without breaching security? Finally she found a way. "It's experimental and top secret, and that's all I can say about it, Nathan. Except that it doesn't have anything to do with Douglas. I give you my word on that."

His whole attitude changed, and Nathan let go of the device. "Then you'd better let Home Base know we located it." He turned to swim to the boat.

Kate tucked the device into her fanny pack, then turned to join him—and slammed smack into his shoulder. Pain shot through her chin and her breath swooshed out. "Oomph!"

Nathan didn't seem to notice. "Kate, look."

She rubbed at her chin and followed his line of vision. Their boat was gone.

Chapter 8

Twilight threatened.

Kate gently kicked her legs, scanning the horizon one more time, but the boat hadn't drifted or been carried by the tide.

It was nowhere in sight.

Her tired muscles cramped. She and Nathan had been at this for hours, treading water, working against the tide and current, trying to fight being swept out to sea. She glanced over at him. He was solemn, hurting and doing better than she. Off and on, she'd flirted with using emergency egress—the procedures were in place—but this close to GRID without a tactical team in place and ready to take down the compound could jeopardize the entire effort. They had to keep trying to get out of this on their own.

A flicker of movement caught her eye, about seven feet off her right shoulder. She strained to see what it was, but the glare of setting sun conspired with her nearness to the surface of the water; she couldn't make it out. Whatever the object was, it was dark, large enough to disturb her, and it was floating closer.

"It'll be dark soon," Nathan said. "If we aren't rescued before then, we're going to have a big problem."

"The tide's coming in. I feel the shift in the current. That will help." It would aid them in drifting toward shore. "With luck, by morning we'll be there." If they managed to stay afloat that long. She lifted a weary arm and pointed. "Nathan, what the hell is that?"

He darted his gaze at Kate, then in the direction she pointed. "It looks like a...oh, hell, Kate. It's a mine!"

"Don't touch it." Kate moved closer to him, positioning herself between him and the mine.

"What are you doing?" He reached for her arm and tugged her back.

She looked over her shoulder at him. "I'm an explosives expert, remember? Let me see what it is. Maybe I can neutralize it."

Roughly sixteen by thirty inches. Drab combat-green. A closer inspection had her skin crawling. "It's a Mark 1. Pressure-sensitive." Could the news possibly get any worse? "It'll float for about an hour—buoy suspension. If we can avoid it until then, it'll sink. We can float above and avoid it."

Nathan stared at the distant water surface over her shoulder. "It's got a lot of company. We can't avoid all of them." He spared Kate a glance. "Is there anything you can do?"

Soon the drift mines would be above and below them. "Not without equipment I don't have. How many do you see?" Kate paddled away from the mine, giving it lots of space.

"I can't count them all," he said honestly. "If these suckers only float for an hour, you'd better check below to see what they've done there. They wouldn't go to all this trouble and leave us a way out in an hour." He reached over and pulled her closer. "Stay near me. I'll keep you clear of them up here."

"Thanks." Kate pulled on her face mask, grabbed hold of Nathan's arm, let her hand slide down the outer length of him, and sank below the surface. Holding firmly to his leg, she spun in a small circle.

Sheer horror flooded her. *Mark 3* mines were everywhere!

Shimmying up Nathan's body, Kate broke the surface and tossed back her headgear. "They're all over down there. Mark 3s—same as Mark 1s but they float suspended about thirty-five feet below the surface." She pulled in a sharp breath. "Jesus, I've never seen so many mines in such a concentrated area. There are hundreds of them." She scanned the water in all directions.

Panic flickered through Nathan's eyes. The same panic Kate felt inside. "What are you looking for? We've got to get out of here. Fast."

"These are launched from surface ships. I was looking to see where the damn thing is." And whose it was. The choice had been taken out of her hands now. She had to invoke emergency egress.

"Does it really matter? If we don't outrun these damn things, or some fish bumps into one, we're going to be blown to bits."

"We might." Kate slid the zipper of her wet suit down to the middle of her chest. She rubbed at her neck, depressed the implanted chip activating an SOS in her personal tracking device. Yes, she was in a no-activation zone. But this was a warranted emergency.

She looked around them, counted fourteen mines then stopped. At most, she had Nathan had three minutes to get out of here. By the fourth minute they'd be dead.

"Kate! Let's move it."

"Don't panic, Nathan," she said, responding to his elevated tone. "You can't afford the luxury."

"Don't panic?" Nathan looked at her as if she had lost her mind. "I'd say panic is warranted. Do the math, Kate. We're going to be dead in—"

"Four minutes," she said calmly.

"Then don't tell me not to panic. Let's move."

She rolled her eyes, making certain he saw it. "Just listen to me. The mines are going to encircle us. They're above and below the water—there's nowhere to go, Nathan." She paused a moment for her words to sink in, then went on. "I want you to try not to move. Float on your back and fold your arms across your chest." As she gave the instructions to him, she also followed them. "We can see the mines around us. We can't see the ones below. This position will best limit our blind exposure. Remember, stay perfectly still."

"I'll sink."

"As still as possible," she amended. "It could be that the mines can bump into us and not detonate. It depends on the amount of pressure they've set."

"The trigger is adjustable?" Some of the worry left Nathan's face.

Kate regretted having to put it back. "Yes, it is. It makes the weapon system more flexible and that makes it a viable option for a greater number of uses. But don't hang your hope on that, okay? I have a feeling GRID meant these mines for us, and considering someone stole the boat to make sure we would be in the water, the detonator setting is probably at low level."

"Do you hear that?"

A dull distant drone thrummed in her ears. Relief washed through her. "Yeah, I do." She'd summoned, but had no idea how Home Base would respond or with what. "It sounds like…a helicopter."

Moments later, a Chinook rounded a distant knuckle, no more than a large speck in the sky. But its shape was distinct with the twin props at front and rear atop. Her mouth went dry and she tore her gaze from the aircraft back to the water. The mines were all around them now. If the triggers were set on system minimums, the Chinook was too late. There was no way they'd get out of this alive.

"Do you think it'll see us?" Nathan asked.

With her face turned away from him, Kate smiled. It seemed crazy to smile in this situation, they were now in the most intense danger of all, but the little-boy hope in Nathan's voice was so alien to the man she knew him to be, she just couldn't help herself. "Yeah, you know, I do."

She watched the chopper's progress and tried to block out the fact that within three feet of her floated seven mines.

"They're heading straight for us," Nathan said, wonder in his voice.

"I'm sure it just looks that way. More than likely they've picked up the mines on their scanners and they're investigating them." The aircraft neared and Kate saw it clearly. It was a Sea Knight assault transport for combat troops.

"Kate," Nathan's voice sounded strained to the breaking point. "I've got about two feet and then we're going to know the trigger pressure levels."

"Ditto." She watched the gawky-looking chopper move closer and closer until it was hovering right above them.

"I'm seeing a lot of heads up there."

So was Kate. The side door was wide open and men filled the hole, peering down in the water. "It's okay," she assured Nathan over the roar of the beating props. "It's a CH-46E. They have tons of room."

"They've got at least a dozen on board."

Kate scanned her memory. "It holds fourteen, plus the aerial gunners."

The wind off the blades whipped at the water. Fortunately, that pushed the mines further away from Kate and, she prayed, Nathan.

A rescue ladder dropped out of the side of the chopper. Two men shouldered their way in to stand in the wide opening, monitoring Kate and Nathan's location.

Kate lifted her arms, but the ladder was still just out of reach. Nathan grabbed hold of the ladder, then grabbed her by the hand and reeled her to him.

"Hold on." He slid an arm around her middle, his fingers digging into her flesh. "I've got you, Kate. I won't let go."

Quickly removing her fins, her foot slid onto a ladder rung. She hugged Nathan tightly. "Okay. Okay, I'm good."

"You sure?"

She looked up at him and smiled. "Yeah, I'm sure."

He smiled back. "Climb on up."

"I can't." Worry flickered across his face. She didn't like it, and wanted it gone. "You've got to let go of me, Nathan."

"Oh." He rolled his eyes back in his head, then smiled. "Details. Details. You're such a nag about details, Kate." He gave her a squeeze.

"Yeah, that's me. Resident detail nag." She squeezed back, her fingers digging into his side. "Um, Nathan. Let go now, okay?"

He released her. "Post-mission stress. Like the flirting."

"Right." Kate let him have the lie and took one last look at the water.

Hundreds of mines littered the surface and hundreds more lurked in the clear water just below it. GRID didn't just mean to scare them away from the cave. It didn't just mean to slow them down from exploring the cave.

It meant to kill them and to buy itself a healthy chunk of needed time to clear out the compound before anyone else could contemplate an attack.

And, damn it, it looked as if GRID had succeeded—but only with half their goal.

While Forester glad-handed their rescuers, Kate contacted Home Base to notify them of the mine dump and to put high priority on getting minesweepers in to clear the area.

Maggie manned the desk. "Okay, Bluefish, I've put it in the system and Intel is working the chain."

Every minute that passed was in Thomas Kunz's favor. Enough time and he could have GRID clear the cave of any evidence of a compound. The hostages, if they were there, would be moved to yet another undisclosed location.

"Damn it." Kate mumbled her feelings on that thought and leaned back against the vibrating side of the chopper. "We need uninterrupted observation on the landside of those hills, Home Base."

"Understood, Bluefish, but we've got three high-priority target missions currently under way. We don't have—"

"Find a way, Home Base. Or get ready for a Fourth of July that will light up your world." That was the phrase. The one that cued Maggie on the weapons cache. Kate prayed her instincts were right or she was going to be in deep and serious trouble over the claim. It was logical, to be sure. The compound, the chatter about bio and chemical weapons. The boats riding low in the water and high when they arrived in port. Every bit of it fit.

But it wasn't conclusive proof.

And she'd just warned Home Base that it was.

Colonel Drake would have her rank for breakfast and her ass for a snack.

"Roger that, Bluefish. I'll get Intel on it and resources claimed right away."

"Thanks." Kate shut down communications and opened her eyes.

Nathan sat on a bench beside her, but spoke to a small group of men seated beyond him. "We were damn lucky you guys came along when you did."

That remark snagged Kate's full attention. He had no idea she'd summoned the chopper by activating her locator system. The crew did a double take, but Kate silenced them with a warning look and a few telling words. "It was a blessing, all right. We were at the point of no return."

They got the message and played dumb. "What happened to your boat?" a sergeant with more stripes than Kate had ever seen on his sleeve asked.

Kate took that opportunity to shut down questions. "A couple opium freaks stole the damn thing." She turned to Nathan. "Commander, you should get that theft reported."

"Right," Nathan said before moving toward the cockpit.

One of the crew, dressed in fatigues with his face greasepaint-smeared, sat beside Kate. Her mind was on a thousand things, mainly on getting the mines cleared before Kunz could clean out the compound.

"Hello, Kate."

She swung her gaze around to really look at the guy. It took a long second for recognition to sink in. When it did, she gasped. "Gaston?" What the hell was a CIA double agent doing in *this* Sea Knight?

Maybe it wasn't a U.S. Sea Knight.

Her stomach sank to her knees. Oh, no! No, it couldn't be that. Adrenaline streaked through her like the tail off a comet. She swallowed hard as she watched Nathan walk back toward her, looking calm and content.

He had that luxury. He didn't know Gaston. He didn't know Gaston worked for the CIA, or that he'd been undercover and inside GRID for over a year. Nathan didn't know Gaston had been at the Iranian compound when Kate had blown it up and Douglas and his tactical team had handled the mop-up operation.

And Nathan had no idea that, gauging by all the signs, they had just been rescued by the very people trying to kill them.

GRID.

Chapter 9

Kate unsnapped the strap on her knife sheath.

"Wait." Gaston stayed her hand, brushing it off her thigh. "It's not what you think." Leaning forward on the bench, he crossed his hands at his knees.

Nathan walked up, tense and frowning. "Kate?" He looked straight at Gaston. "Everything okay?"

She stared at Gaston, wishing she knew how to answer that honestly. He shot her a look telling her that she was fine. Since she had no choice, she went with it, giving him a warning glare that she'd better be right, and then swung her gaze to Nathan. "Everything is fine." She managed a thin smile.

"Major Forester," a young lieutenant came up behind Nathan. Unlike the others, he wore no greasepaint. His face was clean. "The captain wants a word with you, sir."

Nathan nodded, then walked toward the cockpit.

Deliberately separating them? Kate slapped her hand back on the sheath. "Okay, Gaston," Kate whispered, "you've got five seconds to answer me. Are these people GRID or American?"

He did a quick check to make sure that no one else was within earshot. "American," he whispered back. "I've been extracted."

Suspicion still ran rampant through her. "How do I know you're you?" It was a reasonable question. Kunz had doubled U.S. employees in virtually every segment of government service. The CIA definitely wouldn't be exempt. And Gaston had been with GRID for a long time. In a year, he'd surely had many opportunities to screw up and blow his cover. Lord knew he had been able to report very little to Langley, though in fairness she had to admit that wasn't for his lack of trying or taking risks. It was Kunz's fault. He kept everything humanly possible to himself, keeping even his own high-ranking GRID members in the dark. As long as their fat paychecks kept coming, apparently they could not have cared less, though she couldn't say that applied to his new second-in-command. Since Amanda had killed his old one, Paul Reese, S.A.S.S. assumed Kunz had replaced him, but so far, the new mystery man's identity had remained under their radar.

This was S.A.S.S.'s main problem with fighting an enemy who wasn't fighting for a cause. GRID operatives fought for greed, and Thomas Kunz kept them well fed and dumb. With that, they were happy.

Considering what they were doing—selling weapons to anyone with the money to buy them and who'd pay for them in the cursed American dollar—being in the dark probably helped some of them sleep better at night. Unfortunately for Kate's side, it also meant anyone who wanted money could be an enemy, and that left the door open to Kunz recruiting a lot anonymous people with no history or previous arrests to help tag them. "Well?" she asked Gaston again.

"It was an emergency extraction, Kate." Gaston looked half embarrassed, half furious. "Moss was suspicious of me. He has been for a while, but when I lost the black box, that was proverbial nail in my coffin."

"Meaning?"

"He took his suspicious up the ranks to a guy named Marcus Sandross."

Already, Kate didn't like this. She'd never heard of the man. "Who is he?"

"Kunz's new right-hand man. I don't know where he came from. Interpol had nothing on him. All I can tell you about him is that he's so vicious he makes Paul Reese look like a gentle kid that played at being a terrorist."

That rattled Kate. Paul Reese had been a greedy, blood-thirsty bastard. A coward himself, but he could sure issue the orders for others to commit horrendous atrocities.

Gaston leaned closer, then dropped his voice even lower. "The first day Sandross was with my cell, he killed three operatives."

Was that unusual? Gaston's tone made it seem extremely out of the ordinary. "For what?"

Gaston sent her a look that said it didn't really matter. Sandross would have used any excuse; he was establishing himself as a hard-ass. "One wasn't paying attention when he was talking. Another slumped while standing in formation. The third one happened at lunch. A guy spilled a glass of water. Sandross shot him and kept right on eating."

Definitely making a point. This guy needed to be reported to Home Base. Kate added it to her mental list, which was unfortunately getting to be quite lengthy. Considering it prudent, she'd restricted comments on the chopper to the urgent and essential.

Studying the faces of the men around her, she wondered if Darcy had come across anything in the intel reports on this Sandross guy. "Do you have art?" she asked, seeking a photo of the man.

"No. Kunz is more than a little camera shy. Carrying one inside GRID is an automatic death penalty. I couldn't risk it with Moss already suspicious. But I've reported a physical."

"What is it?"

"Medium height, medium weight and build, medium-brown hair and eyes. No visible scars or other identifying marks."

"Hell, you're describing half of the men in the U.S., Gaston." Frustration crawled through Kate. Why did it seem the bad guys got all the breaks? "There has to be something distinct about him."

"There is," Gaston agreed. "His temper." Worried, and not bothering to hide it, Gaston looked over at Kate. "I only know one other man alive who loves to kill as much as this guy, Kate. Only one."

Disgust rippled through her, turned the taste on her tongue bitter. "Thomas Kunz."

Gaston nodded.

Kate remembered Nathan finding the black box in the water outside the cave, the red bow wrapped around it. "You made sure Forester found the C-273."

"If the C-273 is that black box near the cave, then yeah. Well, actually, I was making sure you found it. I knew you'd be back for it." Gaston smiled. "The red ribbon was a nice touch, don't you think?"

"Hmm." She'd thought Kunz was lording it over her actually. "So GRID didn't get access to it?" Kate was afraid to dream it.

Gaston shook his head. "I was pulling guard duty, posted outside the cave. I saw you attach the box to the rocks. I went back and removed it. That's what landed me in hot water with Moss. When you went into the cave, I didn't warn him. I thought you might get lucky and take him and Parton out, since there were only two of them."

She nearly had. Unfortunately, Moss had escaped with a gut wound. "You were on the boat that chased me?" Kate didn't know how to feel about that, so she just waited to hear his explanation.

"No, I was dragging Parton's dead ass back to a second boat."

"The one dropping the mines."

"I don't think so."

Then there were three GRID vessels out there and yet she and Forester hadn't seen any of them. They could've come and gone while they were under water, though, so that need not be significant. "Is there a GRID compound at the other end of that cave?"

"Maybe," Gaston admitted. "I honestly don't know. I've never been allowed anywhere near it. Today is the first day I've been permitted to dive there, and it wouldn't have happened now except that Sandross got the flu." Gaston shrugged, lifted his palms upward. "You know how tight Kunz holds the reins. No one knows anything about an operation—even when it's over. Only what's essential for their part in the current mission."

Kate leaned against the wall of the chopper, letting the vibrations massage the exhausted muscles in her back.

"So if you weren't there, working at the compound, what were you doing?"

Again, Gaston checked to make sure no one was listening. They weren't. The men were busy gabbing between themselves and keeping an eye out down below. It was post-mission decompression. Premission, they'd been in focus mode. You'd have been able to hear a pin drop. Now, the drone of chatter combated the drone of the chopper props.

"Two suspected GRID operatives were aboard a vessel the Navy searched late this afternoon," Gaston said. "Before word came down through the chain of command to hold them, the men were gone. They disappeared not far from where we found you. No sign of another vessel, no sign of them in the water. They just weren't there anymore."

Divers intercepted them, she figured. What else could it be? She asked the clean-faced guy for a drink of water and then looked back at Gaston. "So you've had a busy twenty-four hours, too."

"Oh, yeah." The bags under his eyes proved it.

Still not sure she had Gaston and not a double, she held back, keeping her distance and her information to herself. But she thought she knew now who had attacked her and Nathan in his tent.

Red ribbon on the box. Red scarf.

Black box found and returned in the water. Black box supposedly stolen from the compound. Douglas hadn't done it to prove he'd changed sides. Gaston had fired on her and Nathan.

The question was, had he meant to kill them?

The tent pole had been cut in two near the top of the tent, but nearly everything inside had been shattered and destroyed. Still, the gunman had fired a lot of rounds into the sand, endangering no one.

"Commander Forester and I will check things out," she said, reserving opinion until she had time to absorb all the facts. "I'll let you know if we come up with anything."

Still unconvinced that Gaston truly was Gaston, she searched for a way to prove it, and finally lighted on one. She dropped her voice yet another pitch and then put him to the test. "Exactly where are we?"

"Don't answer that." Nathan glared down at her, not bothering to even pretend to be subtle or not be disappointed. "You know better, Kate."

She hadn't heard him return. Now he towered over her. She glared at him. She did know better, which meant he should have given her credit and known she had a damn good reason for asking.

"Walked right into the middle of that one, Kane." Gaston laughed. "Not that I could tell you, anyway."

Anger heated her neck and flooded her face. She shrugged and slid Forester a chilly half smile. "No offense, Major. Just doing my job."

He wasn't amused, and still didn't see that she'd had just cause for requesting the information. "Ask again," he said, "and I'll do mine and court-martial your ass."

Gaston grumbled a curse.

Kate turned up the wattage on her smile. "Don't worry," she told him. "The major and I actually get along very well. We have a lot in common."

Nathan looked more stunned than Gaston.

By a hair, Gaston managed to keep his chin up off the floor. "You're kidding."

He clearly remembered that Kate didn't get along well with anyone. She always held back and went it alone. She was damn prickly around other people, and Gaston as well as most others thought she liked it that way. Truthfully, she did. Alone was safer. She was used to it. And being just like every other human being on the planet, she liked what she felt most comfortable with. Everyone opted for whatever felt normal. Not that Gaston or anyone else knew what her normal was like, or ever would know. "Kidding? Me?" She gave him a look that said he should know better. "No, I'm not kidding. Not at all." She spared Forester a look laced with unbridled challenge. "Isn't that right, Major?"

Nathan looked mortified and, considering his policy about female subordinates, she imagined he was mortified. Apparently the few breaches he'd indulged in with her weren't destined for public knowledge. "Um, yeah. Absolutely. We have a lot in common."

Definitely uneasy as hell. But he covered for her. And Kate decided right then that he might be a pig, but he was a pig who'd stepped over his own personal/professional line to back her up.

It was the nicest thing any man had ever done for her.

And that she was deeply touched was also a secret that would never be told.

The last twinkles of dusk lay on the sand at the outpost. The temperature was cooling, as it did at night, and the wind was no more than a gentle stir.

Men with shovels were scattered throughout the encampment, still digging out from the storm, hollowing the drifts that blocked tent openings and the shower stall. Walking by with Nathan at her side, she glanced over. Sand had blown inside and half covered the waist-high spigot.

Nathan's order for the men to prepare to bug out hadn't been ignored. Everywhere Kate looked, there were stacks of boxes. But moving day apparently hadn't yet arrived in the form of orders coming down from headquarters reassigning the unit to a new location. The outpost was functioning on a war footing, meaning it was ready, willing and able to exercise any interdiction orders that might come in.

Near the command post, Nathan slowed his steps. "Kate?"

He'd been awfully quiet since they'd left the chopper. She looked over at him and waited.

A frown creased his brow and he shoved a fist into his pocket. "What do we have in common?"

"What?" He sounded odd, maybe even a little wistful, though it was hard to imagine Nathan Forester wistful. She didn't have to imagine that he felt he was under pressure about this, though. His left eye's twitching proved it.

That surprised Kate. "Oh, you're talking about what I told Gaston on the chopper."

"Well, yes." Nathan's frown deepened and his footsteps slowed even more. "I am."

She let him see amusement in her eyes, turned her voice caustic and laced it with sarcasm. "One thing comes right to mind. It isn't pretty, but it's accurate, I think."

That had him curious, and she preferred that over wistful. "More often than not, we want to shoot each other."

He stared at her a long second, then chuckled. "I should have known."

"Gee, Nathan. You look relieved." She feigned a frown, but her heart wasn't in it. "If I were the sensitive type, I'd think you didn't like anything about me."

"But you're not." He stopped outside the command post. "So, being a nonsensitive type, what do you think?"

"Truthfully, I have no idea." He was a complicated man. Who could decipher him? And around him, she felt complicated, too. "Sometimes I think we connect. Sometimes I feel like we're from different planets. But most of the time, I just don't know what to think."

"Neither do I," he confessed. "You annoy me, Kate. Actually, you infuriate me—and you rub my nerves raw."

That hurt. More than it should. "Don't hold back, Forester. Tell me what's really on your mind."

He stilled, stared at her long and hard, then sighed as if he had just gotten godawful news. "I like you."

Her heart seemed to stop, then skipped a little in her chest and ricocheted off her ribs. "Annoyance, infuriate, rub raw nerves…" She repeated his words back to him. "Goodness, with all those wonderful attributes, how could you not like me?" She waved an expansive hand, more than a little ticked off. "Hell, it could be love."

He had the grace to blush. "You don't understand, Kate." Staring at the ground, he turned serious, then looked up at her, letting the truth shine openly in his eyes. "I really like you."

He did. She felt the truth of it ripple across the distance between them and seep into her body, filling it full. She willed her heart to jumpstart and felt it thump with a pinch of relief. Now definitely wasn't the time to die from heart failure. No man had liked her, not like this. Alan had wanted her, he'd desired her, but he hadn't liked her because he couldn't control her. Nathan didn't want to control her. He just wanted her.

This was new and different—and scary as hell. "I like you, too."

Nathan's expression clouded and closed. "Don't."

"Excuse me?"

"Don't, Kate," he warned her. "I don't want to like you or any other woman ever again."

His wife. Some pains were too deep to ever heal. "I see." It figured. He was still married to her in heart and mind. She'd known that. So why had she been so stupid as to let him get under her skin.

As if she'd really had a choice?

Hell, he'd waylaid her. That's what he'd done. He'd made deliberate moves to sidetrack her, to focus her defenses on work, and then, *bam!* Waylaid her with the personal stuff.

Nathan watched her reaction and obviously didn't like it. "Just gauging by your expression, I don't think you see at all." He seemed to be standing on really shaky ground emotionally, and he clearly hated it. "I know I don't."

"That makes it challenging for you to explain it then, but I'd appreciate it if you'd give it a shot."

"Have you ever loved a man, Kate? Really loved him?"

She could lie. If she had any sense, she would lie. But the idea of lying to Nathan, especially about this, seemed beyond offensive. It seemed repugnant. "No, actually I haven't."

"Then I can't explain. It's like trying to describe color to someone who can't see, or sound to someone who can't hear. I'm a simple man, Kate. I'm just not gifted enough to be able to do that."

Simple? There was nothing simple about Nathan Forester.

Riley came barreling out of the command post tent. "Sir?"

Nathan swung around. "Is it Douglas?"

Riley stopped so fast he dropped his pen from his clipboard. "No, sir," he said, genuine apology in his tone.

"There's been no sign of him anywhere." Riley grabbed his pen, then changed topics. "Headquarters is on the horn for you, sir. They say we're to stay put."

Nathan grunted his disbelief. "Did you tell them we're doing time as sitting ducks in a GRID shooting gallery?"

"Yes, sir." Riley held the pen poised above his board, awaiting a stream of orders. "HQ said to sit tight for now. This comes straight from Secretary Reynolds."

Nathan glanced over at Kate. "Thank you, Captain Kane."

"Hey, it's not my fault."

"Did you file a report on the compound?"

"The potential compound, of course."

"Like I said, thank you, Captain Kane." Nathan walked off, toward the command post's tent flap. "And welcome to the shooting gallery."

He stepped inside and his voice carried back out. "Riley! Get in here and get me Search and Rescue on the line."

Riley shot Kate a "sorry" look, then disappeared inside the tent.

"Pig." But at least his major concern was Douglas. That redeemed Nathan a bit in her eyes. Still, she muttered a little more on the walk to her tent.

First, she contacted Home Base. Maggie took the report and then got Darcy on the line. In her mind's eye, Kate could see Darcy sitting alone in a room that deprived her of noise and other sensory input, files stacked three deep on her desk. Worldwide intelligence reports, all of which she would read and put into perspective with all the others, choose what significance each one bore, and who needed to know.

They dispensed with the courtesies, caught up quickly on events and then Kate asked Darcy about Marcus Sandross.

"Not a word on him has crossed my desk."

The instant recognition she'd hoped for didn't come. "Strange." A GRID member, okay. She could understand never having heard of him. But a second-in-command replacement for Reese. He couldn't be a rookie. They should have something on him.

"Very strange," Darcy agreed. "I can't believe he's that high in GRID's organization and he's stayed under our radar. You'd think someone somewhere would have something on the guy. It just doesn't make sense."

"Well, I guess there's no rule that says it has to, but I'd hoped it would." Good thing sense wasn't a requirement, considering. "See what you can find out for me, okay?" She paused and then switched topics. "Now, what about Gaston?"

"Officially, there is no Gaston. He doesn't come up on anything, anywhere. No computer entry, nothing. We don't officially know he exists."

This could be great news. If they didn't officially know he existed, then neither did GRID. Net result: Gaston had no double. But Maggie had said *officially*. "What about unofficially?"

"He's in a unit under presidential lock and key called S.A.S.S. Confidential. No intermediaries and no influence. It's them and the president. That's it. Simply put, it doesn't exist."

Neither did S.A.S.S. so this didn't amaze Kate, but the name being so similar tossed her for a loop. "Modeled after us?"

"And adapted to the special needs of the CIA." Darcy

grunted, amused. "Imitation is the finest form of flattery and all that rot."

"What does S.A.S.S. Confidential do?" Kate dropped onto her bed, hoping she got a grip on this soon. Her head was starting to throb.

"Anything it must do to protect our national security interests. Discreetly. Quietly. And always without notice."

"Pretty much on our footing." Kate rubbed at her left temple, trying to convince the jackhammer banging away inside it to knock it off. "So how are we different? Why not just bring the unit into S.A.S.S."

"Nonmilitary, my dear. Whole different set of rules. They're CIA. Limited to protecting our interests outside the country."

"Okay, so the official call is it's safe to assume he's okay and not a double."

"Officially or unofficially?"

Kate sighed. She couldn't help it. "Both?"

"Officially, no. It's not safe to assume anything," Darcy said. "Unofficially, your orders are to trust your instincts."

They were honed from her years of field experience, but this order ticked her off. If her instincts were wrong, she'd be left hanging out to dry alone. "S.A.S.S. has no official position?"

"Afraid not. The colonel was specific. She's relying on your instincts."

The latitude intended to be a show of support had now become a liability. But Kate couldn't have it both ways and that sealed the envelope on the matter. "Got it."

"I spent a few hours checking out the coordinates you beamed up, and did a fairly thorough study of the topography. I'm guessing there are a substantial number of air pockets in the caves that most interest you. Ran a few diagnostics and those pockets stretch quite high into the hills. Not high enough to get nosebleeds, but certainly above water level. You might want to run a complete check there for your missing man."

"Will do," Kate said. "Anything else?"

"Just one thing. Insignificant really, but our friend insisted I pass it on."

Kate braced, all too familiar with Amanda's insignificant messages. "She said to tell you she's having a banana split—double chocolate syrup and extra nuts."

Kate's stomach growled and her mouth watered. Her favorite food in the whole world. Banana splits with extra chocolate and nuts—and Amanda's way of telling her everything was going well with her and Mark Cross. Like Kate, he had no family to speak of, so years earlier they'd pseudo adopted each other, though they'd both kept most details of their lives to themselves. Still, it was a known body across a table at Christmas dinner, when that dinner wasn't pre-packaged meals being eaten in the field. She was thrilled Amanda and Mark were together. "Tell her she's a bitch," Kate said, knowing it was expected.

Darcy laughed. "That's exactly what she told me you'd say."

"Later." Kate paused, then pulled off the mike. Darcy was a good woman. Having perfect recall was a royal—and isolating—pain for her, but rather than taking a medical retirement, which she could have, she worked to keep S.A.S.S. informed. Definitely hard on her, but it had been a gift straight from heaven for the other members of S.A.S.S.

And maybe this time Darcy's recall and considerable talent for putting seemingly dissimilar bits of information together to gain the very insight needed to make all the puzzle pieces click into place would be just the magic needed to help Kate and Nathan.

And maybe it'd be the miracle needed to save Douglas.

Chapter 10

Kate returned to the command post and looked around. It was quiet inside, but then it usually was whenever the mess tent was noisy. When Kate had walked by it a few minutes ago, it had been hopping. Getting that fired up over powdered eggs just wasn't on her list of things she could easily do.

As expected, Nathan's cubicle was empty. Still, she scanned the tent, but he wasn't in the command post. Riley was seated at his desk, his nose buried in some report.

She walked over. "Hi, Riley."

"Ma'am." He looked up at her, his eyes glazed and not yet refocused. "Yes, ma'am."

"I need to see maps of the area where Douglas went missing. Preferably ones that chart water currents."

He looked up at her, wary and unsure of what to do. "Our location is classified, ma'am."

She stared straight into his lenses, though she couldn't see his eyes, only her own reflection, and didn't back down an inch. Let Nathan court-martial her ass. It'd be worth it. "Yes, it is. But if you don't get me those charts, by the time I can get to Captain Douglas, he might just be dead."

Torn, Riley's eyes stretched wide behind his rounded glasses. "But, ma'am, I have orders—"

"Riley, stop it." She'd had enough of this. "I'm declaring this a matter of national security. Code Two priority. Got it?" A stray thought hit her. "You know what a Code Two is, right?"

"Yes, ma'am." He shrugged. "Of course."

"Then get me the damn charts."

"Can you do that?" Riley looked over her shoulder obviously wishing Nathan would suddenly appear.

"Kramer said he's in the shower," she said, letting Riley know she was aware of what was on his mind. "But don't worry. I can do that, and your commander will have no objections to me reviewing the charts." At least, he wouldn't after she shared her last Home Base report with him.

"Yes, ma'am." Riley walked to the far end of the tent, skirted around a long, flat table and then opened a wooden crate full of rolled-up maps. "There you are, ma'am."

"Thank you." She turned away from him, bent down at the crate and went through the maps, not seeing anything inside that surprised her. Iraq. Iran. Kuwait. Pakistan. India. The Persian Gulf. Maps of all the countries surrounding the Gulf were rolled up inside.

She pulled the one on Iran, pressed it flat across the long table and started studying it, using Bubiyan Island as a point of beginning. It had been the insertion point on many a mission in the region. It was the perfect place for an outpost.

After giving the maps to her, Riley had eased out

through the tent flap, presumably, Kate sighed, headed toward the showers.

She couldn't blame him. When Nathan learned she knew their location, he would indeed be on a tear. But he'd have to get over it, just as Riley would have to get over his fear of Nathan's reaction. It was a shot at saving Douglas, and they could just accept it. Supposedly, the entire reasoning for keeping her blacked-out on knowing the location was to protect her. Well, she had no choice at this point but to take on any additional risks.

Putting them both out of her mind, she plotted Douglas's coordinates and focused on the current patterns.

The initial results looked promising. She worked another thirty minutes, and things still looked promising. She permitted herself to feel encouraged but no more. She'd been down this road before too many times and had the outlook turn on a dime and head south. Not on this. It was too important.

Another twenty minutes and she was still encouraged.

Unfortunately that's when Nathan came in, looking ready to kill. "Captain Kane."

"Don't bother, Nathan. I know the drill." She stood, crossed her chest with her arms and frowned. "Write me up, if that's what's in your mind to do. I'll even sign off on it. But give me a few minutes before you have me shipped off to the nearest brig. It looks like I'm on to something important."

"Excuse me?" He had a full head of steam and didn't look eager or even inclined not to unload it.

"Look." She pointed to the map. "Douglas went down here. Look at the proximity to the cave. I mentioned this when we were in the water, but it's even closer than I suspected then." She hoped he picked up on the potential

GRID cave without her having to mention it specifically. They were in the same spot. "There are air pockets inside. I've been there."

"What's your point?"

She looked up at him, hoping to hell she was right and not engaged in wishful thinking. "My point is that Douglas could be in there."

"In one of the air pockets?"

She nodded. "They were about to end the dive, right?"

"Yes, but—"

"He was low on oxygen." She shrugged. "What if he saw something and went to check it out? What if he got there and he didn't have enough oxygen to get back out?"

"He wouldn't do that. He was an experienced diver."

"What? Experienced divers can't make mistakes? Maybe he misread the gauge. Maybe he saw something he *had* to check out. Maybe he had to hide and didn't have a choice, Nathan. There could be a hundred reasons, but the only one that matters is that it's possible he's stuck in there without sufficient oxygen to get out." Her theory would have fallen apart of course if he'd gone missing at the beginning of the dive, but he hadn't. "According to the incident report, the team had less than five minutes left in the water before mandatory surfacing."

"It's possible." The starch went out of Nathan's shoulders and the heat left his voice. "He could've been lured there."

"Or trapped," Kate said, warming up to that theory. It seemed far more likely that Douglas had gone hunting and what he'd found had kept him pinned down and unable to move without being exposed to GRID. "Maybe when I came in, I surprised him. Maybe he observed the trouble between me and the two GRID agents and stayed put. Maybe he's still down there, waiting for us to rescue him."

"Sure are a lot of maybes in this, Kate. Supposition is rarely an asset in our line of work." Forester didn't dispute her, he just wasn't sure they'd made an accurate conclusion.

"True, but sometimes supposition is all we've got and it can lead us to the facts." She hated to be brutal, but this was a time to be totally frank. "His body should have surfaced by now, Nathan."

"Unless GRID has him."

"Unless GRID has him," she conceded. "But what if it doesn't? What if he's just stuck and waiting?"

"Do you really consider that possible?" Nathan grimaced, his finger tracing the points on the map. "Search and Rescue have every piece of electronic equipment known to man at their disposal, and they're using every resource they've got to locate Douglas. If *they* can't find him—"

"Nothing takes the place of human intelligence and you know it, Nathan." She pointed to the map. "Look at this." She let her fingertip flow over the paper, marking a trail on the map. "These caves are constantly flooded. We think GRID is off-loading illegal cargo at sea. Now look at the currents. They'd bring the weapons right up to the caves and they're heavy enough. They could be gouging the rocks."

"Weapons are heavy. They would sink," he said. "For Christ's sake, think, Kate. A crate of metal weapons wouldn't float."

"What if they didn't sink and they did float? What if GRID receives the weapons, moves them through the caves and then moves them out through the other side that's on dry land? From there, they could truck or fly them to the end buyer."

"The crates would've been seen at sea. The Navy would have gotten a visual."

"What if they didn't?"

He was losing patience fast. "It's pretty damn hard to hide crates of weapons floating in the gulf, Kate."

"But what if GRID somehow did it?" she persisted. "Look, you're thinking like a normal human being. Don't. Think like Thomas Kunz. He hid at least sixty men and women—high-ranking, top-level, security-clearance, card-carrying people—in plain sight. If he could do that, then he could find a way to move weapons, damn it."

"Okay, okay." The fight went out of Nathan. He lifted his hands, giving up on simple reason. "What do you want to do?"

"I want to explore these caves." She pointed to them on the map. "At dawn," she added. "That's when the current is strongest."

Forester stepped back from the table. Legs spread, he folded his arms across his chest. "And GRID is just going to let you walk in there and take a look around."

"Of course not." She stared up at Nathan, wondering if he'd be nonplussed or repulsed by what she next said. "I'm going to have to kill the men guarding the gate first. Then explore the caves."

"Oh, I see. That simple. You think?"

"That difficult," she contradicted him. "Which is why I need you to come with me."

"Kate, I'm good, but I'm not an expert diver. You need an expert."

She stared at him a long moment. "I don't need your diving skills, Nathan. I need someone to watch my back. But if you'd rather not, just say so. I can just as easily go in alone. I've done nearly everything in my life that way and watched my own back. I can certainly do it again now."

He gave her a stoic look. "Then why did you ask me?"

"Honestly, right now, I have no idea."

"Five minutes ago, then."

She looked up at him. "Because I trust you and I know what I'm walking into down there. I've infiltrated GRID compounds before." She shifted on her feet, half turned away from him. "Just forget it. I'm fine on my own."

"Whoa. Hold on." He softened his voice and clasped her arm. "I never said I wouldn't go, Kate. Only that one of my divers might be better."

"He can't."

"Kate, they're more experienced. They're the experts. I'm just the man who commands them."

"I said he can't, and I meant it."

"You're not listening. You don't know—"

"Yes, damn it, I do know." She exposed a stubborn streak a league long.

"How?"

Her gaze softened and she tilted her chin up to look him in the eye. "I know because it's you I trust, Nathan." It was hard to say and harder to feel. But it was right and it was time to say it out loud. Maybe then her feelings for him wouldn't seem so strong and powerful.

"Trust is a fragile thing," he said. "It shouldn't be put at risk needlessly."

She nodded.

"I could fail you, Kate."

"I could fail Douglas, too." She hiked her chin. "But just because I know that doesn't mean I'm not going to try."

Nathan's expression turned sour, but he didn't pop back with a witty or even a dry remark. "All right. You win, and

I hope to hell you don't regret it. I hope neither of us regrets it. At dawn we explore the caves."

She smiled, lifted a hand to his face and stroked his jaw, earlobe to chin. "Thank you."

He grunted, not at all happy with developments. "Thank me tomorrow—if we live."

Chapter 11

A shoe scuffed the dirt at the tent flap.

The noise startled Kate awake. *The gunman was back!*

Adrenaline rocketed through her veins, but she forced herself to stay still. A man. She smelled his sweat. He had feather-light footsteps, a short stride. At most, he had to be medium weight, medium height.

Curled up on her cot in her underwear, she eased her hand to the floor, retrieved her gun and then whipped around rapidly to take aim on his hulking shadow. "Hold it right there."

"Don't shoot, Kate! It's me." The man moved closer in. "Gaston."

"Are you stupid?" She blew out a rattled breath. "What the hell are you doing, sneaking around like some idiot rookie? You want to wake up dead?"

"I need to talk to you."

She turned on a battery-powered lantern that filled the

tent with a soft gold light. "Try knocking, for pity's sake." He'd scared ten years off her and nearly gotten himself killed. It was an outrageous mistake for a seasoned operative. "Never mind. Just tell me what you want."

He walked over, stopped short of a full approach. "I want to know why you're here."

"You sneak into my tent in the dead of night and risk getting shot to ask me *that?*"

"Yeah." Lean and wiry, he shoved his hands into his pockets, assuming a nonthreatening pose.

His sheared hair was nearly nonexistent. She hadn't noticed that earlier; he'd had on his hat. "I'm updating my diving certification. The instructors authorized to sign off on it are over here, so here I am." She lied, and didn't feel a second's worth of remorse about doing it.

Gaston clearly knew it. He pointed an irritated finger at her. "If you're here for GRID, I'm warning you, Kate. Stay out of my way. The last thing I need is you coming in now and screwing me up."

"Exactly what would I be screwing up?"

He clenched his jaw. "I hate it when you play dumb. You're not good at it." He wiped his hand across his head as if he still had hair. "I need those weapons."

"And I need the hostages—if they're here—*and* the weapons." Kate sat up, pulled the blanket over her legs and let her feet rest on the cool dirt floor. "Are the hostages here, Gaston?"

"I don't know. I haven't seen them, or heard anything about them being here." He shrugged and his jaw went tight. "Unfortunately that doesn't mean diddly squat. They could be right under my nose and I wouldn't know it because Sandross would kill anyone who mentioned it anywhere. Kunz's orders, of course."

Clearly, Gaston was being truthful. That level of bitterness was impossible to fake. You felt it or you didn't, and Gaston definitely felt it. "I shouldn't have to remind you that we're on the same side, you know."

"Listen, you haven't been here," he said. "You don't get the big picture, and I can't explain it. But if I don't get those weapons, I'm a dead man, Kate, and that's a fact."

She believed him. He was too shaken up for it to be anything but the truth. She pushed a hank of hair back from her face. "Who's going to kill you?"

Gaston shook his head, refusing to answer. He couldn't, or wouldn't, tell her. And that had suspicion rearing its ugly head, invading and nibbling at her. Regardless of what Darcy had said about Gaston not existing on paper, and because he didn't, Kunz wouldn't know of him to double him, Kate still had to double-check to make sure that the man standing in front of her wasn't a GRID double posing as Gaston.

One of the first intel secrets Kate learned was to never ask a question that she couldn't already answer. It was time to take that lesson out for a run and put it to the test. "Okay. Then tell me why it's okay for you to know the location of this outpost, and not me."

He hesitated before answering, then lifted a supplicating hand. "It's for your own protection, Kate. There's nothing more to it than that."

A flat-out lie—and he'd looked her right in the eye while doing it, too. "I don't believe you." She couldn't get more frank than that. "Try again."

He lifted his arms, palms up. "You can't tell what you don't know. I know you're assigned to S.A.S.S., and I know every S.A.S.S. mission carries lousy odds. It's almost statistically impossible that you'll complete this mission without being either captured or killed."

Kate took his comments in stride. He hadn't said anything she didn't already know, and he couldn't be more frank than that.

"That's enough, Gaston." A man's angry voice boomed from the door. "From everything I've seen, you're not doing a damn thing here to make her odds any better. All you're worried about is covering your own ass." Nathan walked into the tent, looked from Gaston to Kate, and radically altered his tone from outraged to concerned. "Do you need anything?"

Clothes would be nice, since it appeared they were going to have a midnight convention in her tent. But she couldn't very well ask for those. "I don't think so, thanks." She tucked the edges of the blanket tighter around her thighs and studied Nathan, hoping he hadn't jumped to the conclusion that Gaston had been here all night. But he didn't seem in the least surprised to find Gaston in her tent. The trip wire. Gaston must have set it off. The only logical reason Nathan knew he was here, Kate surmised. "Gaston was just leaving."

"Ah, good." Nathan got between the man and the exit and looked down at him. "Don't make the mistake again of coming into this tent during the night. If Kate doesn't shoot you, I will."

"Back off, Commander," Gaston said. "I needed to talk with her."

"Fine. Then talk outside, preferably during decent hours—unless you're in a life-threatening situation." Nathan crossed his arms. "Are you in a life-threatening situation, Gaston?"

He rocked foot to foot, pissed but not willing to overtly cross Nathan in his own outpost. Here, he ruled. "Not at the present moment, no."

Nathan had a satisfied look on his face that amused Kate and frosted Gaston. "Well, then, there's no reason for you to be here." His jaw tightened. "Good night."

Summarily dismissed and totally peeved about it, Gaston turned to leave, but he couldn't resist firing off a parting shot. "Don't forget what I said, Kate."

She stared at him and said nothing.

He left the tent, and when the flap closed behind him, she looked at Nathan. "Are you in a life-threatening situation, Nathan?"

"Around you?" he asked. "Always."

"Commander?" Riley called from outside.

Kate let out a huffy sigh. "Doesn't anyone sleep in this damn unit?"

"Sorry to disturb you, ma'am." That from Riley, standing on the other side of the tent, who then added, "General Shaw will call back in forty-five minutes, sir."

"Thanks, Riley. I'll be there. Put on a pot of coffee, will you?"

"Yes, sir." The sound of Riley's retreating footsteps faded.

General Shaw? Kate's boss, Colonel Drake, answered to General Shaw. He was in her chain of command, not Nathan's. So what was going on here? And why had Kate been omitted from the need-to-know loop? She hiked her eyebrows, silently putting the question to Nathan.

He ignored it and walked over to her cot. "Mind if I sit down?"

Surprised he had deviated yet again from his distance policy and stayed in her tent, Kate nodded that she didn't mind.

He sat beside her. The cot creaked under his weight and the scent of his soap tickled her nose. "You said you trusted me, Kate. Well, the truth is, I trust you, too." He looked up from the floor to her. "It's time."

"Time for what?" She wasn't playing coy. She didn't have a clue what he was talking about.

"For full disclosure," he said, asking her to enlighten him in a roundabout way uncommon to him.

Normally, Nathan Forester was very direct. But coupling Douglas's disappearance with Gaston's comments about her survival odds, would give Nathan serious concerns. For one thing, he was her host, responsible for her, and for another, he had full disclosure authorization. There was no valid reason for her not to tell him everything. And she trusted him.

Until now, she had disclosed topical bits she had felt compelled to disclose. But now, with everything that was happening, it was time for her to fill in the substantial gaps she'd deliberately left in place.

"Okay," she said. "Full disclosure. But, Nathan, swear to me you'll never make me regret this. I'll believe you because you've proven that you're a good man. Still, I want your word."

"You've got it, Kate."

"On Emily's soul," she said, looking him right in the eye, knowing that any vow Nathan Forester made that put his dead wife's soul on the line was a vow he'd never break.

"On Emily's soul."

Satisfied, Kate licked at her dry lips and started at the beginning. She put all the proverbial cards on the table. Disclosed everything about Thomas Kunz. About witnessing the remnants of some of his tortured victims. About Amanda being taken hostage and doubled, and running into the woman face-to-face in a GRID replica of her apartment that matched her real one down to the brand of salt in the kitchen cabinet. All of her things—even her toothbrush and articles of clothing—had been duplicated and put in their proper place.

Kate told him about the sensory-deprivation chambers and the surgical clinics discovered in the three GRID compounds S.A.S.S. already had taken down. The clinics that were better equipped than most top-notch U.S. hospitals. And with a hitch in her chest and a knot in her throat, Kate told Nathan about a nanny named Rosalita, who loved Jeremy, a child not even her own, so much she had sacrificed her life to save him and his parents, Dr. Joan Foster and her husband, Simon.

And the more Kate told Nathan, the more there seemed to be to tell, including S.A.S.S. fears that there were many more GRID compounds scattered throughout the world, many more doubled operatives already inserted into positions within the government that would be nearly impossible to expose. She told him specifics that S.A.S.S. had discovered about the people doubled, that the doctor, Joan Foster, a victim herself, had used psychological warfare techniques, including memory manipulation, to prepare GRID doubles for their roles as U.S. employees. It was a comprehensive process so successful that even the doubles didn't know that they were doubles unless Kunz wanted them to know.

Nathan listened intently, not once interrupting Kate, but his expression grew more solemn by degree, more grim with each disclosure. And while Kate talked, she imagined how hard it would be to assimilate all of this at once. Even aware that Black World operations had held the technology to do all of these things for years, that someone would deliberately subvert that technology and use it for such inhuman purposes would slay Kate.

Clearly, it bothered Nathan, too, and that made his assimilation of all the nasty tentacles in this even more challenging. Watching him, his body language, the look in his eyes turn from haunted to bleak, she realized how much of an advantage it had been to learn of all these things in segments. And she wanted to say something to let him know she understood the difficulty for him. "Nathan." She pressed her hand lightly against his forearm. "This truly is a complex mission. It has more facets than a cut diamond, and that makes it enormously complicated."

"Yes," he softly agreed. "It certainly does."

"But it's not hopeless." Her mouth dry, she licked at her lips. "The minute we give in and feel hopeless, that's the minute Thomas Kunz wins. If he wins with us, what will he do to the rest of the world? We're the last superpower, Nathan. If we can't stop him, no one can. So we don't dare to feel hopeless or helpless. It's just too high a price for all of us to pay."

He stared at her a long second, then blinked hard three times in rapid succession. His expression remained grim, but it wasn't horror that reflected in his eyes now. It was resolve. "What about GRID itself? I know the basics. Fill in the blanks for me. How does it operate?"

Relieved by his change in attitude, Kate relayed everything she remembered about GRID's structure and organizational philosophy. Like every other S.A.S.S. member who learned to what extent greed drove GRID, Nathan was repulsed. And when she told him about GRID's new second-in-command, Marcus Sandross, Nathan didn't bother to hide his contempt.

"It's hard to believe any man could justify what they're doing in his own mind."

She agreed. "Dr. Joan Foster, our psyche specialist,

says they don't try. She's convinced Kunz knows right from wrong, he just doesn't consider that perspective in his decision-making. He wants what he wants and that's all he wants. For him, that's where it ends."

Nathan's brows shot up on his forehead. "He can't be pushing that perspective to recruits. It doesn't make sense to a rational person, not even one motivated by greed."

His deduction was insightful, and correct. Kate shared with him the tripe Kunz fed new recruits. "One man's terrorist is another man's liberator."

Nathan rolled his eyes. "But for him, it is all about money."

"Absolutely. Money can liberate, Nathan," Kate said. "Kunz was an abuse victim, remember? With money, he's not reliant on any other human being to fulfill his basic needs or his desires. Maggie says he equates having money to being free."

"That makes a twisted kind of sense. But the costs of that kind of freedom, you would think, would make it clear it's a false premise."

Kate countered. "Not to him. To him it holds together just fine."

"Which is why we're in the spot we're in."

"According to Maggie, yes," Kate said. Then going beyond what she knew, she did something totally alien to her. Something she could never remember doing before in her life. Something she could hardly believe she was doing now.

She shared with Nathan her personal fear.

Fear that, through his doubles, Kunz would compromise the country, that he would successfully destroy the economy, that he would kill not hundreds or thousands, but millions of Americans.

And encouraged by quiet acceptance, his receptive concern for all she revealed, she took a huge leap of faith and revealed her greatest fear of all.

That she would try her best and still fail to stop him.

Nathan's shoulders slumped, he leaned forward, bracing his hands on his knees, his feet on the floor. "Do you think the Kunz you saw here is the real Thomas Kunz, Kate?"

"Nathan, I—"

"If he is, then you have to know Gaston is probably right. Going toe-to-toe with Kunz…he'll likely kill you."

"It's not out of the realm." She had accepted that long ago.

Nathan clasped her hands in his. "I'm not ready for you to die."

She squeezed his hand hard, amazed at how comforting it felt to have someone so strong and capable of crushing her bones, be so gentle with her. "I don't want to die, Nathan. I'm not a martyr or a saint. But I can't know all of this and not do something. It's my job. It's the way of life I chose to live."

"You didn't answer my question."

She thought back, remembered the question. "I don't know if he's the real Thomas Kunz. I can't know that without a DNA test. He's done very well substituting records, and his plastic surgeons do nothing short of brilliant work. The saving grace is that it's difficult to change someone's voice. You can get close, but it's impossible to get a perfect voice print match. Yet he's substituted some of those records, too."

"Then what's left?" Nathan looked outdone.

"Not much," she admitted. "We have an accurate DNA on him and an accurate intel audio intercept. I've studied that audio intensely, Nathan, and the man I heard here sounded like the real Thomas Kunz. Inflections, phraseology—all of it. But he's been too damn cunning too many times for me to believe it without hard evidence proving it."

Nathan dropped his gaze for a long moment, working through all she'd told him. Finally, he finished processing, then said, "With all those substitutions, even hard evidence has to be treated as suspect. And Gaston was right about something else, too. Your not knowing your current location is for your own protection."

Nathan dropped his voice, his tone calm but serious. "The CIA and Navy are involved in this, Kate. They know our location, but they have the protection of working in teams. You work alone. As your host, I have a responsibility to you. You need every edge that I can give you." He paused, turned to her on the cot, lifted an unsure hand and stroked her face as if she were the most fragile thing he never touched. "As a man, I need to give you more, and it's killing me that I can't."

She cupped her hand over his. "I'm a big girl, and a professional. I can take care of myself."

"I don't doubt that. But what I'm feeling has nothing to do with your abilities, or your job. It has to do with you, the woman. Is it so hard to believe that a man who cares about you wants you to be safe?"

Kate wasn't sure she wanted to answer that. In fact, she was certain she didn't want to answer. But the worry in his eyes was for her, and that was a rare gift she couldn't ignore and wouldn't pretend didn't exist. "Yes, honestly speaking, it is hard for me to believe."

He stood, turned back around to look at her, his arms at his sides. "Are you married?"

"Why?" What difference could that possibly make?

"Just answer the question, Kate."

"No." She shrugged. "I'm not married, never have been married, and likely never will be married." She wondered if she was the only woman in the world whose parents didn't nudge her to the altar to provide them with grandchildren. Her parents likely wouldn't notice any grandchildren existed until their college graduation. She should be sad about that, but frankly, she'd grown too accustomed to their indifference to waste the energy.

"Good."

"Good?" That she'd never been and likely never would be married?

Nathan Forester smiled. A wide, open, genuine smile that lit up his face and warmed her heart. "I don't know how to play games. I don't want to learn." He paced the length of her cot, rubbing the back of his neck, his left eye doing that telltale twitch. "The truth is, you're the first woman who's fascinated me since I met my wife. She still fascinated me the day she died." He paused and really looked at Kate. "Emily would have liked you a lot, Kate."

Confusion rippled through her. "Is that why you like me? Because Emily would have?"

"No, of course not. But I trusted her judgment. She had an uncanny way of seeing through the garbage right into the souls of people."

So it was a respect issue for him. Kate liked it that he had respected his wife and her judgment. So many men talked their wives down when they weren't around. She hated that. Nathan was relying on what he found comfortable, but his feelings for Kate were all his own. And that was what she most needed to know.

She stood, letting the blanket fall away, and walked

over to him, stopping so close that she had to crane her neck to look up at him. "I'm not into games, either. I've never been inclined to play them, and I've rarely cared enough about a man to want to bother." She lifted her arms, curled them around his neck and whispered close to his chin. "I'm going to kiss you, Nathan. If you don't want me to, you'd better tell me now."

Nathan swallowed hard. "Tell me you didn't walk back from the shower dressed like that."

Kate smiled and captured his lips in a kiss that was soulful and searing, sweet and seductive.

He shuddered against her, pulled her closer, winding his arms tightly around her. "I'm taking that as a no," he whispered against her lips, and then deepened the kiss.

Kate wasn't prepared for her reaction, for the weakening of muscle and melting of bone. She had kissed and been kissed, but this…this was more. Different. Enticing, exciting and terrifying. Each cell seemed to awaken and take him in, and while she loved the sensations, the liquid heat, the fire thrumming through her veins, she worried, too.

Having once known this kiss, would she ever again be content with less?

Chapter 12

Shortly after dawn, Kate and Nathan climbed into the jeep and headed for the shore. Not a word had been mentioned about their kiss last night, though Kate had had trouble holding two thoughts together about anything else ever since. What should she make of that?

Mulling it over, she was almost convinced it was best forgotten and definitely safer. Feeling a little pang of disappointment, she looked off toward the sandy horizon and allowed herself a wistful sigh. Some things should be mourned.

Nathan reached over, clasped her hand and brought it to his lips.

A warm glow lighted in her chest and spread to settle low in her belly. Her breathing hitched. Why would anyone choose to forget these tender moments? They were the jewels in life, all the more rare because she knew that, and she'd known so damn few of them. She couldn't forget that or this moment, and neither could be best forgotten.

Acknowledged or not, rare moments are still treasures and a jewel still gleams.

"You okay?" Nathan asked.

"Yeah. Never better." Meaning every word, Kate smiled.

When they pulled in at the docks, Riley had the boat ready and waiting, as promised. After another scan for bugging devices and explosives, Kate dumped in her gear, while Nathan removed the mooring ropes. She slipped behind the wheel, cranked the engine and, when Nathan was seated, headed out across the open water for the caves.

Looking for Douglas was dangerous and she wasn't fooling herself about that. But the sun sparkling on the calm water, seeing Nathan in the seat beside her, his hair slicked back by the wind, his face lifted to the sun…well, there was a moment of joy here, too, that had nothing to do with premission anxiety. She didn't have the slightest inclination to flirt, though she wouldn't object to another kiss. Yet considering how her body had reacted to Nathan, maybe that was wisest left for after their mission—a reward for surviving.

"I'm going to give them a little space," she warned Nathan. Best to see how GRID would react to their return away from the cave where they could have a stash to protect.

"You're not going to lull them into complacency, Kate."

"I know that," she told Nathan. "But we need to explore the vicinity. What if all the mines were a diversionary tactic?"

Nathan thought for a second and then answered. "Doubtful, but better to *know it* than to *suppose it.*"

Her feelings exactly. She'd bet her next paycheck it'd be question three or four on Colonel Drake's list.

Within an hour, they were in the water and meticulously exploring several caves. When they'd gone through half a dozen and run only into dead ends, Nathan tugged at her sleeve and pointed skyward.

Kate kicked upward, broke the surface and caught her breath. They'd found nothing. No gouges, no open passages, no signs of any type of inhabitation.

"Have we taken sufficient precautions to satisfy S.A.S.S.?"

Kate nodded.

"Then let's press on and check out the compound cave."

More than ready to do so, Kate swam for the boat. "Better make sure the minesweepers have done their thing." If not the mines, Kunz and Sandross would have something else waiting for them. She'd brought as much gear with her as possible, trying to prepare for anything. But the bottom line was, she could never prepare for everything. Her stomach gave a little lurch as she climbed into the boat.

Within minutes Nathan radioed Riley, who in turn relayed for the necessary verifications from the sweepers. When Riley got them, he'd report back.

"Okay," Nathan said. "He's on it."

"Good." Riley was a gem, too, and Nathan clearly knew it.

It seemed relatively apparent that Douglas had been hijacked and wouldn't be found unless GRID wanted him found. Though without hard evidence, she had no choice but to keep an open mind. His drowning remained a possibility, just as it remained a possibility that her theory was on target and he had been lured into the cave when low on oxygen and had gotten stranded.

When she assessed the facts objectively, any of the three possibilities were viable. Of them, she considered Douglas's drowning to be the most remote and GRID snatching him to be the most likely, though it chilled her down to the marrow of her bones.

Riley radioed Nathan. "Sir, verification just came in. The minesweepers have finished mopping up. You're good to go."

"Thanks." Nathan turned to her. "We've got the all-clear."

Kate hit the throttle, steering the boat toward the knuckle of land above the cave. "Where is everyone?" she asked Nathan. "Has the search for Douglas been officially called off?"

"No. General Shaw ordered all units to take up distant positioning."

"Why?" And why hadn't Home Base relayed the order to her?

"He wants GRID to consider everything business as usual."

Kate guffawed. "Nathan, that's absurd. Kunz and Sandross aren't going to buy into that. I was in the damn cave leading to the compound and they know it."

"And you killed Parton and gut-wounded Moss," Nathan said. "Yes, I know."

"Well, nothing is going to take their focus off that."

"I know that, too." Nathan frowned. "The only thing I can figure is the secretary has some other information that we don't have. That, or his synapses are misfiring, in which case, we have more serious problems than just this."

Kate accepted the inevitable and obeyed the order. Nathan's agreeing with her helped take out some of the sting. Steering left, she passed the big rock that had saved her neck when outrunning GRID the first time she'd explored the cave. On the far side of it, she tapped the throttle to idle the engine and checked her position relative to the compound cave. Anyone guarding the mouth of the cave from the water near it wouldn't see the boat.

Nathan double-checked her, then dropped anchor.

Within fifteen minutes they were suited up and in the water. Another twenty and they were near the rocks where she'd first seen the gouges. The spiking temperature hovered at the hundred and ten degree mark, but the water felt cold.

"Nathan, take a look at this." She pointed to that same telltale section of rock she'd first noticed. "Fresh gouges."

Nathan swam over for a closer look. Treading water, he backstroked hard to keep the water from pushing him into the rocks. "Current's really strong here."

"Strong enough to pull something heavy into the rocks?"

"Oh, yeah. No doubt about it." He ran his fingers over the face of the gouged section above the waterline where the rocks were dry, then slung crumbled bits from his fingers into the frothy white water. "These weren't here yesterday. High tide would have taken the water up. It would have cleaned out any loose particles of rock."

It would have. Kate swam out a little, retrieved her binoculars from her fanny pack and zoomed in for a closer look higher up on the rocks. "Wait. Nathan, there are new gouges above those, too." A bubble of getting close to something burst low in her belly. "Maybe whatever gouged the rocks came in *with* the tide."

"Weapons are too heavy to float. We've considered that. And anything substantial enough to float weapons would be so buoyant it wouldn't gouge the rocks, it'd bounce off them."

Valid point. Damn it. *Something* was here, just waiting for her to find it. Kate felt it in her bones.

Fighting the current was wearing Nathan down. He stroked back over to her, his breathing a little labored. "Didn't you say that when you first went into the cave, Gaston had been outside it, pulling guard duty?"

"That's what he said, but I didn't see him." That rankled Kate, too. How had he watched her and remained unobserved? She'd been all over the area, above and below water. Surely she would've noticed something. Never before had her instincts been on hiatus when she was on full alert.

"Something's not making sense. GRID isn't going to guard the mouth of this cave 24/7, not unless something extremely important is in it. And if they were suspicious enough of Gaston to keep him out of the cave, then why have him guard it?"

"He said he was a last-minute substitution," Kate said. "Sandross got sick, so Gaston had to fill in."

"Is Gaston high up in the chain of command?"

"No, he isn't." Where exactly was Nathan going with this?

"Then to use him, they had to have been really short on manpower and feel they couldn't leave the mouth of the cave unguarded. Put that together with the fresh gouges and it means they had to have been waiting for something."

Kate followed his logic, expounded on it. "Or maybe that something was already inside." Could be Douglas or whatever had caused the gouges. "Maybe they knew Douglas had located the cave and feared he'd come back."

"Or they knew he came back and thought someone else could stumble on to the cave looking for him."

"Could be either—or neither. Could be whatever gouged the rocks needed protecting and Douglas hasn't been detected."

"Possible," Nathan agreed. "Especially since they didn't abduct the entire team. They might not have gotten Douglas."

The potentials were numerous and the facts to knock out erroneous ones were too few. A swell crested and hit Kate right in the face. She shook her head, slinging water, then hiked her chin to keep from getting popped again. "Let's take a look to see if we can find out what's in there."

Nathan shot her a level stare. "Technically, we're supposed to have backup Tactical with us."

"If Douglas was available, and your other teams weren't deployed, we would have backup Tactical. But we don't." She reminded him of the obvious. "GRID knows we're on to them, Nathan. I killed one of them and wounded another. We had an attempted assassin at the outpost. They dumped hundreds of mines right outside the cave to kill us and slow down backup forces to keep them out of here as long as possible. This can't wait any longer. Kunz isn't going to put operations in Park and wait for us to pull together tactical backup. He's going to bug out." If he hadn't already.

Knowing Kunz, he'd left the compound for safer digs the moment she'd escaped. Him or his double, it didn't matter. Whichever had been there would've hightailed it out of here before the heat ratcheted up. He'd run like the coward he was and leave his minions behind to do the dying.

"I wish I could disagree with you, but I can't." Nathan raised and lowered his brow, pinched his lips, his left eye twitching. "Let's move."

"Stick close, and be prepared for anything." Out of

long-term habit, Kate checked her sheath, then her thigh holster and finally her waist belt and fanny pack. Knife, secure. Dart gun, secure. Darts, secure. The tips were poison-tainted and stored properly in their clip at her waist. The snub-nose .38-caliber pistol resting between her breasts inside her wet suit couldn't move unless she moved it. Fanny pack of tools, including a brick of C-4 explosives, secure. And prayers that she wouldn't have to use it, and sacrifice herself and Nathan, whispered and reiterated. Satisfied she had done all she could to prepare, she dove down toward the mouth of the cave.

Nathan followed, wearing matching headgear so that they could continue to communicate under water.

Kate swam along the perimeter of the formations, but she couldn't find the one that had been so obscure she'd nearly missed it. She swam back and tried again. And again, failed to find it. "Damn it."

"What's wrong? Don't you have the coordinates?"

"No. S.A.S.S. plotted my course after I entered the cave."

"Can you plug those in, and go from there?"

"No, I can't. This is a black zone. No activation." She kept looking, straining to see, scouring the rocks.

She again swam the length of the formation, dipping into and out of crevices. "There." Finally she spotted the telltale gouges. "This is it." With a strong kick, she made the tight bend and entered the narrow cave.

With Nathan following, they began moving through, staying as close to the ceiling as Kate had the first time she'd explored it.

"Low-level light only," Kate whispered, warning him to control the beam on his flashlight. "Otherwise, they'll pick it up. Watch for trip wires, too. I didn't hit any before, swimming close to the ceiling, but they know that now, too. I'd expect them to adapt to make it more difficult for us."

Nathan nodded, swept the low-level beam of his flashlight along the cave wall. "These walls have taken plenty of hits."

"Yeah, they have." They were beaten down smooth in places.

"This cave wasn't easy to find. If you hadn't led the way, I'd have missed it."

"I did miss it the first few times I checked the formation."

"Too much work for recreational divers. They couldn't do this kind of damage to the rocks." He swam a little further. "Incoming tide could be responsible for part, but not all of this. Something beyond the hand of nature is definitely going on in here."

"That's the way I see it, too. Weapons cache, compound or something else entirely—but something manmade." Kate motioned to the right wall. "You check that side and I'll check this one."

Nathan veered to the right. "I thought you said there were air pockets in here." He looked over at her, his eyes shadowed by his headgear. "Where are they?"

"Further up. When we round this next bend, the water level drops. We can surface there, and save our oxygen. But remember the audio wiring. Talk only when necessary."

They swam on, looking for signs, for some small piece of evidence that would prove this cave was a GRID compound or a holding tank for GRID weapons.

When they rounded the bend and the water level dropped below the ceiling, Kate motioned to Nathan to surface.

Kate went first, barely breaking the water with her head

and stopping when the water level fell to just below her nose. She looked around, saw nothing unusual, no signs of life, then shoved back her headgear, took another look, and motioned to Nathan to join her.

Nathan came up and removed his headgear. "Wow, that's potent stuff," he whispered, conscious of the audio wiring Kate had mentioned.

"What?" Kate asked in the same low whisper.

He swiped at his face. "My nose burns like fire and my eyes are watering so bad I can hardly keep them open."

"It gets worse deeper in."

He looked up, then forward. "I see what you mean about the lighting. It's a perfect fit, all right. I'd bet it's square center in the narrow spectrum."

She knew it, of course, but hearing him verify it made her feel more confident of her observations. When it came to GRID or Thomas Kunz, it never hurt to have validation. Actually, validation was essential. So much under their domain seemed real, but wasn't. "Notice anything else?" She wanted him to specifically mention the salt. He'd noted the burning, but not the salt itself.

"Yes," he whispered. "I realize we're dealing with salt water, but it's not stagnant in here, so that can't be it—"

"It?" she asked.

"The reason the tang is all wrong." Perplexed, he frowned. "It's not typical for salt water. That's all. Maybe it's a reaction with something else in here."

"Tang?"

"You know, the salt tang," he said. "It doesn't smell salt water salty. It smells…different."

Exactly. Kate's heart thumped hard. "Saline saturation is off the charts. Maybe that's the difference?"

"Maybe so."

A bit disappointed he'd let go of it that easily, she walked on, mindful of trip wires, alert to the slightest sounds and movements.

Kate stopped near where she'd been the first time, when she'd killed Parton. "This is about where I was when I ran into trouble." She looked over at Nathan.

He paused beside her. "They came up from out of the water?"

"Yeah." Kate nodded, and moved on, edgy, afraid of getting waylaid again.

Minutes later, she stepped down.

Something bumped into her foot.

"Oh, God!" She came to a dead stop. If it was a pressure mine, she'd tripped it.

"What is it?"

"Back up, Nathan. Now."

"Why?"

"Now!" she whispered harshly.

He moved back.

She waited a few beats, half expecting it to explode, but it didn't.

"Kate, damn it, answer me!"

"I hit something." Looking down, she spotted a cylinder. An oxygen tank.

Her stomach pitched and rolled over. "Nathan, tell me this isn't Douglas's." If he'd been trapped this far inside for days and there were fresh gouges in the rocks outside, then GRID operatives had been through here. The odds of his evading them would be astronomical. Surely they had found him.

Nathan bent down and double-checked Kate's search for wires or any type of explosive device that could've been attached to the canister.

"It's clear," Kate said.

Taking her at her word, he flashed his low-level light on the tank and saw the markings he'd hoped not to see. "I wish I could tell you it's not his." He looked down at her, the dread in his voice reflecting in his eyes. "But I can't. It's Douglas's tank."

"I'm so sorry." Bitterness and regret thickened Kate's voice. She didn't have to say it. Nathan's upset proved he already knew it. Their mission to find Douglas had changed.

Odds had increased dramatically that their search and rescue mission had now become a recovery.

Kate moved through the cave, every instinct remaining on high alert. She steeled herself, fully expecting to come up on Douglas's body at any moment.

Normally focusing all of her energy on the task at hand was easy. But finding Douglas's tank, fearing it signaled his death, had upset her.

It had more than upset Nathan. He had issued the order: Douglas had been in this cave because Nathan had authorized him to investigate. And, gauging by Nathan's expression and body language, the responsibility at having done that bore down hard on him. Merciless. Unrelenting. Unforgiving.

"Are you okay?" It was a stupid question. Of course, he wasn't okay. But she had no idea what to say to make things any better. She couldn't offer false hope. That would be the worst kind of insult, and Nathan deserved better. "I didn't mean it like that," she tried to explain the unexplainable. "You know what I mean."

Gratitude shone in his eyes and he clasped her upper arm and gave it a gentle squeeze. "I know, Kate. I've been in similar positions many times. You want to help, but never know what to say."

She nodded.

"It's a damn shame, but it never gets easier." He shrugged. "I don't know. Maybe that's a blessing. What kind of people would we be, if it did?"

"You wouldn't be the man you are." She lifted a hand and stroked his jaw. "And the man you are is very special."

He brushed a kiss to her cheek. "Thank you."

They moved on, silent now, dragging their feet to avoid splashing and continuing to watch for traps. The water dropped down to chest level and calmed to the rare ripple.

Something felt strange, different, and it pricked at Kate's instincts. She looked over at Nathan, feeling the need to warn him. About what, she had no idea. But he was already looking at her.

He nodded in silent agreement, that he, too, sensed something amiss, and they kept moving.

Far beyond the portion of the cave Kate had explored, they approached another bend, and Kate sensed the danger growing stronger. She lifted a hand to Nathan, opened her senses and felt someone lurking in the darkness. Motioning, she swept the left wall with her light. Nathan swept the right, as tense and wary as she. Still nothing appeared out of the ordinary, yet dread dragged at her stomach, warning her to retreat. Her heart rate kicked up a notch and she pushed on around the bend.

A man's voice came out of the darkness. "Don't move."

Chapter 13

Nathan grabbed Kate's shoulder, pulling her behind him. Endearing gesture, but totally unnecessary. "Nathan."

His gaze fixed on the darkness, he didn't seem to hear her. "Nathan, I think it's okay," she whispered again, a smile tugging at her lips.

He darted her a glance, saw her smile, and looked at her as if she'd lost her mind.

"The voice," she said. "He sounds like Douglas!"

Shock widened his eyes, then his Adam's apple bobbed hard and the fear to believe settled on his face. "Douglas?" Nathan whispered loudly. "Is that you?"

"Commander?"

"Yes!"

Douglas moved out of the darkness through a deep shadow and stepped into the beam of Nathan's light. "It's me. Don't move. You're about to trigger a heat sensor in the warning system. It'll let them know you're here."

Nathan let out a sigh so full of relief it warmed Kate's chilled body. She felt it down to her toes. Douglas moved closer, walking in the beam of light.

Nathan gave his back a healthy whack, the sound lightly echoing. "Damn, I'm glad you're not dead."

"Me, too." Douglas grinned. "Did you find my tank?"

"Yes," Kate answered, considering that an odd question. *How did you find me?* That would have been a more typical thing to ask. Him asking about the tank set her teeth on edge. "What happened?"

"High tide. Knocked me right off my feet and into the rocks. I hit my head. I'm fuzzy from there, but I wasn't knocked out. Anyway, the next thing I knew, I was stuck on a rock ledge over there—" he pointed into the darkness from which he'd come "—with no oxygen tank. I knew it had to be too far to swim out without one, so I waited for Search and Rescue to come get me." He smiled. "I don't suppose you have a cold beer or a cheeseburger in that fanny pack."

That smile had Kate examining him closely. It seemed too cheerful and, well, too rested. "Afraid not." Suspicion seeped deeper into Kate. Douglas didn't look dehydrated or half-starved. He didn't look haggard. If he'd spent the better part of three days in this cave, wouldn't he look all those things and more? And Douglas had been bringing up the rear, diving with his team. He hadn't been on the surface swimming, susceptible to the tide and rocks, and he hadn't been inside the cave exploring, he'd been outside of it, still with the team.

Too many inconsistencies. Too many aspects of his story just didn't fit the facts. A hollow pit formed in her stomach and fear filled it. And the inevitable question smothered the joy she'd felt on seeing him and replaced it with doubt. Doubt that carried regret because it would soon sink its hateful talons into Nathan, too.

Was Douglas really Douglas?

She had to know the truth—the sooner the better. "We need to get out of here and get you some food and water." She sent Nathan a pointed look, silently insisting he go along with her suggestion. "We should get his report now, while it's fresh in his mind." And before they ventured any further. "And notify Search and Rescue."

A strange look crossed Nathan's face. "Right. That's appropriate protocol." He shifted his attention back to Douglas, now cautious. "We'll share my tank."

The shift in him was subtle but distinct to Kate. She watched closely to see if Douglas picked up on it. He didn't. And that had the hollow pit in her stomach expanding. The real Douglas wouldn't have missed that. He knew Nathan well; the change would have been glaringly obvious to him.

Nathan buried his notice adeptly. He reached into his pack, pulled out a spare hose, attached it to the emergency valve on his tank and then passed the loose end to Douglas. "Try to conserve. We should be okay, but it could get close."

"I'll lead the way," Kate said. "Give me two minutes."

"I'd feel better if we all stuck together." Nathan didn't like Kate's going ahead of them, but nodded slightly to let her know that he would respect her decision.

Douglas wasn't as amiable. "We'll come, too."

Her deep suspicions, now strengthened to certainty, signaled a warning. She was damn good at her job, and the real Douglas knew that. She outranked him and he'd never question her orders, even if they'd been issued in a conversational tone.

Trust no one.

In her mind, she again heard Colonel Drake's warning, and listened to it. "You heard what I said. Two minutes."

Douglas looked ready to object. Nathan interceded with a hand at Douglas's shoulder. "We'll wait."

Given no choice, the man backed down. Nathan paused, the lines in his face deeper than they had been only minutes ago. "Two minutes, Kate. No more."

They exchanged a look that told her his concerns about Douglas matched her own and his worry about her leaving. "Be right behind me," she said, then headed out.

Before reaching the entrance, Kate noticed another smaller chamber off the main cave. Ducking inside she quickly noted the sensor. She moved closer for a better look. Embedded in the rock wall, there was nothing high-tech about the sensor, but it was effective. If it picked up on a heat source, it triggered a flashing red light and foghorn. Kate imagined the sound, if not the light, would echo through the entire cave.

Something splashed behind her. The noise was far too loud and distinct to be the seasoned Douglas or Nathan. Kate stiffened, stilled.

"Son of a bitch, get them!"

Gaston? He'd issued the order, but to whom? Were Nathan and Douglas being pursued, or were they pursuing someone else?

Unsure, she sank down until the salty water threatened her nose, then slid deep into the shadows to the darkness and waited, her heart thudding, adrenaline punching through her veins, her mind skittering in a thousand different directions at once.

"Damn it, Douglas, explain this screwup?" Gaston shouted. "He's supposed to be dead. What happened? And where the hell is Katherine Kane?"

Oh, God, no! No! Kate's stomach revolted and her chest went tight. Gaston, a double agent for the CIA who had been inserted undercover inside GRID for a year, who had access to senior levels of top-secret information that Thomas Kunz would—and had—killed to get his grimy hands on, had fallen into the biggest trap carrying the highest risks possible for a covert operative positioned with hostiles long-term.

Gaston was a traitor.

Chapter 14

A battery of fear rammed through Kate's body; more fear than she thought she could hold. She'd been in tight spots, bad situations with minimal survival odds, but this was worse. A thousand times worse. Her heart pounded, her hands shook. Nathan. They had Nathan.

"I asked once. This is your last chance to answer me. Where is Katherine Kane?"

"Kate is dead, Gaston," Nathan said sharply. "Your man Douglas here killed her outside the cave."

Nathan knew for fact Douglas was a double? Or was he so repulsed by Douglas's turning traitor like Gaston that he just wished it so?

The Douglas with Gaston didn't deny it. *Why not?*

"Do you realize how pissed Kunz is going to be?" Gaston asked, obviously talking to Douglas. "Fifteen months of surgery and intensive training, and you didn't even make it out of the damn cave before blowing it."

"I didn't blow it," Douglas said. "You just blew it for me, you stupid bastard. You just confirmed Forester's suspicions." A scuffle, splashing. The sound of fist hitting flesh. "I could kill you."

Kate moved, bent on seizing the opportunity to intervene and free Nathan, but the splashing stopped.

"Instead, explain why you killed Katherine Kane. You know Sandross wanted to talk to her. Kunz specifically ordered her not to be killed until after Sandross talked to her."

Listening to Gaston talk about her murder so blandly made her queasy. At least now she knew what Kunz had in mind. Torture à la Marcus Sandross and then murder.

Odd. Kunz really had it in for S.A.S.S. and for Kate specifically, since she'd blown up his Iranian compound. So if he loves to torture and he hates her, would he pass up the opportunity to torture her himself and give the pleasure over to his second, Marcus Sandross?

Only if he wasn't here.

Kunz must have used the time with the mines to bug out. Definitely leaving the dying to his minions. The coward. Yet Kate was happy she wouldn't have to face his torture, too.

"I can't believe you," Douglas's double said. "You ruined me—totally ruined me—and then act like it's nothing. Do you realize what you've done to me? When I walk back inside Sandross is going to take one look at Forester and blow my frigging head off."

Disappointed that the distraction she needed from the scuffle was over, Kate sank back into the shadow to the darkness and swallowed hard. Douglas had been sidetracked by his exposure. That could be why he hadn't denied killing her, but more than likely, he didn't dispute Nathan's rendition of her whereabouts to try to save his own ass. Kunz and Sandross would be more ticked about her escaping than about Douglas's exposure. And, she remembered Kunz telling Moss not to kill her unless he had no choice, Douglas need only say that he had no choice. Since she was dead, he brought Forester for Sandross to interrogate.

Damn. It sounded too good. It would work. If Nathan cooperated by keeping his mouth shut. But to resolve all their problems, they only had to kill her and Nathan. A "killed him first" and then "she gave me no choice" would do it.

The simplicity of it terrified Kate.

"Just shut up and let me think." Gaston was afraid. Kate heard it in his voice. "Okay. Okay. Kane's dead and we've got Forester. We can pull this out." Then he said to Douglas. "She pulled a knife on you. You took her out, kept Forester alive for questioning. Keep your mouth shut about exposure and we're on point. You open it and Mr. Kunz has no further use for you. Mr. Sandross will kill you just for the fun of it."

"And I have you to thank for that."

"Done is done, man," Gaston said. "What do you want?"

"What the hell difference does it make now?" Douglas shouted. "Just radio in the frigging report and let's get out of here. Caves give me the creeps."

Nathan interceded. "I want to make a deal."

Deal? What kind of deal could Nathan possibly be making with these jerks?

"Talk fast."

"Okay, Gaston, here it is," Nathan said. "You tell me where my Douglas is, and I won't tell Kunz or Sandross that Douglas's double has been exposed."

"What's to keep me from just shooting your ass right here? You're supposed to be dead, anyway."

"Nothing. But I'm inside the cave. Don't you think Kunz might want to know who else knows about the compound? Obviously someone has alternate plans for me or I would already be dead."

"Take the deal," Douglas said.

Détente between Nathan and Douglas's double. Nathan wouldn't expose Douglas's double to Sandross and Douglas's double wouldn't reveal Kate wasn't dead. As deals went, it wasn't bad. Mutually assured destruction was on the line.

"And neither of you so much as mentions my name on any of this. It was all done before I got here," Gaston said. "Otherwise, Mr. Sandross gets the whole story from me."

The whole story included the fact that Kate wasn't dead. Gaston suspected it, but Nathan knew it and so did Douglas's double. So bottom line, Nathan had traded Kate's life for Douglas's double's life.

"So where is my Douglas?" Nathan asked.

"He's in the compound," the double answered.

"In this cave, right?"

"Yeah. You'll be seeing it soon enough." The double then told Gaston, "Call it in."

Kate held her breath. If Gaston did it, Nathan had given her the greatest gift that in her present situation she could be given. Dead women don't attack. GRID wouldn't expect her to enter the compound. She'd have the advantage of surprise.

Dead, she stood the best chance of rescuing Nathan and the real Douglas alive.

"Mr. Kunz?"

"Is unavailable. It's Sandross. Go ahead, Gaston."

"We've got a floater outside the gate, sir. Female. Bringing one in upright. Male. He was inside. Interrogation on compound status with the enemy is suggested, sir."

"Is this tangent of the mission secure?"

"Yes, sir," Gaston said. "It's secure."

Could Sandross hear the tremor in Gaston's voice? It came through loud and clear to Kate, but Sandross was on the other end of a radio transmission. If he did hear it, he'd likely blame it on the equipment.

"Retrieve the floater and bring in the upright," Sandross said.

Gaston replied, "Yes, sir." His relief was as obvious as the tremor.

Now Kate could move. Now she could take out Douglas's double and Gaston and rescue Nathan. She retrieved her dart gun and loaded it with a poison-tipped dart, then moved out. She'd have to get around the bend to get off a decent shot.

Just before she was to make the turn, heavy splashing echoed through the cave. She stopped, pulled back, hugging the rock, and then peeked around the edge of the rocks.

Six lantern lights came through the cave, stopping when the men reached Nathan, Gaston and Douglas's double. Frustration set in. Eight-to-one odds sucked, and Gaston was holding Nathan's weapon. He had a knife, unless they'd gotten that, too, but a knife against a gun still gave her lousy odds. Especially factoring in that the real Douglas was still inside.

"Good timing, men," Gaston said. "Moss, you and Carson retrieve Kane's body. It's somewhere outside the cave. We'll meet you back at the compound." Gaston pushed at Nathan's shoulder. "Let's move it."

They started moving toward her. Kate dropped back into the darkness. Douglas wouldn't dare to so much as glance her way; it'd mean his death. She could follow them in, but the way their luck was running, Marcus Sandross would be waiting for Nathan's arrival. That meant his guards would be with him. Better to wait for the two men retrieving her body to return. That would up her odds a little.

Seeing Nathan surrounded by GRID operatives and traitors had her heart in her throat, launching a battle with her brain. Maybe she should take them out now. *Damn it, why hadn't she carried a sound suppressor for her gun?*

"It's going to be interesting," Nathan said. "To see what's going on down here."

A cue to her not to do it, to be patient, let them pass and later follow. How had he known her head and heart would be at odds? Would his have been?

Gaston harrumphed. "Don't get your hopes up, Forester. You won't be seeing much of anything down here."

"Probably not," Nathan said, deliberately sounding defeated. "Probably not."

He knew Kate would come after him.

Clearly he also believed they'd both end up dead.

A shudder rippled through Kate, warning her he well might be right.

Kate stayed hidden in the shadows, her back to the rock wall. It'd been more than two hours since Nathan had left surrounded by GRID members and traitors, and during each minute of that time she had imagined a thousand things—all fodder for nightmares—that could be happening to him. Unfortunately, every damn one of them was a real possibility, considering what was known about Kunz's brutal tactics and Sandross's violent tendencies.

In the distance she finally heard the awaited sound of

men moving through the water, coming closer. Minutes later, two of them made the bend and came into full view.

The one on the left had to be Carson. Lean and muscular, he outweighed her by at least a hundred pounds. Any hand-to-hand combat with him would have to be short, fast and lethal. Otherwise he'd clean her clock. The second man on the right was Moss: big and beefy and, unfortunately, hard to kill.

Having inflicted a gut wound that should have killed him but had failed to even knock him out of commission, she'd be an idiot to engage in hand-to-hand combat with him again. Avoiding that, she raised her dart gun, took aim, and was about to squeeze the trigger when Moss spoke through his lip mike.

"Command Center."

"Go ahead, Moss," a man said.

"We're inbound."

"We, who?"

"Carson and me, sir."

Sandross, Kate thought. Sounded like him and Moss had called him "sir." He had done the same thing during their first encounter.

"You're clear."

Remembering the heat sensor, Kate lowered the gun. Rather than return it to its holster, she held on to it. It would save her seven seconds of reaction time. She couldn't kill either of them without the remaining one sounding the alarm to Sandross. She'd have to follow them into the compound proper and hope that Sandross assumed the heat sensor was picking up warmth from her corpse. Sandross hadn't asked if they'd located her body, and Moss hadn't volunteered the information.

Moss and Carson passed by. She gave them a little lead,

as if they were pulling her body by a rope, and then followed, submerged just beneath the surface.

Minutes later, the men entered a well-lit, open area.
Kate hesitated, knowing she was taking a huge risk either
way—if she went into the light or if she hung back in the
shadows. Certain she could inflict more damage before
being caught from hiding in the shadows, she slid into the
darkness and examined the vicinity to get her bearings. In
case of battle, she needed to know her options.

Several steps led out of the water to a flat, concrete deck
about forty feet long and twenty feet wide. Along the left
wall, metal spikes had been driven into the rock wall.
Dozens of wet suits and diving gear hung from them. To
the right, down the wall, a line of twenty or more oxygen
tanks rested in cradles formed by a metal rack that had
been bolted into place. A long plastic sign hanging above
them read Full Tanks Only.

Carson and Moss stood on the deck, stripping off their
wet suits. Carson hung his on a peg, near the others. Moss
was slower, but finally moved and hung his, too.

Nervous, Gaston appeared at the door to the right of the
oxygen tanks. "Well, where's the body?"

Carson answered. "Tide must've taken her out. We
didn't find a thing."

"You're not serious."

"Yeah, I am." Carson shrugged. "If she's there, she's
been swept out into the open gulf already."

"Damn it." Gaston turned and started to walk down
what appeared to be a major exit point.

Beyond the exit, all Kate could see were doors. Looked
like a typical wide hallway.

Gaston paced and cursed, then finally spoke to Carson
and Moss. "Well, we can't put it off. Let's go report it."

"I hope Mr. Sandross is in a good mood."

"Don't be stupid," Moss told Carson. "Would you be in a good mood if you were told this?"

"No," Carson admitted. "Just wishing, man. Sandross doesn't have good moods, anyway."

Gaston sighed. "All I can say is, she'd better be dead or Sandross will rip out our throats."

They were afraid of him. Clearly, all three of them were terrified of telling Sandross they'd failed.

Kate rubbed at her nose. It was already raw and she swore it had to be about to bleed from the strong salt smell. The scent had been potent where she'd waited for Moss and Carson to return, but near the deck, it was stronger still. Salt water is salt water and it filled the place. So why did the salt smell so much stronger here than in the tunnel of the cave? Overwhelmingly potent and strong.

The question ran rampant through her mind and caused an avalanche of others. Was the real Thomas Kunz in this compound? Did he have a double inserted here? Gaston appeared to have turned traitor, but appearances could be deceptive. Had he changed sides or was he a loyal CIA operative? She just couldn't be sure. Were there any hostages here? Where were Nathan and the real Douglas? What was happening to them?

And toppling onto all those questions came yet another. One that had her shaking down to the soles of her feet.

Was she savvy enough to figure all this out?

All those old fears of not being good enough rose up in her like a phoenix from ash and she silently cursed, silently swore she'd give her left boob right now for a tactical team to assist her.

But none came. As always, she was on her own.

She scanned the walls for cameras or other signs of

monitors or alarms, and saw none. Kunz and Sandross had to feel substantially secure here or they'd never agree to be in the same compound at the same time. It was customary to keep the head honcho and his second-in-command apart for security reasons, to ensure the organization's ability to continue ongoing efforts in case one of them was killed.

If neither of them felt secure, the place would be wired from ceiling to floor. That was highly unlikely, considering the remote probability of the cave being found. If Douglas hadn't summoned her and then disappeared, this compound never would have been found. That scared her, and she prayed for their sakes that Kunz hadn't been this clever with all his GRID compounds.

She stepped into the light and moved to the steps. They were scraped, the edges rounded, as if heavy items had been dragged over them repeatedly, and the smell of salt burned so strong it nearly knocked her to her knees.

Leaving the water, she listened for warning sounds that she'd tripped some alarm. But there weren't any sounds of that or of anyone approaching, and no one was in sight. Actually, there was no activity whatsoever. Was that normal?

Having no way of knowing, she quickly removed her oxygen tank, fins and headgear and placed them near the end of the tank rack, hidden. Then, keeping an eye on the door, she moved over to the line of tanks and opened the valves on most of them, emptying out the oxygen.

If she got lucky enough to find Nathan and Douglas, and then got lucky enough to escape with them, they would all need air to get out of here. If she were really lucky and found any of the detainees inside, they would need more air. Otherwise, she would have emptied all of tanks in the rack to eliminate GRID's ability to give chase. Not knowing, she couldn't risk emptying any more. She quickly moved the full tanks to the end of the racks, placing them in front so there'd be no confusion.

Heading toward the door, she paused. An oddity on the floor caught her eye. It looked like part of a wooden plank.

She walked over to give it a closer look. It was part of a wooden plank—a cracked sliver of oak. Two slight indentions marred it about ten inches in toward the center from either end. She tested the depth of the indention with her thumb. These were the kinds of marks that came from metal bands being cinched tightly around wood. What could Kunz be doing with…?

Gouges.

Salt tang.

Scraped steps.

Oak with metal band indentions.

All of the pieces slid into place and Kate gasped.

Suddenly the truth was as clear as the water off the coast and she knew *exactly* how Kunz was getting the weapons into the compound. And because he was, he then had to be trucking the weapons over land to his end buyers.

She had to give the devil his due. It was, simply put, a brilliant plan.

Damn him.

Voices from the tunnel carried to her over the water. Several voices, and the people attached to them were heading her way and just beyond the last bend. She'd be in full view!

She rushed through the major exit and then down the dimly lit hallway. It was narrow and white-walled. This area had to be above ground—it had Sheetrock walls.

Water had no mercy on Sheetrock, and there were no signs of any damage. Neither were there any damn doors, offering her somewhere to hide.

The men had ditched their gear and were coming closer. She couldn't turn back. She had no choice but to move forward.

Running to the fork in the hallway, she paused and scanned left, then right. Nathan's voice sounded. She jerked back to the left. He was somewhere down there. Somewhere close.

"I don't know, I said," Nathan shouted. "I can't tell you what I don't know. What part of that don't you understand?"

He didn't sound hurt, he sounded angry. Glad to hear it, she took the left fork, dart gun in hand, moving with caution, wary of being discovered, certain if she were, it would be an automatic death sentence for all of them.

Six doors down, a guard entered the hallway.

Oh, spit. Her heart nearly stopped. She darted her gaze, looking for somewhere to go. The guard was turning toward her—she had no choice. Ducking into the first open door, she slammed her back against the wall, her breathing hard and heavy.

The room was empty. Bare walls and floor. In a cold sweat she waited, praying this guy wasn't on his way to this room for some untold reason.

Finally, shuffling footsteps cleared her doorway and then faded beyond the hallway fork. The guard stopped there to speak to someone. Their words sounded muffled from inside the room, but the tone of their conversation seemed cordial not frantic. They clearly considered everything to be normal.

When she no longer heard voices, she peeked out and checked the hallway. Empty. She listened intently, hoping to again hear Nathan's voice. Moving door to door, she paused to listen. But at each step, she heard only silence.

Outside the sixth door—the one to the room the guard had come out of—she heard someone talking. A man. She stopped, hopeful, but it wasn't Nathan.

"You can spare us both this distasteful ordeal, Major," the man said.

He wasn't Nathan, but he could be talking to him. Him or another major held captive. There were several.

Her heart beat faster and she willed it to slow, resisting the urge to rush into the room.

"Simply answer my questions and I promise you'll have a painless death."

Kate had no idea who the interrogator was, but he definitely wasn't Kunz. He didn't sound like Sandross, either, offering mercy. Silently grateful to be spared a direct confrontation with either of them, she eased the door open a few inches and peered inside.

Nathan was the victim.

Across the wide room, he sat naked, strapped to a metal chair, his arms and legs restrained with leather bindings. He was wired to the rafters. Monitors were stacked up along the wall, and wires from the machines had been attached to various parts of his body: his heart, his temple, a clip on his fingertip, monitoring his pulse. His cheeks had inch-long slices over his cheekbones and nodes had been inserted into the cuts.

Electrico-shock therapy. *Pain. Severe pain.*

Anger burst from deep inside her and it was all she could do to keep from barreling in and ripping out the interrogator's heart.

The man keyed in something on a keyboard attached to the machine nearest Nathan.

His face contorted in agony, his body jerked tight against the restraints, and Nathan screamed.

Chapter 15

Kate nearly hit the floor. Nathan's scream chilled her to the bone, fueling fear that filled her every cell.

His body stretched tight as a wire and then, just as suddenly, went lax. He slumped from the waist and didn't straighten.

Kate could barely breathe, barely focus on anything other than Nathan being in pain.

Think, damn it. You can't help him if you don't think!

She forced her mind to function. The man standing over him was about forty. He wore a white lab coat and he'd spoken with an indistinct accent. Maybe Russian; she couldn't be sure. But she didn't recognize him from the S.A.S.S. watch list.

"Refusing to answer will only delay the inevitable and cause you more pain, Major Forester. You will tell us what we want to know. I suggest you make it easy on yourself. Now, where is Captain Kane?"

No answer.

"What is Captain Kane doing here?"

No answer.

"Does Captain Kane know what is happening here?"

No answer.

"Who did Captain Kane tell about this compound?"

No answer.

Kate eased the door shut behind her and lurked behind a white privacy curtain hanging from the ceiling.

Nathan sensed her there, but he didn't look over. How she knew that, she had no idea, but she was as certain of it as she was about her own name.

The interrogator sighed, weary of this one-sided conversation. "You must answer or you leave me no choice but to increase the pain, Major Forester. I am not a proponent of torture. I am a man of science. But Mr. Sandross insists you answer these questions. Unless you do so now, you leave me no choice—"

"Bullshit." Nathan spat the word out, furious and somewhat recovered. "Everyone makes choices. Good or bad, and they own them. Don't peddle your trash to me. I'm not buying."

"Very well, Major Forester."

Kate's stomach clutched. Her temper rising, she eased her knife out of the sheath and watched the man move from in front of Nathan back to the machine he used to inflict the torture. When he reached for the keyboard, Kate rushed across the room. Her knife arced to strike, she warned him, "Touch him again and you'll die slowly."

Shocked at her being there, the man turned toward her. Kate sliced the air and he walked right into her swing. The knife caught him midthroat.

He collapsed, dead before he hit the floor. Bright red

blood spilled from his neck and pooled on the floor at her feet. She stepped over his body to get to Nathan.

"I thought you'd never get here." Nathan shivered and pushed against the straps banding his arms. "Get me out of this damn thing."

"Sorry I took so long." Kate loosened the leather straps at his arms and then his legs, freeing him. She deliberately avoided checking out his body, though she was tempted. But under the circumstances, it felt like a violation, and he'd been violated enough. "Are you okay?"

"Hell, yes." He pulled the nodes out of his face, off his chest. She grabbed two sterile strips from her fanny pack and bandaged his face. "Better than all right. I'm freaking phenomenal."

Impossible. "Nathan, did they do something to your head?"

"No," he said, clasping her arms and giving them a shake. "Douglas and at least two other Americans are here. I was with them, Kate. Come on." He rushed to a coatrack near the door, stole a lab coat and tugged it on. "This way."

They ran through the corridor, took the first right through a second one, and then entered yet another hallway. "They're down here," Nathan said without looking back. "Sandross won't consider you dead without a body. He instructed the men that if you tried to get into the compound, to let you. But not to let you leave it."

Kate stayed close on Nathan's heels. "What about Gaston?" She still couldn't believe he had turned traitor. Yes, it happened, but she had expected better from him. "Is he with us or GRID?"

"Damned if I know. I see it both ways, and that rattles the hell out of my confidence in him."

"That's how you're supposed to see him. In his job, that's an asset."

"Maybe." Clearly grasping Gaston's status as a double agent, Nathan added, "But maybe not."

"What about Kunz? Have you seen him?"

"No. But I heard him on the radio with Marcus Sandross. Gaston was right about that man. He's one mean son of a bitch, Kate."

"Is Kunz not here, or is he in another part of the compound?"

"Sorry. No idea." At an intersecting corridor, Nathan slowed and then stopped, looked up and then down the cross hall. "But Sandross is heavily armed. The compound's a veritable fortress."

"Where are the weapons?" She stopped beside him and ran her own visual check of the cross hallway.

"There in two rooms the size of warehouses," he said, breathless and weary from the torture. "To the right. Four guards posted outside—two of them on each door. The weapons are stacked ceiling-to-floor, Kate. Row after row of them. It's the biggest cache I've seen in my career, including ours."

What the hell was Kunz planning? To overthrow the governments of a couple of countries? She wished she had more of her own arsenal with her. "Did you get a look? Are any of them tagged?" Bio and chemical warheads were tagged with a yellow band—a visual warning to anyone who came into contact with them that special handling was required.

Nathan's expression turned grim, the sterile strips crinkling over his skin. "All of them."

Shock stole her breath. Her voice came out as a ragged whisper and acid roiled in her stomach. "*All* of them?"

Chapter 16

The compound was a maze of corridors and Kate followed Nathan down yet another one. So far, they hadn't seen a soul.

When Nathan paused, Kate motioned with a shrug. "Where is everyone?"

"Scattered. It's a huge place."

"Did you see Sandross personally?"

He nodded. "He had the doc rig me up and told him what Kunz wanted to know."

Which was all about her. "I'm sorry, Nathan. I heard the questions…"

"No, it wasn't your fault. Don't even go there."

"Where?" It was her fault. Kunz wanted information on her.

"Guilt." He shook his head. "Forget it, Kate. Kunz and Sandross—all of GRID owns it."

True, but when she was the object, dismissing it just wasn't that easy.

Nathan pointed to a few doors down and swung his finger right. "Cell block. Douglas and the others are in it."

She nodded and stepped in front of him to take the corner and get a look. Midway down, two guards stood near a vacant desk. Shooting them where they stood would be effortless but, without a sound suppressor, the gunfire would alert the entire compound. Better to try to keep it stealth. She held two fingers up to Nathan, pointed to her chest and then right. He could take the one on the left. When he nodded, she passed him her dart gun and three darts, then mouthed, "Poison tips."

Giving her a thumbs-up, he loaded the dart gun.

Ready to move, she unsheathed her knife, then unsnapped the strap holding her gun place in case she had no choice but to use it. The desk backed into an alcove, leaving her staring at the back of one of the guards. At any moment, he could turn, and her intention to stay stealth would be obsolete.

Hoping to hell he was right-handed, she hugged the right wall where, if turning, he'd see her only at the last second. Nathan fell in behind her and motioned with two fingers to move slowly. Kate disagreed. They needed to rush them. That gave them better odds of the guards not having time to sound an alarm.

Kate signaled back and then counted down, her arm at her side, her fingers where Nathan too could see them, then she took the corner in a dead run. Hearing Nathan behind her, she pushed, rammed into the closest guard and knocked him off his feet.

The second man hurled himself across the desk.

Nathan fired.

The dart stuck square in the man's chest.

The guy on the ground threw a right cross that landed square on Kate's jaw. Her head jerked back, her jaw throbbed. She dropped her knee on his throat, crushing it, then turned her attention to Nathan. He was retrieving the cell keys from the dead body of the guard. The dart still stuck into him, midchest.

Kate didn't recognize either of the men. Not from personal experience going against GRID, and not from the S.A.S.S. watch list. That had her stomach curling. They were insidious, like rodents. Take one down, and two more appear.

Nathan tried to unlock the cell door. "Damn it. Kate, none of the keys work."

Unzipping her fanny pack, she pulled out a minibrick of plastics and spoke to the three men inside the cell. "Back up and turn around. Don't move until I tell you to. Got it?"

The three were pretty beaten up, but one sure looked like Douglas. Wondering if he was, she wired the cell door with C-4. "It's going to explode. It'll be loud, but you'll be safe. Nathan," she added, without pausing or glancing his way, "get to the desk and see if there are any audio sensors you can knock out."

"Don't you have anything quiet in there?" Nathan waved toward her fanny pack. "They'll be all over us in minutes."

"Quiet explosives?" she asked, busily working. "Nathan, does that sound remotely logical to you?"

"Okay." He grimaced, went to the desk and examined the panels. "Found it, Kate." Something clicked. "Go for it."

"Just do what I told you," she said to the men through the bars. Glancing back, she saw Nathan, standing two steps off her right shoulder. "Back off."

He moved away.

"Three, two, one…"

The plastics exploded. The cell door rocked off its hinges.

"Hey, not bad. I thought you'd take the place down."

"I know what you thought," Kate said, a little affronted. Not too loud, her ears weren't even ringing. "I'm a pro. You forgot that."

"Yeah, I guess I did," Nathan admitted, his eyes gleaming male appreciation. "I was thinking…"

"Later, Romeo." She thumped his chest. "Your timing sucks. But don't lose the thought."

Haggard and weary, Douglas started out of the cell.

Kate blocked his exit with a hand to his chest. "What have you mailed lately?"

"Figures, Kane. You're a pain in thc ass, but I like having you around when I get in trouble." He smiled at her through cheeks split like Nathan's. "Sand."

Kate smiled her relief. He was Douglas. The real Douglas. "Story of my life. When their asses are in a sling, men love me. When they're not, I'm forgotten." She nodded toward the other two men in the cell. "Who are they?"

"Field Intelligence officers," Douglas said, pointing. "Andrews and Mathis."

Andrews was bruised up, half his lean face was purple with hints of green. New and old wounds. "You ambulatory, Andrews?"

"Damn right, I am."

His voice sounded strong; his will, stronger. He'd be fine. She rolled her gaze to Mathis. The poor guy's nose was splattered halfway across his face and the tattered rag that was left of his shirt showed cuts all over his back. *Sorry bastards were into mutilation, too.* Her stomach kicked, rebelling. Before she could ask how he was, he told her.

"I'm mobile, ma'am. My leg's screwed up, but I can move."

Admiration for him swelled in her chest. "Then let's get the hell out of here." She stepped back from the cell door.

Douglas swung an arm around Mathis. "Come on, buddy."

"Nathan."

He stepped her way. "Get them to the tunnel. Use the oxygen tanks on the ground at the end of the rack. The ones in the rack are empty."

Andrews stopped, looking shocked. "What about the women? You can't just leave them here."

Surprised, Kate rounded on him. "What women?"

"The two women with JAG. I haven't seen them, but I heard the guards talking about them."

"Do you know where they are?" Nathan asked.

"About ten cells down," Mathis said. "I was with the guards when they brought them back to the cell after their session."

"What session?" Kate asked.

"That's what they call their interrogations." Anger burned deep in Mathis's eyes. "They look like the rest of us."

"Nathan, Douglas. Get the women and then get to the tunnel. Douglas, you get the others out of the cave. You'll have to share oxygen tanks." She turned to look at Nathan. "You'll need to wait for me or I won't have a tank to get out."

Torn between worry and surprise, he didn't bother to mask either, but nodded agreement. "Where are you going to be?"

"We won't go undiscovered much longer." She rigged a charge for the women's cell door and handed it to him. "You can handle this, right?"

"Yes," he said, then put a hand on her forearm. "But where will you be?"

She lifted her gaze to meet his. "I've got to get a look at the weapons."

"No, Kate." He took the charge from her. "We leave here together."

"We will," she assured him. "Send them with Douglas, you wait for me, and then we'll leave together." She turned and headed down the hall.

"Damn it, Kate." He shouted after her. "I don't like this."

He didn't like it? She was walking into the inner sanctum of Kunz's lair. She *hated* it. "Me, either." Truer words had never been spoken.

Kate followed Nathan's directions and located the corridor with the weapons rooms. That she and their group remained undetected amazed and concerned her. It seemed impossible, and yet with the location and security measures in place, it was entirely within the realm of reason that they wouldn't be detected. Still, Kate didn't trust it.

She passed an open door in the hallway and looked inside. Four desks in the wide room, all neat and pristine with nothing seemingly out of place. Computers, data-gathering and transmitting. And a wall full of monitors. Images feeding in from various locations within the compound. None of which currently had images of Nathan, Douglas or the group.

This was a minioperations center, she realized, stepping inside around a cartful of files.

A plan bloomed and she moved to the main computer, sat and took a look at the incoming data on the screen. "Holy cow, it's the mother lode!"

She scrolled down the screen, seeing file after file of U.S. government employees who had been substituted by GRID operatives. Unwilling to risk losing the information—a disk successfully surviving the dive was questionable at best—she checked for Internet access and found it. She could transmit all this to Home Base, to Darcy. Of course, if she did transmit, Kate would never get out of here alive.

Her muscles clenched and the decision weighed on her. If it had been just her life, she wouldn't have been eager, but she'd made that call a ridiculous number of times before. But this time, it wasn't just her life being decided. It included Nathan and Douglas, Andrews and Mathis and the two women with the JAG corps. They would all die with her. And making that call was a bitch of a decision.

What decision? Do you really have a choice?

Kate wanted to groan. Now was not the time for her conscience to butt in. She was having enough problems with this because of Nathan.

Think, Kate. Two warehouses full of weapons. All of them banded or marked with the emblem that they're bio or chemical.

She loved Nathan Forester. He didn't know it. Hell, she'd just realized it herself. She was willing to forfeit her own life, but his?

Bio or chemical, Kate. We're talking mass murder on a scale the likes of which have never been seen. Hundreds of thousands murdered at once—and somebody loves every one of them. Can you live with that?

She couldn't. Kate squeezed her eyes shut, prayed she

was doing the right thing, and typed in the code to upload the data files to S.A.S.S. systems Darcy would be monitoring. She'd be on this like glue. In less than two minutes, Colonel Drake would activate and elevate GRID to Code One status, and all the honchos would know who the GRID operatives were inside the government.

"Nathan, all of you—forgive me." A tear filled her eye, blurring her vision. Signing their death warrants, she hit the button to send.

Kate's heart felt too big for her chest; part homesteaded in her throat. Too antsy to move, she forced herself to stay put in the squeaky chair until she saw that the files were actually transmitting.

The icon appeared, then the bar, and as soon as it started filling with blue, clicking off seconds left to finish and percentages of the file processed, she hit the floor running, snagging a white lab coat from a rack and the cartful of files.

Her plan was brazen, likely stupid, but it was her best shot of getting a look inside the weapons room. And if she was lucky—very, very lucky—she would get to transmit her findings back to S.A.S.S., as well, before they killed her.

Two guards stood outside the weapons room door; one on either side, just as Nathan had said. They were both the size of mountains and looked about as approachable as Mount Everest was climbable in the dead of winter.

Kate steeled her nerves, rolled the cart up the corridor, trying her damnedest to look as if this was standard operating procedure and she was bored half out of her mind.

Between the two men, she turned to enter the first weapons room.

Neither spoke nor moved to stop her.

She didn't acknowledge them or look directly into their eyes, just walked between them into the room, scanning frantically to see if there were files anywhere. If there weren't, she would die in this room.

But there, across the concrete floor and against the far right wall, stood a line twenty feet long of open shelves, all crammed full of file folders. *Eureka!*

She turned toward them. God, the information would be invaluable to S.A.S.S. It was all just stacked here, six rows deep, waiting for her. If only she had a way to get it out of here!

Pushing the cart into position, she stopped at the closest end of the shelves, grabbed a file from the cart and thumbed through it. She glanced at it—a dossier on an FBI agent in New Mexico—then skimmed the shelf, as if looking for the proper place to file it. But her focus was on the weapons filling the room.

Nathan had accurately described the place. Ceiling to floor, metal warehouse shelves, all carefully labeled and all bearing bands or emblems.

There was no way in hell all of these weapons could be laced with bio or chemical agents. Kunz had to have a system to identify those purported to be WMD and those that actually were WMD fortified. She rolled the cart down a few steps and took another look. Shoulder-held rocket launchers.

The guard on the left of the door stuck his head inside to see where she was. Locating her at the files, he ducked back out.

She watched him from the corner of her eye and when he returned to his post, she scooted further along the file shelf. She wanted to take a serious look at those launchers.

They were banded and had the emblem—and, damn it, they were bio or chemical capable. She slipped around to the next shelf of weapons and did a quick examination. The warheads were neutral. They, too, had bands and emblems, but they also had the initials T.K. engraved on the casing.

T.K. for Thomas Kunz, of course. Kate grimaced. The sadist was apparently also an egomaniac who relished the perverse pleasure of knowing that regardless of who launched the weapon system against America, his signature was on it. Every system bearing his initials was his personal gift to the U.S., a country he hated.

Kate returned to the files, checked the guard, who was still blissfully ignorant that she'd moved to look at the weapons. Quickly, she had made a supposition about the meaning of the initials on the casings. Did they signal that the warheads were laced with WMD agents, or that they were not?

She had no way of knowing without running labs on the contents, and field tests usually netted spotty results. To be sure, she'd have to take the systems to a lab, and that just wasn't going to happen.

Shoving files onto the shelf, she continued to take a mental inventory of all she saw. By the time she got to the end of the file row, she had a decent grip on what the arsenal contained.

It gave her the creeps. It turned her stomach. Kunz had to plan to take out a few countries—or to sell enough weapons to a few countries to make them capable of taking out each other.

He'd probably like that better. Détente, and he got paid huge sums of money for it.

One thing she didn't see was any type of replica of the C-273 communications device. Maybe Gaston hadn't turned the black box over to GRID. Maybe he hadn't actually turned traitor. If he had, she felt certain those communications devices would be on the shelf. With a model in hand, duplicating them wouldn't be a complex process and Kunz, the sick son of a bitch, would feast on knowing he had a system to market that the U.S. developed but hadn't yet made available to its military and field operatives.

She had to get out of here. At any moment someone was going to notice something was wrong. A silent alarm would be triggered, a guard not reporting in on time would be noticed.

Pushing the cart, she headed back to the door, turned to return to the minioperations center where she'd found the cart. Her heart felt stuck somewhere between her rib cage and backbone. Any second, she fully expected one of the guards to put a bullet in her back.

She kept moving, pressing on down the hallway, warning herself to slow down and not run, to just stay calm.

Finally she turned into the computer room, and fear spiked through her like rocket fuel.

A man stood at the desk, watching the screen. The wheels on the cart squeaked and he looked up at her. "Who the hell is running a virus check on this?"

Kate shrugged. Virus check? God, could she be so lucky? Was it possible the man didn't know what he was looking at?

No, the world didn't hold that kind of luck. Darcy! Kate's heart lightened. Darcy was doing this, making it appear on this end as though the computer was scanning for a virus. God bless that woman!

"Who's been in here?"

"I don't know." She mumbled to disguise her voice, then turned for the door.

"Where the hell are you going?" He braced an arm on the desk and looked at her hard enough to crack his leathered face.

He had to be Marcus Sandross. He had that killer look about him. "The doc just told me to bring the cart down."

"Then get the hell out of here." He turned his back on her.

Kate walked to the door, but hit the hall in a full run. She was at the bend nearest the receiving dock where Nathan was to be waiting for her when she heard Sandross's voice boom over a loudspeaker.

"Captain Katherine Kane is alive and inside the compound. Repeat. Captain Katherine Kane is alive and inside the compound. Dead or alive, I want her taken down—now!"

Footsteps poured out into the hallway behind her and Kate pushed for speed, her legs pumping hard, her muscles screaming.

Then a foghorn that rivaled the one on the Golden Gate Bridge blasted the air, piercing her ears. Red lights flashed in every direction.

"Security breach." A man's voice sounded. "Maximum response. Repeat. Security breach. Maximum response. Shoot to kill. Katherine Kane. Female…"

He went on, giving her physical description. Kate made the last turn and saw Nathan through the red flashes, standing at the steps waiting. She ran blindly to him.

And then she saw Douglas, Andrews, Mathis and the two JAG women. They were as battered as the men. Fury rose inside Kate. "Damn it, Douglas, get them out of here."

"Kate." Nathan grabbed her arms. "Calm down, Kate. We can't get out," he said. "Look." He nodded toward the water.

Kate swerved her gaze and despair threatened to knock her off her feet.

Between them and freedom, blocking any possibility of passage above or below the water, was a steel grate.

"Kate," Nathan said. "We're dead."

"Not yet, Nathan." She stepped into the water.

A thunderous rumbling sounded in the distance, far beyond the doorway.

"What the hell?" Douglas swirled around.

"Get in the water!" Kate shouted. "Go to that ledge, get down on the bottom and stay there. Use one tank. Do not come up." The roar grew louder. She shoved at their shoulders. "Hurry! Give me your other tanks! Nathan, grab some in front of the rack. Move it!"

They scrambled into the water, passing the tanks to her. She grabbed them by the straps, then swam for the grate. Nathan followed with four more. She positioned them between the bars in the grate, concentrating them in a small area. Certain they were secure, she motioned to Nathan to rush to the ledge. The alcove where the others gathered would give them the most protection.

A horrendous explosion split through the cave, jarring her teeth, rattling her bones. Her ears popped from the pressure, and Kate groaned from the pain, but kept pushing to get into the alcove.

Nathan surfaced, grabbed her shoulder and pulled her to him. Looking past her shoulder, his eyes stretched wide. "Oh, God!"

Stumbling into him, Kate looked back and gasped.

A giant fireball burst through the wall and rushed toward them.

Chapter 17

Kate's stomach brushed the sandy bottom under the water.

Nathan lay beside her and she prayed what she expected to happen would happen. Otherwise they were all going to be burned alive or buried in rock when the tunnel collapsed.

Douglas and the others lay stretched out like corpses, hugging the cave floor, holding their breaths. She looked up. Fire licked at the surface above them, shattered slivers of debris punched through the flames, plunking into the water, and then floated and sank. Some of the slivers were actually fist-size chunks of debris.

The salt water stung her eyes, but she kept them open and fixed them on the oxygen tanks she'd shoved into the weakest section of the grate, straining to see the explosive charge she'd attached to it. It should give the tanks an extra kick she prayed would be enough to blast a hole they could get through.

It should be enough.

She hadn't gotten back to the computer in the mini-command center to tell Home Base what she'd learned about the weapons. The extra kick *had* to be enough.

She hadn't even told Nathan. Nathan, who held her hand and though in crisis at this critical moment, still seemed strong and comforting. He believed they were going to die.

And he wanted to die touching her.

Deeply moved by the gesture, she felt the emotional burn, in its way as wild and unfettered as the fire raging over their heads above the water. It started in her chest, spread out and crawled up the back of her throat, seeped through her nose and stung her eyes. It was the most loving gesture she had ever experienced. And that it came from a man who had earned her respect and admiration, a man she craved to make love with, to be loved by, made the sensations all the sweeter, made the man only more endearing.

Above, the fire rolled over them, crackling and hissing so loudly the sound carried through the water. It blazed on toward the grate. Nathan squeezed her hand, pulled her closer, trying to shield her with his body. She looked over at him and stroked his face. He blinked once, slowly, deliberately, letting her know her unspoken message had been received and her feelings were returned.

Something heavy crashed. The ground beneath them shook. Andrews panicked and started to stand. Four sets of hands grabbed at him and pulled him back down.

The fire swept through to the grate, and Kate prayed harder than she'd ever prayed for anything in her life, calling for intercession by God, angels, guides—even Nathan's former wife. *Emily, if you can help us, please. Please!*

The oxygen canisters blew.

The charge fired.

And the bellow nearly shattered their eardrums. Debris flew, the gushing water turned to froth and the pressure lifted them all up off the cave floor. Grabbing and snagging, they helped each other, pushing and pulling one another back down to the bottom.

When things calmed to a roar, Kate motioned to Nathan that she was going to check. He reluctantly let go of her hand and she crept along the cave floor to the grate.

There was a hole in it below the waterline. A hole large enough for any of them to get through!

Hope soared in Kate's chest and she rushed back to get the others. They surfaced, gasping to fill starving lungs. But the air churned with smoke and smut, offering little relief.

"Hold hands," she said, moving to the front of the line. "Stay low to the bottom. It's safest from falling rock and whatever else has been cut loose in here… Mathis, you doing all right?" In the worst shape of all, he looked ready to collapse.

"Yes, ma'am. I'm fine." That will in his voice still sounded strong.

She nodded, and they sank in the water, then she led them through the grate.

On the other side, where the cave broadened and the water level dropped, they surfaced. Bits of rock were still falling from the cave walls. She took a breath of polluted air and choked. It was still thick and heavy with smoke, and likely would be for hours. She just hoped Kunz and

Sandross hadn't released anything laced with bio or chemical weapons. Dealing with weapons of mass destruction right now was just more than she could take.

Kate looked back. "Is everyone still okay?"

"Yes."

"Yes."

The two women answered simultaneously. Kate looked at Douglas. "We're all okay, Captain."

"Fine." Nathan looked up at the rocks. Pebbles and baseball-size rocks peppered the water, signaling stress from the explosion had led to a serious amount of crumbling overhead. "Let's move, Kate. This place isn't stable."

"Kunz is obliterating it," she said, certain it was just a matter of time before it collapsed. Unfortunately, his obliterating also meant he wasn't inside. Was Sandross?

"He doesn't want S.A.S.S. to know what weapons he had here."

Kate thought of the files, stomped through the water, and whispered to Nathan, "He had more than weapons stashed in this compound."

Nathan looked over at her, silently asking.

"Files." She stepped around a large rock that had fallen right in the middle of the passage. "Lots of them."

"The doubles?" Nathan asked. When she nodded, he let his head loll back on his shoulders. "Damn it."

"Maybe not," Kate whispered cryptically.

He snapped up, looked at her. "Tell me."

"Later," she promised. She needed all of her attention and skills to tell him she'd sacrificed his life to transmit the files to Home Base. That wasn't something you told someone in passing.

"Maybe the explosion didn't blow up the weapons. Maybe it just got us. Kunz isn't likely to blow himself up."

Douglas answered Nathan. "The blast was too powerful, Commander. He took out the compound and half the damn hill."

"Or more," one of the women said.

"At least," the second JAG agreed, scrambling around a ragged boulder. "But I'm with the major on this. Thomas Kunz isn't going to blow himself up. The brutal bastard thinks he's invincible and too damn smart to die."

History would side with that woman, Kate thought.

"If he was here, he's toast," Mathis said. "And he was here. I talked to him." He rubbed a cautious finger around his broken nose. It was bleeding again.

"Are you sure the man you talked to was Kunz?" Kate asked.

Mathis hesitated and then grumbled. "No. It could have been one of his clones. I talked to Douglas—or a guy I thought was Douglas who wasn't. Maybe Kunz has a clone for himself, too. Hell, he probably has more than one."

Oh, boy, did he. Kate kept her mouth shut, but felt strongly that odds favored the real Kunz never setting foot in this place. Yet, just as strongly, she believed only he could authorize blowing up such a significant arsenal. So he had communications with the cave compound. And she could've sworn he came after her while she was buried in the shallow grave. Kate was more confused than ever.

Nathan stopped dead in his tracks. "Kate." He swung around to face her. "The weapons. The bio and chemical."

"Were fake," she said. "I saw launchers with capability to carry them, but there were only three warheads. None were marked with his initials."

"But they had bands," Nathan countered. "I saw them myself."

"They have to be empty or fake, Nathan. We're still

here," she clarified and then shrugged. "I guess he wants GRID to think he has more firepower for sale than he actually does. They feed on greed, remember? More money inspires more loyalty. The weapons with WMD capability had T.K. engraved on the casing. None of the warheads did."

"Thank God."

"Nathan, we'd have been dead within minutes of the blast." If not within seconds.

"Yes." He looked relieved to have realized it, shoved a hand through his hair. "You're right. I just hadn't gotten that far in my thinking yet."

Tenderness swept through her. Maybe she had always known better than to hope for love. But whatever this was, this bond with Forester, it felt an awful lot like how she imagined love would feel. She gave him a gentle smile and caressed his arm. "You know GRID will be waiting for us when we leave the cave."

His eyes grew solemn and he nodded. "We need a miracle."

"Yes." A miracle, a touch of luck, and damn good aim, Kate thought, and then spoke to the group. "Okay, everyone. Rest a minute and breathe deep. We've got a long haul out of here with no oxygen."

"Kate, no," Douglas objected. "We can't do it."

Several others mumbled their agreement. When they quieted, she went on. "Yes, we can. It won't be easy, but it can be done, Douglas. And we're going to do it."

Douglas turned to Nathan. "Commander, do something."

He looked from Douglas to Kate, held her gaze a long, unwavering moment. "She's gotten you this far, Douglas. If you want to live, I suggest you shut up and continue to follow her."

Douglas sighed deeply. "Yes, sir."

Mathis turned to Kate. "In case I can't make it, thanks, Captain."

"You'll make it, Mathis." She shook his outstretched hand. "Even if I have to breathe for you."

"There are more of us, you know." This, from one of the women, the little redhead in her mid-thirties with two black eyes and choke marks ringing her neck.

"Where are they?"

"I don't know. But they can't be far. They took them out yesterday afternoon. Sandross did. He was back within an hour, so it can't be far."

Douglas had an arm around Mathis's waist, helping him move. "What do we do at the mouth of the cave?" he asked.

"Focus on getting everyone to air," Nathan said. "Kate and I will take care of the rest."

Kate nodded, and again they were all under water, swimming.

Just before the last bend to the cave's mouth, Andrews stopped stroking. Kate swam back, grabbed his arm. Douglas had his hands full with Mathis, who couldn't kick with his bum leg. And Nathan was scouting ahead, trying to clear the way of GRID assassins.

Kate held on tightly, moved to position Andrews so she could haul him, but he put his hand atop hers and shook his head, a grateful look filled with resignation.

Weak and worn, he couldn't go on.

Kate emphatically nodded, refusing to accept that. He would go on, and they would make it out of here. She covered her mouth with his, pushed her breath into him, then dragged him with her through the remainder of the cave.

Her lungs burned, her muscles cramped, craving oxygen. Finally, they arrived at the mouth. She passed off Andrews to Nathan, swam out, and saw three divers waiting in ambush. Firing in rapid succession, Kate shot all three.

They'd never seen her coming.

Damn grateful for that, she motioned for the others to hurry. They swam out of the cave and kept swimming, passing her and Nathan.

They verified that the GRID operatives were dead—more men she didn't recognize—and then started up to the surface together.

About fifteen feet down, Kate knew she was in trouble. Sharing her breath had been too much. She could see the surface, see the spangles of the sun playing on the water, could see…

Oh, hell. She was sinking.

Not now, please not now. She tried to kick, but had no strength. Struggling, she commanded the meager threads of everything she had left to bind together and fight. She wanted to live. Her muscles gave out. She wanted to stretch and reach the surface. It was so close. So very close.

But there was nothing left in her. No energy. No threads. Nothing.

Her muscles shut down; she couldn't kick or make her arms move. She couldn't do anything but float. The light dimmed and her mind seemed to film with gauze she couldn't tear through. Yet her last thought formed crystal-clear and held.

She was drowning.

Chapter 18

Kate drifted in nothingness.

She no longer struggled or tried to focus. There was no pain, the burning had left her chest and her lungs had stopped aching. It was too late…

Something snagged her arm. She lacked the strength to look to see what it was. The something pulled at her, dragging then pushing, shoving her upward. No one shoved her! Angry, she opened her eyes—and looked into terror. Nathan's eyes. Nathan's face. Twisted in terror. *No. No, not Nathan. Not Nathan. He couldn't lose Emily and then be forced to watch me die, too. He couldn't!*

The urgency in his touch, the fear in his eyes penetrated her malaise. He didn't want her to die. She didn't want to die. She especially didn't want him to see it happen.

Fight, Kate. Fight. You know how to fight. You've al-

ways had to fight for everything. If you want to live, then fight!

Yes, she knew how to fight. She could do it. She could. She shook the cobwebs from her mind. Failed. Tried again. Failed again. And kept trying until something inside her broke through and a spurt of energy miraculously appeared. She kicked hard, a feeble move, but to her, one that required Herculean strength.

Nathan cupped her bottom and shoved her hard.

She shot up, breaking through the surface, and sucked in a sharp gasp. Kate struggled to catch her breath while coughing up the water she'd swallowed, not at all sure she could keep herself above water.

Nathan popped up beside her, spewing water and gulping air. His chest heaving, he stared at her, clutched her arm and patted her on the back to help her stop coughing.

"Kate. Kate?" Nathan rubbed a hand over her head, smoothing back her hair. "Are you all right? Kate?"

He had saved her life. Tears gathered at the corners of her eyes, trickled down her face. She looked over at him and their gazes met. They shared a look acknowledging what had happened, a look of gratitude that puzzled Kate. She knew why she was grateful, but why was Nathan? "I'm okay," she said, her voice husky.

Pulling her into his arms, Nathan hugged her to him. He shook from head to toe and his heart beat hard and fast against her chest. "My, God, Kate." His ragged voice broke against her ear. "I thought I'd lost you."

Awed by the force of his emotions, she circled his waist with her arms, pressed her face against his hard chest and clung to him. "Thank you, Nathan."

His eyes red and overbright, he sniffed, and Katherine

Kane saw the tenderness in his eyes she had so envied with Emily.

Amazed by it, she lifted a hand to his face, tears washing down her face. "Oh, Nathan."

Perplexed, he wiped a tear from her cheek. "What is it, sweetheart?" The skin under the bandages on his face crinkled and worry lines deepened at the corners of his mouth.

She heard the others, spared them a glance. "Everyone made it? Andrews?"

He nodded, and relief joined the other tumultuous emotions coursing through her. "I'm okay, Nathan," she assured him. "I've just never felt this depth of caring from a man before—and I've never felt it for a man, either." She swallowed a lump in her throat. "And never in my whole life has anyone looked at me the way you're looking at me right now. It's…it's humbling, Nathan. It's just…so humbling."

"A moment of grace," he whispered softly, almost breathlessly.

"Yes." That was it exactly. How had he… "Emily, right?"

He nodded.

Oddly comforted by that, Kate smiled. "I think I would have liked your Emily very much, Nathan."

"She'd have loved you."

She just might, Kate thought, recalling asking for her help in the cave.

An engine whined, stealing everyone's attention.

A boat rounded the finger of land extending into the gulf, heading their way. Nervous chatter erupted.

"It's GRID. It's GRID!"

"No, Andrews, it's okay," Douglas cut in. "It's my team."

"Thank God." Kate let her forehead fall against and rest on Nathan's shoulder. She just didn't have the steam to slay one more dragon. Not one more today.

"Kate?" Nathan whispered so only she could hear, his breath warm on her face.

She looked up at him, a ghost of a smile curving her lips.

"You said one time that you knew better than to expect love."

Odd, that he would choose now to bring this up. "It's the way I was raised, Nathan. I'm all I've ever had."

"Not anymore." He clenched his jaw, clearly half expecting her to rebuff him.

Kate wasn't sure whether to laugh or to cry. She adored this man, admired and respected him, and she damn well thought she loved him. Though she couldn't be sure, she knew that this man had changed forever the way Katherine Kane saw men.

More so, he had changed forever the way she saw herself. Kate was good enough and worth loving.

The question had changed to: was she capable of loving?

As she climbed into the boat, she was perplexed about the lack of GRID operatives pursuing them. Kate was certain Kunz would blow up the compound as he'd done others before, certain he would sacrifice his mother, but not at all certain he would sacrifice his new second-in-command, Marcus Sandross. And what about Gaston? That question, too, remained unanswered.

Chapter 19

The outpost hummed.

Nathan's men rushed in and out of the command center, from desk to desk, phone to phone, conversing with multiple people simultaneously on a host of pertinent topics.

Everyone understood the urgency of moving fast: to prevent GRID from making a successful land-based escape from the compound—with, or without, the weapons. Those in the need-to-know loop wanted to investigate the damage and to retrieve any and all surviving evidence.

Kate sat in Nathan's clear cubicle in the center of the command tent, using a secure-line telephone to report to S.A.S.S. Waiting for authorization approval, she looked up at Nathan and Douglas, who had just walked in.

"Did you get them to the medic?"

Nathan nodded.

Douglas stuffed a hand into his fatigue pants' pocket. "They're having to medevac Mathis to Germany for his leg and his nose."

Medical evacuations were a way of life when you were this deep in the field, so the news didn't surprise Kate, but she felt bad for Mathis because he had to wait for treatment. The poor guy had been through a hell of a lot. "But he'll be okay, right?"

"He'll be fine, Kate," Nathan said, dropping onto the edge of her desk. "And Andrews told me what you did for him."

Having no idea what to say, she kept quiet.

"He said he had given up, but you wouldn't let him. You breathed for him."

Nathan had an odd catch in his voice. She didn't know what to do with it. "Andrews and the JAGs are okay, too?"

"They're fine. They're all a little bruised and battle-worn, but they'll recover."

Glad to hear it, Kate took the cup of steaming hot coffee Nathan passed to her. It was black. He remembered that she liked her coffee black.

That warm sense of being cared for spread through her chest again. It settled in her stomach, soothing her, and while she had no basis to conclude it was love, she knew beyond a shadow of a doubt that feeling cared for like this was addictive.

She also knew she'd shoot anyone who considered offering her a detox.

Maggie's voice cut through her thoughts. "May I help you?"

Damn it. Why couldn't Amanda have answered the phone? Hell, the one she really needed to talk to was Darcy. "Home Base, it's Bluefish."

"What the hell is going on over there? The phones have been lighting up like Christmas trees around here for the past two hours."

"We found another compound." Kate wiped her hair back from her eyes. "Listen, I need to talk to Intel. Pull her in, okay?"

"Sure. Stand by one."

Nathan sat behind his desk and signaled Douglas to pull up a chair.

Riley came in, carrying a tray of food. "Captain Douglas?"

"Is that for me?" He looked at the food on the tray and his mouth watered. He swallowed hard.

"Yes, sir," Riley said. "The doc said liquids would be best for twenty-four hours, but the cook said you'd starve to death before then, and he wasn't having it." Riley passed the tray. "He said to put this into your hands myself. And I'm also supposed to tell you that he knew you were too mean to die."

"Thanks, Riley." Douglas smiled. "And thank Max for me, too, will you?"

"Yes, sir." Riley shoved his glasses up on his nose and looked across the desk at Nathan and then over at Kate. "Can I get either of you anything?"

Kate's stomach was too full of knots to consider putting anything in it. "No, thanks, Riley."

"Sir?"

Nathan refused, then thought better of it. "Maybe a sandwich. I don't care what kind."

"Yes, sir." Riley left the cubicle and then the tent.

Douglas dug into a bowl of beef stew that smelled pretty darn good. And the bread sounded crunchy. It was probably more stale than crunchy, though if Douglas's expression was a decent gauge, he was dining on a feast fit for a king.

Smiling, Kate sipped at her coffee. She'd been that hungry. More than once.

"Bluefish?" Darcy's voice sounded through the phone.

"Hi."

"What's up?"

"Everything." Kate turned her attention to the report. "We located the compound, four detainees and Captain Douglas. Everyone's out alive. The detainees had been tortured, though I'm not sure the extent, so you need to have special investigators on hand ASAP to check that out. Three are ambulatory and suffered minor injuries. One is en route to Germany for treatment."

"How bad is he?"

"Banged-up leg and a nose that needs a new one jacked up under it." Kate glanced over at Nathan, and asked. "Do you have names and serial numbers on Mathis, Andrews and the JAGs?"

"Riley?" Nathan shouted.

He popped in his head. "Yes, sir?"

"Name, rank and serial numbers on the hostages we rescued."

He flipped through his clipboard and passed a sheet of paper to Nathan, who then passed it to Kate. She read them off to Darcy and then passed the paper back to Riley.

"Oh, boy."

"What?"

"Do you realize the first woman you mentioned is a major contract negotiator? She acquires weapons systems for the DOD at Pentagon level."

The Department of Defense. Military. All branches. Oh, joy. Wasn't that just great news? "Well, you'd better have her damn double arrested pronto."

"Did you get that?" Darcy asked Maggie.

"I'm on it," Maggie answered.

Kate then relayed information on the weapons observed in the compound. From the looks on Nathan's and Douglas's faces, they were either impressed by her memory or awed by the sheer volume of weapons in the GRID arsenal.

Likely the volume of weapons. Even Kate, who had been exposed to far too much to impress easily, had been struck by it.

"So," Darcy said. "You've connected the active weapons with his initials engraved in the casings."

"No," Kate corrected her. "I can't verify any of the weapons were bio or chemical, just capable of carrying bio and/or chemical. I also saw rocket launchers capable of delivering them and they were marked with our guy's initials."

Kate paused, giving Darcy time to key in everything she was telling her, and then told her about the files. "There were hundreds of them. Maybe even more."

"That's chilling."

"It was—is." Kate licked at her lips. They were parched from all the salt water. "Did you get the transmission?"

"I got twenty-three names and records. The OSI and FBI are working jointly. They formed a task force and are rounding them all up."

"Only twenty-three?" Disappointment washed through Kate and she sipped at her coffee to give herself a second to get a grip on her emotions. "There were hundreds of files on the computer."

"Things were coming in fine," Darcy said. "I fed back so it appeared a virus checker was on the screen there, and we were swimming along great."

"Well, what happened?"

"All of a sudden I got a skull and crossbones on the

screen, and it locked up my system. Fortunately, I had safeguards in place—extra firewalls—or I'd have fried the entire unit."

"Big Fish."

"Him or his second-in-command, I figure."

"Could have been him. He was at the computer when I last ran into him."

"You ran into him? Did you take him out then?"

"No opportunity."

"Too bad." Darcy's sigh crackled through the phone. "I ran a trace. It's still zigzagging around the world, country to country. I figure it's on a terminal loop and will never stop, but you don't know, if you don't try."

Douglas swallowed a steaming bite of stew and lifted a finger in Kate's direction.

"Just a second." Kate hiked her chin for Douglas to go ahead.

Riley returned with Nathan's sandwich. It looked like turkey, smelled like chicken. Bits of lettuce were falling out from between the slices of bread.

Kate leaned around Riley to see Douglas. "What?"

"Tell Darcy I saw two new boats with the same MO. Both flew French flags. They were riding low at sea and high on reaching port." He spooned up a carrot. "I know they're dumping weapons, I just can't prove it."

"Intel, Douglas says—"

"I heard. Any idea what's happening?"

Nathan passed Kate half his sandwich. She shook her head, but he pushed it over, insisting, so she took it. "I know exactly what's happening," she said, shoving bits of lettuce back between the slices. "In fact, when I have a minute where I'm not in the middle of a crisis, I'm going to give myself hell for not figuring it out immediately."

Nathan perked up. "You know how they're moving the weapons?"

She nodded.

"How?" he, Douglas and Darcy asked simultaneously.

Kate set the sandwich down and sipped at her coffee before responding. "GRID used a method popular during the war between England and France, back when champagne was banned from England."

"Come on," Douglas snorted.

"Stow it." Nathan frowned at Douglas and then looked at Kate, his curiosity clearly piqued. "That's been a while."

"Indeed it has, which is precisely why I didn't think of it." She snagged a bite of lettuce and chewed it up. "GRID puts the weapons in an oak barrel. Then they set the barrel into a larger barrel and fill the empty space between the two with rock salt."

"Rock salt?" Douglas rolled his eyes.

"Hey, genius," Nathan said. "If GRID dumped barrels packaged like that, they'd sink."

"Exactly," Kate agreed. "The Navy searches the vessel and finds no contraband, nothing illegal. The ship goes on."

"So who retrieves the damn barrels?" Douglas emptied his bowl and hand-signaled Reilly that he'd like more.

Riley shot back a thumbs-up and headed out of the tent.

"No one retrieves them." Kate paused to take a bite of her sandwich, chewed slowly just to drive Douglas nuts.

Darcy was chuckling in her ear, enjoying this. That alone made it worth it to Kate to drag it out. Darcy spent most of her life isolated and didn't often have a chance to laugh with anyone else.

Douglas mulled over the information, then slapped at his knee. "Son of a bitch." He flipped his hands up. "The rock salt melts."

Kate nodded, a smile curling her lips. "It melts, and the barrels float. The tide takes them in, they crash into the rocks—"

Nathan chimed in. "Leaving the gouges."

"And someone steers them into the cave," Douglas said.

"Yes," Kate said. "Then they float through the cave to the steps, where they're removed from the barrels and the weapons are stored in the warehouse rooms until Big Fish sells them. Then he moves them out over land."

"Damn it." Douglas grunted. "Damn it."

"We never considered he might use methodology so obsolete." Nathan frowned. "We should have."

"Obsolete but effective," Kate said. "But don't worry about it. The second you develop an opinion about the way Big Fish thinks or works, he takes a one-eighty and does something like this to prove you're wrong. The man reinvents himself every time he turns around."

The skin between Nathan's eyebrows creased. "The two operatives who disappeared off the ship—divers were waiting for them in the water, and they took the men into the cave. That's how they seemingly disappeared."

"It fits, Commander," Douglas said.

Stew in hand, Riley appeared at the door to the cubicle. "Sir, Search and Rescue needs for all of you to come down to the dock. They've found a floater they want you to take a look at."

"Who do they think he is, Riley?"

"They're not sure, sir. But they believe he's Thomas Kunz. They know he's in Leavenworth, but the guys there insist the floater looks just like him."

"Let's move." Nathan slid out of his seat.

Douglas grabbed the bowl of stew and bottle of water, then headed to the tent door.

Kate dragged her weary body outside and slid into the jeep, beside Nathan. "You realize this is an exercise in futility."

"Yes. At best we'll be looking at a double, and I'm thinking it signals Sandross skipped out of the compound, too, and they left Kunz's double to blow things up. Whether or not he knew it, that's another matter." Nathan cranked the engine and gunned the gas. "But we can't very well refuse to take a look."

They couldn't. It'd be like sending out an ad that Kunz wasn't Kunz. And believing Nathan was right about Sandross, as well, had Kate in a totally foul mood.

When they parked at the shore and Douglas hopped out, Kate put a hand on Nathan's, silently telling him to wait.

"We'll be right there, Douglas." He shouted to him over the hood of the jeep.

"Yes, sir." He walked on toward the dock.

Nathan looked over at Kate and fear flickered through his eyes, but he just waited for her to say what was on her mind.

He sensed it was personal, she realized. And it was. How did he do that? Tune into her that way?

Her mouth suddenly dry, she moistened her lips. "When this is over, I want to spend some time with you." Her face felt as hot as an oven. What was wrong with her? "Alone, I mean. Well, not alone. Together. With you. Just you and me, I mean."

The fear left him and a teasing twinkle she might just love replaced it. "Why?"

So much for his reading her. She frowned. "Are you going to rub my nose in it?"

"No, of course not." He raked a thumb on the steering

wheel. "I just want to make sure we don't have crossed wires here."

"I am... I think..." She couldn't talk because she couldn't think. Nothing sounded right inside her head. It certainly wouldn't, if she said it. This was insane.

Actually she supposed it wasn't. He mattered. That was the problem. If a man didn't matter, you had nothing at stake. But Nathan mattered. A lot. Enough to take the risks. So she plunged in. "I'm crazy about you, Forester. I want to be alone with you. I want us to do something normal, like normal people do. That's the picture."

He gave her a slow smile that rivaled the twinkle. "Oh."

"Oh?" What did he mean by that?

"I thought maybe you wanted to jump my bones." He sighed. "Well, we can do the normal thing, too."

He was teasing her! "Jumping your bones is normal."

"Good." He nodded, looking totally pleased with himself. "Okay, Kate. We'll spend some time alone together and do the normal thing, which includes you jumping my bones."

She didn't trust him on this. With her life, yes, but not on this. "You're razzing me, right?"

"I'm serious."

"Look, Forester, a few days ago you wouldn't step inside a woman's tent. You made me stand out in a damn sandstorm."

He got out of the jeep, opened the door for her, leaned over and whispered close to her ear. "But I wasn't in love with you then, Kate."

She couldn't move. Didn't dare move. He was in love with her? Impossible. Outrageous.

"I figure with your attitude about love, it's going to take a while for you to accept it. I'm sorry about that, sweetheart." He stroked her cheek. "But it's true. I'm not razzing you, and you're not crazy—you're asking yourself that, right?"

She nodded, not together enough to consider not telling him the truth.

"You're not. Sometime when we have time, I'll tell you exactly when I fell in love with you. You'll be surprised."

"Nathan, I don't think I could be more surprised than I am at this moment."

"You can be, and you will." He laughed, hard and deep. "Come on, they're waiting."

Kate got out of the jeep and, doing her damnedest to focus, walked down to the shore to the small cluster of men. All she wanted to do was to grab Nathan in a ferocious hug and kiss him until his lips were numb.

But duty called. And celebrating would have to wait. She pulled herself back, kicking and screaming, to the reality of what they were doing at the shore, and joined the men.

A tall guy, about forty-five with gray hair and a pug nose nodded. "You Captain Kane?"

"Yes, I am." Kate extended her hand.

"Sergeant Baker." They shook, and then he motioned east. "We've got the floater over here, ma'am."

"How long has he been in the water?"

"M.E. says a couple hours at most. He thinks the guy died from a blunt force trauma to the head."

Kate stopped in front of the body, which was laid out on a stretcher. The medics were preparing to move him.

Sergeant Baker pulled back the sheet.

And Kate stared at the face of Thomas Kunz.

"Is this man Thomas Kunz, ma'am?"

Kate sighed. "It could be," she admitted. "The truth is, I can't verify that without his DNA."

"You can't go on a visual?"

"I'm sorry, no." She couldn't say any more.

Nathan stepped forward. "Kunz has a team of men who act as doubles for him, Sergeant. Like most leaders do. This could be one of them, or it could be Kunz. The only way to be certain is to run his DNA."

"Damn," the sergeant said. "Sorry, ma'am. Sir," he said to Nathan. "I've run into this before with politicians, but I never thought about an arms dealer doing it."

"Let us know when you get the DNA, would you?" Nathan asked.

"Yes, sir." He nodded. "I'll have a copy of the report sent over to your clerk."

"Thanks." Nathan turned back to the jeep.

Douglas was already halfway there. Kate walked with Nathan. "It gives me the creeps to see Kunz's face."

"I can certainly understand why." Nathan dropped his voice. "Kate?"

"Yeah." She glanced over.

"For the record, I want to jump your bones, too."

She smiled. "Yeah?"

"Yeah."

The ride back to the outpost was calm and quiet. Kate and Nathan seemed content to just ride and unwind, and Douglas slipped into a doze shortly after climbing into the back seat.

About halfway to the outpost, Kate got a strange feeling. Shivers crawled up and down her backbone. Warnings.

Serious warnings.

Wary of snipers, she scanned the terrain, but saw nothing that shouldn't be there. Nathan had a field phone; Riley hadn't called. Everything had to be okay at the outpost. Maybe something was going on at Home Base…

You're exhausted, Kate. You've been on the go for four days now. You need rest. That's all it is. Your body is telling you to take a break and give it some rest.

Kate just about had herself convinced to ignore the warnings when they passed the guard post at the camp perimeter. It was empty. "Nathan—" she started.

"I know, Kate."

A man didn't leave his guard post upright or willingly. That this one was vacant had Kate tense as strung wire and withdrawing her weapon.

Nathan drove into the outpost.

Not a soul was in sight.

They searched the entire post. TVs were on in the recreation tent. Food was burning on the stove in the mess tent. The shower was on, the stall empty.

"I don't understand this." Kate paced between two tents. Worry, thick and hot and nerve-racking, burst and strengthened inside her, souring her stomach. "It doesn't make sense, Nathan."

"No, it doesn't." His worry matched her own. "No sense at all."

Checking every tent, every possible place where anyone could be, they found no one.

The outpost was deserted.

Chapter 20

Kate stood in the center of the outpost compound, wearing her lip mike. For the first time, when not in the field on a mission, she felt grateful for the ability to connect instantly with Home Base.

"That's right, the entire unit is MIA," Kate said, ruffling the hair at her nape. It was hot and her hair was soaked. "I'm all but positive GRID has them."

"Roger," Maggie said. "We'll be on standby—the colonel's orders. Keep us in the loop on developments."

"Will do." Kate shoved the mike back away from her mouth, and tapped her earpiece.

Nathan stood beside her, seemingly dazed. Strain lined his face. He clearly was having a hard time wrapping his arms around what had happened.

Blessing or curse, Kate grasped it immediately.

"Where the hell could they have gone? My men didn't just vacate the premises."

"They were taken, Nathan." She spoke softly, hoping to ease the blow. "This is why we met so little resistance on leaving the cave compound." Three divers. She should've expected something like this. Damn it, why hadn't she suspected something like this? "While we were there, they were preparing to come here."

"But sixty men?" Nathan lifted a hand skyward. "You don't just walk in and take over an armed unit of sixty men."

"You do, if they're taking orders from a senior officer."

Realization struck Nathan and he clamped his jaw shut. "The bastards posed as us?"

"I doubt they had time to prepare doubles, Nathan. That usually requires about three months. But some senior officer showed up here and issued orders to the men. That's my suspicion, anyway, because it would give GRID the least amount of resistance."

Kate felt sweat roll down the sides of her face and pool in her bra between her breasts. The air was so hot it almost burned to breathe it, and the glare from the sun had her head pounding. "Remember what the JAG woman said back in the cave about GRID taking the other hostages out? They said Sandross couldn't have gone far with them because he returned to the compound within an hour or so."

"Yeah, I remember that."

"Well, maybe they took your unit to the same place they took the hostages."

"Logical." He dragged a forefinger across his damp brow. "But how the hell do we find them?"

"Same way we always do." She edged her voice with grit and determination. "One clue at a time."

The distant sound of a helicopter approaching breached the ominous silence. Kate and Nathan took cover behind the jeep, pulled their weapons and waited for it to land.

Douglas walked out of a tent situated closer to the landing pad and waited for the helicopter to set down. "He must have called it in," Kate said.

"He did." Nathan holstered his weapon then walked toward the chopper. "Or he damn sure wouldn't be approaching it."

Kate did the same and watched five men in fatigues disembark. She recognized them. Douglas's tactical team. They had been temporarily reassigned to another mission while Douglas was waiting to be thoroughly debriefed. "Reinforcements, finally!"

"Bluefish?"

Hearing Maggie's voice in her earpiece, Kate lowered her lip mike into position. "Yeah, go ahead."

"Has the major gone up the chain of command on this latest issue?"

Kate watched the team greet Douglas and couldn't resist a smile. They were genuinely happy to see him. "Douglas's escape, the weapons cache being located and the explosion in the cave have all been reported up his chain of command." Kunz and GRID and the doubles, of course, hadn't been mentioned. That was selective intelligence and reported only to S.A.S.S.

The chopper stayed on the pad, its props whirling. Douglas and the team came over to where Nathan and Kate stood.

"Commander." The most senior, a lieutenant with huge blue eyes and perfect teeth, saluted. "Good to see you, sir."

"You, too, Carlisle." Nathan nodded toward the chopper. "What is he waiting for?"

"You, sir." Carlisle cleared his throat. "The colonel wants you to go to the hospital to get checked out. The chopper is supposed to take you."

"Thanks." He turned to Kate. "Would you please get Colonel Drake on the horn?"

Kate recognized the steel in Nathan's voice. He wasn't a happy major. She pulled down the lip mike. "Home Base?"

"Yes."

"The major would like to speak to the colonel."

"Stand by."

Moments later, Colonel Drake's voice sounded through Kate's earpiece. "Just a second, Colonel. I'll get the major for you."

Kate passed him her headgear. He plopped it on and adjusted the mike. "I appreciate your concern, Colonel, but I don't need medical, I'm fine. And I'm me, if you know what I mean."

A pause, then, "The captain will verify."

Yet another pause while Colonel Drake responded, and then he added, "I need to be at outpost, in case we make contact with my men."

A moment later he passed the handset back to Kate. His expression was tense, his mouth pinched tight, and his left eye twitched harder than ever before. "She wants you to vouch for me," Nathan told Kate.

Oh, boy. The commander was supremely offended. Kate put on the gear. "I'm on, Colonel."

"Are you certain he's himself?"

And not a double. She looked at Nathan. "Yes, ma'am."

"Okay, then. I don't expect he's going to like these orders much, but if he has a problem with them, he can take them up with General Shaw. He issued them. I'm merely the messenger."

"What orders, ma'am?"

"The outpost is off-limits to all personnel. Tactical's positioned to guard the perimeter. No one is to enter the camp until forensics is done with it. They're on the way there now."

Why would Nathan have a problem with that? "I'm sure—"

"I'm not done yet," Colonel Drake interjected. "The general has also ordered the two of you to get on that chopper—the one that dropped off the tactical team."

"Whatever for, Colonel?"

Colonel Drake ignored the question. "You'll eventually be taken to a hotel where you're to remain sequestered on quarters until the preliminary investigations are done. That should be late tomorrow."

Kate swallowed hard. "Sequestered? Is that necessary, Colonel?"

"The general says yes, and the secretary agrees with him. I'd say it's a done deal, Bluefish."

"Yes, ma'am." This bit of news, Nathan wouldn't appreciate or take lightly. *Both* General Shaw and Secretary Reynolds. "I'll tell him." She dreaded it, but she would pass the order along.

"Anything else for me?"

"No, Colonel. Nothing else."

Seconds later, Maggie came back on the radio. "Do you want us to remain on standby? I've received notification that tactical is onsite."

"No, Home Base. Thanks. They're here." Kate took off her headgear and attached it to her belt. "Commander, may I speak to you privately, please?"

Noting the formal address and clearly figuring it was due to the men, Nathan stepped away. "Of course, Captain."

They walked over two tents, and Kate stopped and

turned to face him. "Nathan, General Shaw has banned everyone from the premises. We're to go in the chopper to a hotel."

"What?"

"We're sequestered until they finish investigating. At least until late tomorrow."

"Damn it!" Nathan swore. "Why did he do this?"

"Who knows? But he's the general and Secretary Reynolds is backing him up on it."

Nathan stilled, grunted, then looked into Kate's eyes. "Well, you got your wish, damn it. We are going to get to spend some time alone together."

She snorted. "I didn't exactly want to spend time with a raging bull. Jeez, Nathan, you look so very pleased at the prospect. Careful, my knees are knocking so hard they might crack. I can hardly stand this kind of elation."

"I'm sorry, sweetheart." He gentled his tone, softened his expression. "It's just that I want to be here for my men."

"Well, you can't," she said, dropping any pretense of sugarcoating. "Accept that which you can't change, Nathan. And enjoy that which you can."

"You're right." He looked at the still waiting chopper. "That's our ride, right?"

She nodded.

"Let's go, then."

Kate walked over to the chopper, a little miffed and a little bemused. She even liked Nathan ticked off, and if that wasn't enough of a worry, she had to deal with erotic images of him, too. Pleasant though they were, she'd rather have them when she was feeling tender, not ticked.

They buckled into the chopper, and the pilot lifted off.

* * *

The hotel turned out to be a private hotel in Kuwait contracted by the U.S. government to house visiting military. The floors were cool marble. White columns stretched to the ceiling, three stories above, and ornate murals of gardens and oases adorned the walls. Colorful silk sofas littered the lobby in intimate groupings, shielded by strategically placed potted greenery. Few people in the lobby were not wearing some type of U.S. military uniform, though most were a far cry more tidy than Nathan's or Kate's.

It was also a far cry from battlefield conditions. Looking scraggly and worn in sweaty fatigues, Kate felt out of place and self-conscious. Nathan, who honestly looked worse with dusty bandages on his face, seemed perfectly at ease. She envied him. Was it a woman thing—to want to feel appropriate to her environment? Or a Kate thing—never feeling good enough? And at this point, did it really matter?

A man in his fifties dressed in a gray suit led them to a private room, where the concierge checked them in. Seated at a delicate desk, the concierge stood to greet them. He had a slight build, a belly, a round face with glasses and a jovial smile. Unsure exactly why, Kate liked him.

"I am Abdul," he said. "Your rooms are ready." He motioned to an elderly man near the door who came over and retrieved the keys to their rooms. "We were informed that your personal belongings had been stolen so we took the liberty of providing you with some things you'll need until you have sufficient time to replace them. If we've missed anything, please just let us know." He nodded at the man with the keys. "This is Sattar. If you're ready now, he'll show you to your rooms."

"Thank you." Kate moved to follow Sattar. Walking a few steps behind him, she got an uneasy feeling. Normally, she was shuttled to a third-rate hotel that might or might not have air-conditioning and running water, where someone shoved her a key and she found her room on her own. If her personal items were not with her, she went without them. Period. This was strange, and, while it was pleasant, she wasn't sure if she should like it. She looked over at Nathan. "Why are we getting this kind of treatment?"

"I suspect General Shaw had something to do with it." He winked at her. "We've had a rough few days."

Sattar moved slowly, and Kate didn't rush him. They took the elevator to the fourth floor, then walked about halfway down the east hallway.

He stopped and turned to Kate. "Your room is here. No money, please."

When she nodded, he opened the door, and Kate took the key. "Thank you."

"My privilege."

Privilege? She looked at Nathan. "Where will you be?" The corridor light caught on his wedding ring and its gleam mocked her. As much as things had changed between them, he hadn't yet finished dealing with Emily. That was essential before the relationship between them progressed, wasn't it? It felt essential, reasonable. Logical.

Love isn't logical, Kate.

"Major Forester's room is next door." Sattar moved to open Nathan's door. Then he walked back and passed Nathan his key.

"Thank you." Nathan took it. When Sattar returned to the elevator, Nathan turned to Kate. "What's wrong, Kate?"

Her heart beat hard and fast. Emily aside, them staying together would be a stupid thing to do, personally and professionally. Sad in a way she probably shouldn't be, she walked inside her room. "I'm totally exhausted," she told him. "I need a shower and a nap, then I'll be fine." She said it, and prayed it was true.

Nathan frowned, clearly doubting her. "I'll be next door if you need anything."

Kate nodded and closed the door. She stripped off her top and let the cold air cool down her body. The desert was a wicked place to be in summer. She checked the room for listening devices and found none. But she did find three sets of fresh clothing. All were made of high-quality silk, bold colors and styles that flowed. In a dressing room next to the bath, she found everything she could possibly want in the way of cosmetics and toiletries, including an exotic blend of patchouli oil. The footed tub was large enough to swim in, and she debated between a shower and a long soak in the bath. They both won.

She showered first, washing off the salt and sand and dust caked on her skin, shampooed her hair and knotted a towel around her head, then rinsed the tub and filled it with steamy hot water. She dripped in some of the scented oil, inhaled deeply and sank into the tub.

The rich scent relaxed her, and exhaustion overtook her. Her eyelids grew heavy, then heavier still.

The water cooled and before she fell from a light doze into a deep sleep, she forced herself to get out and dry off. Wrapping a towel around her body, she finger-combed her hair back from her face. Her limbs felt so heavy she doubted she could stay upright any longer than it would take her to get to the bed.

She dragged back the soft, green-brocade spread and

crawled in, then pulled the sheet up over her. Her head sank deep into the cushy pillow and she closed her eyes. "Ah, bliss."

The last image that filled her mind was of Nathan looking at her with that tenderness in his eyes.

"Kate?" Someone smoothed her hair. "Kate?"

Nathan. It was Nathan. She tried to open her eyelids, but they were in full rebellion. Finally one cracked open a slit. "Mmm?" It was all she could manage.

"Are you all right?" He leaned over her, the look in his eyes not tender but worried.

She nodded. "Yes, what's wrong?"

"You didn't answer your door. I knocked and knocked, but you didn't answer." He shrugged. "It worried me."

"I was in the tub." He'd changed clothes. Navy slacks and a subtle print shirt that looked wonderful with his eyes. And the dusty bandages had been replaced with smaller, clean ones.

"You were in the tub for nine hours?"

Frowning, she insisted that her eyes open. "Nine hours?"

"It's nine at night, Kate." He swiped his face with his left hand and she saw a telltale circle of white skin where his wedding band had been.

He'd taken it off.

Her heart skipped a little beat and, silently thankful, she scooted over on the mattress. "Then it's a reasonable bedtime." She tossed back the sheet and patted the empty place with her hand. "Come to bed, Nathan."

"Kate, I don't think… You don't know what you're—"

Alert now, she looked him right in the eye. "Sometimes you think too much, and I know exactly what I'm doing, Nathan."

He frowned at her, shoved his hands into his slacks' pockets. "Do you want me here because of some fear of ending up alone?"

"I've been alone all my life. It's what I know. I don't fear it." She lowered her arm. The sheet fell slack over her hip. This wasn't about her at all. He'd taken off the ring, but this was still about Emily. "Do you love me, Nathan?"

"Yes, I do." He looked anything but happy about it. "I told you I did."

"I know what you told me, but then you thought you were going to die. You're alive now and, at least for the moment, odds look pretty good that you'll be alive for the foreseeable future." She sat up. "Do you love me now?"

"Yes, but—"

Of course there was a "but." Wasn't there always a but? "But I'm not Emily," Kate finished for him.

"No." He looked genuinely surprised. "You're not Emily, Kate, but you're not supposed to be. You're supposed to be you." He let his head loll back. "You've got this wrong."

She scrunched up her pillow. "Then give it to me right."

He caught his lower lip with his teeth, his left eye twitching. "I haven't been with a woman since Emily died. That's what this is about."

She couldn't believe it. He was too virile, too everything. "You're telling me that you've been celibate for five years?"

"Yeah." He nodded, reinforcing his claim. "I don't know the rules in this kind of relationship. I don't like being on unsure ground."

This, she understood. "You're afraid of me."

"Hell, yes." His expression turned frank. "I'm afraid you're going to break my heart." He sighed so deeply it heaved his shoulders. "There, I finally said it."

He expected her to ridicule him; she sensed it. It was hard not to reassure him, but he wouldn't believe her anyway. This was one of those firsthand lessons that he'd have to work through himself, and the only proof that would be of use to him would be time. He'd have to live it to recognize the truth. "I'd never deliberately hurt you, Nathan."

He walked a short path beside her bed. "When Emily died, I thought I'd died, too. I thought that part of my life was over."

"What part?" she asked, settling back on her pillow. Obviously, Nathan needed to talk. "You loving a woman?"

"Yes." He looked her straight in the eyes. "You scare the hell out of me, Kate. You have since I first heard your voice on the radio."

She hadn't talked to him on the radio. "When did you hear my voice?"

"During the first compound raid." He grimaced.

"When I flirted with Douglas?" Now, she was finally getting a grip on this.

Nathan nodded.

"I scared you then?" This, she didn't get. "But I didn't even know you."

"I know." He lifted a hand. "But something inside of me sure knew you. I was so damn jealous of Douglas, I wanted to rip his throat out."

"What did he do?"

"Nothing." Nathan rolled his eyes back in his head. "I wanted you to flirt with me. I didn't want you to flirt with him, and I damn sure didn't want him flirting back with you."

"Ah."

"Yes, ah." He snorted, started pacing again.

"So why didn't you contact me afterward?"

"What?" He stopped. "I'm supposed to call and tell you I was listening in, and the sound of your voice made me a lunatic?"

"I see your point." Infinitely pleased, she rose up onto her knees at the edge of the bed and placed her hands on his chest. "I don't think you're a lunatic, Nathan." She stroked him shoulder to waist. "And you're not the only one afraid of ending up with a broken heart."

"Why are you afraid?" he asked, stunned. "You know I love you."

"I'm not merely afraid, Nathan. I'm terrified."

"I know." His eyebrows knit together. "Of being alone, right?"

"No, I told you before, I'm used to being alone." She looked down at the floor, then forced herself to meet his gaze. "I'm terrified of loving you for the rest of my life and never again seeing you look at me the way you always looked at Emily's picture."

"Kate, no." He stroked her hair, reassuring her. "Oh, honey, no. There's no competition, Kate. Love doesn't work that way."

"See, that's the problem. How would I know?" She sucked in a sharp breath, looked up at him and circled his neck with her arms. "I think I've done something really stupid, Nathan."

"Kate, nothing can be that bad."

"This can."

"What is it?"

She steeled herself and said the words she'd never before in her life uttered out loud except once when she was five, to her favorite teddy bear, Baxter. "I'm totally and completely in love with you." She shook her head. "Love or maybe lust with a kick."

"Love *or* lust with a kick?" He clearly wasn't happy with that.

"It feels like lust—I mean, lust is definitely there—only there's more. It's the *more* that's giving me fits." She shrugged. "I can't explain it, Nathan. I wish I could, but I've never been in love. I've never felt love from anyone else. How would I know it if it fell on me?"

He hesitated and then his expression closed. "I think I understand the problem. I saved your life, Kate. You're grateful to me. That's all. You feel lust and gratitude and that's confusing the issue, making you think it's love. But it's not."

Her arms went slack on his shoulders and she tilted her head to look at him. "How do you know what it is or isn't?"

"It's a logical deduction, sweetheart."

"But everyone says love isn't logical." Yet he feared she had confused gratitude and combined it with lust and considered that love. And he thought that was logical? Sounded damned illogical to her. "No, I'm not buying it, Nathan."

"Why not?"

"Because over the years, many men have saved my life and I've never wanted to sleep with any of them. I've only been in this lust-or-love position once. Now, with you."

She dipped her chin to her chest, weighed her feelings, seeking the truth, and when it settled, she looked up at him. "I am grateful to you for saving my life. I would've drowned, and I know that. But the things I feel for you…"

She faltered, failing to find just the right words, fell back and regrouped, then tried again. "Gratitude isn't enough. Neither is lust. I've known lust. I've felt both of those things, but neither is like…like this."

The fear left his face. His expression softened, the tenderness she craved lighted in his eyes and he cupped her face in his hands then stroked her jaw with a gentle pass of his thumbs. "I think the truth is, we're cowards, Kate."

This, she should find endearing? "What?"

"Cowards," he repeated. "We fight demons like Kunz and Sandross but we run from the ones inside us. I'm afraid of loving and losing again. You're afraid of loving at all. We're cowards."

She frowned and tried to pull away.

He wouldn't let her. "No, listen to me. Just listen."

"Okay, but I have to warn you, Forester, I have issues with cowardice."

He smiled. "Losing Emily was the hardest thing I've ever gone through in my life, Kate. The idea of going through that again—" His voice cracked and he paused. Swallowing hard, he then went on. "Your job in S.A.S.S. really increases the odds."

"I know you're not going to suggest I leave my job, Nathan." Her tone made it clear that would be an outrageous request.

"No, I'm not. I'd never do that to you." He sucked in a breath that heaved his chest. "But I am going to be grateful for you every moment and every day." His hands trembled on her face and his eyes shone bright. "Here's my bottom line. I'd rather have five minutes with you than a lifetime without you." Resolve filled his voice. "I'm not running anymore, Kate. I don't want to run, and I don't want you to run from me."

"I don't want to run from you." She covered his hands on her face. "Together maybe we can do what we haven't been able to do alone."

"What's that?"

"Stop being cowards." Facing men who might kill you was one thing. Openly trusting someone who could break your heart was far more dangerous.

He smiled. "Yeah, I think we can."

She nudged at his hands on her face. "Then kiss me, Nathan."

He brushed his lips to hers and whispered, "I want you to feel all that I feel for you. All of it. All of me."

And she did. With every loving touch, every mumbled whisper and sensuous moan, Kate fell deeper and deeper into the man, sharing intimacies that exceeded lust, exceeded anything she'd known.

Nathan was as greedy as she was, taking and taking, leaving no part of her body or heart untouched. He urged her to open to him, to share her entire self—body, mind and spirit—and this knowing seeped into her pores, obvious, strange and unknown and dangerous, and while it should make her uncomfortable, and it normally would, this time it didn't. She welcomed it, welcomed him, and let passion sweep her into new realms unchecked, unhampered and unafraid. She *wanted* this universal union, this total merging into one. She wanted this man, with all his flaws and memories of a life shared with another before her, confident that his heart was big enough, strong enough, for her, too.

Delving deeper and deeper, sensation upon sensation rippled through her, pouring in heat, awakening desires so well hidden she hadn't known they lived inside her. She was awed by the sheer force of their passion, her body shimmered and thrummed an unfamiliar message that spoke unheeded to his. The unity released a power so fierce that intense emotions tumbled one over the other—passion, pleasure, joy—and pounded through her, forging a new facet in her very core. And recognizing this magnificent change, Kate discovered her strength.

The woman she had been was no longer.

A new woman was born.

A woman both loved and in love.

A rustle awakened Kate.

Sprawled in bed, her face buried at the pillow, she reached for Nathan. The sheets were still warm, but he was gone. She pushed back her hair and looked toward the sound. He was standing at the window, staring out into the night. "Nathan?"

"Did I wake you?" He didn't look back. "I'm sorry."

"No, it's okay." She slid out of bed, wrapped her discarded towel around her and tucked it in over her breasts. "What's wrong?"

"Nothing," he said softly. "Go back to sleep. You're exhausted."

Distant and edgy. Very unlike himself. "Nathan, I asked you a question and I expect you to be honest with me."

He looked over his shoulder at her. "Nothing you can fix."

Kate muddled over that remark. She crossed her arms and moved closer to stand beside him at the window. "Is it your men or Emily?"

He swiveled his gaze from the city lights to her. "I don't want to hurt you."

"I know that, Nathan." She stroked his face. "You're worried about your men, but you feel guilty for making love with me, right?"

"Worse." Agony shone in his eyes. "I feel guilty for loving you, Kate."

"I see." So he didn't feel guilty for making love but he

did feel guilty for loving. Thank God. That, she could help him sort out. She stepped back to the bed and sat on the edge. "Granted, I'm a newcomer to this love business, but as inexperienced as I am, I know that if something happened to me, I would want you to live." She waited, but he still didn't look at her. "I see all the good in you, Nathan. You have so much give. I would die praying you found someone special to love again."

He turned to look at her, his eyes wide and unblinking.

"It's the truth, Nathan."

"But you can't be sure." He shrugged. "You didn't know her, Kate."

"No, but I know you. And I know from you that she loved you." Kate tucked a loose lock of hair behind her ear. "Women are complex creatures, I'll give you that. But love isn't complex. I didn't realize that until you. Love just is, Nathan, and when you feel love for someone, you want that person to be embraced by it. I can't explain it logically—I don't know if that's even possible. Love is too new to me to be sure of much. But I know that I would want you loved, Nathan. I know it as surely as I know I love you."

He swallowed hard, blinked three times in rapid succession. "In my head, and even in here—" he tapped his chest "—I know you're right. It's been five years, but to tell you the truth, Kate, you hit me like a sledgehammer. I think I just need a little time to get used to it." He walked over to sit beside her on the bed. "I fell in love with you without ever seeing you. When you were getting ready to attack Kunz's compound in Iran and you were flirting with Douglas on the radio, I knew it then. I told myself I was crazy, that I thought it was love because I'd been alone so long. But I knew I'd been lying to myself the moment I first saw you. I've known it every moment since. I've resigned my-self to that."

"Jeez, Nathan, your enthusiasm for loving me has my knees shaking. Back off a little on the charm."

"No, quit being sarcastic. I mean, I had accepted that I loved you and I would love you for the rest of my life," he explained. "What I hadn't considered was the possibility that you would ever love me."

"Oh, Nathan." She smiled softly, stroked his knee. "Of course. I get it now." She leaned her head into his upper arm. "You feel guilty because you're alive and being loved and Emily is dead."

"Maybe. I'm not sure." He thought a moment. "Proba-bly."

Kate nodded. "Well, I'll tell you what. Let's make a deal."

He gave her a strange look, one she couldn't fully de-cipher. "We give ourselves time to get used to each other and let things find their natural place. But we talk, Nathan. We're open and honest, and we share what's going on in our minds and in our hearts. We never shut each other out." She hiked her chin. "Do we have a deal?"

He nodded. "We do."

"Okay, then." This stuff with Emily would sort itself out. Nathan might have been a widower for five years, but during that time he'd never shared his body or his heart with another woman. He'd thought that part of his life was over. She'd thought she'd never have it. At love, they were both rookies.

But they wouldn't be cowards.

The telephone rang.

Kate spun toward the nightstand and saw the clock: 4:00 a.m.? Had to be Home Base. She lifted the receiver. "Captain Kane."

"Kate?"

Colonel Drake. "Yes, ma'am."

"Gaston has just reported in. He's found Major Forester's men twenty kilometers west of the outpost."

"That's fabulous!"

"Not so fabulous," the colonel said. "You have to go in and get them—and the other detainees aren't with them. They've been flown to undisclosed locations."

"Another damn GRID compound?"

"I suppose so." Colonel Drake's sigh hissed through the wires. "Gaston wasn't able to determine a location. Tactical will meet you at the border."

"What border, ma'am?"

"Forester will brief you on that," she said. "Kate, move your ass getting there. Transport is already waiting downstairs. Gaston's worried the men are running out of time."

"What does he mean by that?"

"They'll soon be moved or executed."

"I'm on it." Kate hung up the phone and filled in Nathan. "Gaston found out where GRID's holding your men. We've got to go rescue them. He's waiting at the border."

"Thank God." Nathan jumped up, dragged on his clothes. "So I guess Gaston's not a traitor."

"Guess not," she said, bypassing the luxurious silks and slinging on a fresh set of fatigues. "Maybe not." She reached for her gun, then her knife. "Hell, I don't know. But he reported finding your guys. So I guess we'd better be ready for assistance or an ambush."

"Right." Nathan moved toward the door. "Let me grab my gun and I'll be right with you."

"Nathan," she called. When he stopped, she asked, "We're to meet him at the border. What border?"

His expression grim and dark, he answered. "Iran."

Oh, great. GRID *or* the authorities would shoot them on sight. A cold shiver raced up her back and shot through her arms.

What were they going to do? They'd never be able to flush out or to retrieve Nathan's men from a GRID compound inside Iran. Iran wouldn't cooperate with the U.S. in any fashion, including the war on terror. That's damn likely exactly why Kunz is there. And of course Iran would be a lucrative buyer for GRID weapons. Could this situation get any more difficult?

Chapter 21

Douglas sat waiting in the lobby.

On seeing them, he stood, the strain forming deep creases in a face too young to have them. "All your gear is in the jeep."

"I'll need headgear." She had to stay in constant touch with Home Base on this one. And no doubt, every honcho on the Hill would be tuned in.

"You both have it."

They got into the jeep and soon exchanged it for a helicopter that dropped them off in Iraq near the Iranian border. Douglas's team had called in backup and a total of about thirty men stood in small groups, waiting for instructions.

Some didn't look too happy to see Kate.

Used to it, she blew it off. Nathan was senior officer; he'd assume command, but they both knew this was her domain and he would follow her lead.

"Riley?" Nathan said, surprise in his voice.

He stepped forward and saluted, holding the habitual clipboard, though this one was new. The edges weren't worn. "Commander."

"How did they miss you?"

The suspicion in Nathan's voice startled Kate, until she thought about Kunz's doubles. She looked closely but didn't see anything inconsistent with what she knew of Riley, and Kunz hadn't had time to double him—unless...

She nudged Nathan. "At any time in the past, has Riley gone missing for three months?"

He shook his head. "Answer me, Riley."

"I was off duty, sir. I went out on recon, trying to track the guy who broke into our camp during the sandstorm and stole Captain Kane's black box."

Kate hadn't told him that Gaston had returned it via Nathan and that her black box hadn't actually been stolen from the outpost then. "What did you find?"

"A kid saw the man leaving the outpost with it," Riley said. "He was one of ours."

Uneasy, Kate pushed. "Do you know who he was?"

"Yes, ma'am, I do." He pinched his lips together. "Gaston, ma'am. That's who the boy described."

Gaston. Had he switched the boxes on her? He couldn't have. The C-273 communications device wasn't missing. It was safely stowed in her gear. Then there had to be a reason Gaston wanted to be seen leaving with what appeared to be the device. There had to be a reason he allowed himself to be spotted by that kid... Of course!

"Kate?"

She looked at Nathan. "Gaston attacked us at the outpost. Not to kill us, but to convince GRID he was on their side and they had no reason to be suspicious of him. They had been suspicious, so suspicious that Moss had gone to Sandross. Gaston had had to do something, give them something to get out from under intense scrutiny so he could do his job. He didn't steal the device. He gave them a decoy to make them think he had."

"So he's with us?" Nathan asked, clearly uncertain.

"Yes. Yes, he is." Kate considered all angles. "GRID must have discovered he was CIA. I don't know how—he doesn't exist on paper. Hell, maybe he told them." It made sense. "Moss suspected him. Sandross would have killed him for suspicion alone, so Gaston gave him a reason to keep him alive. Gaston convinced Sandross he could be more useful, not less."

Nathan picked up the thread of thought. "So he had himself evacuated to coincide with our rescue so he could find out what we knew—which is what Kunz has wanted to know all along."

"I think so." Kate went on from there. "But Moss and Gaston were in the water when I positioned the C-273 on the rocks. Moss reported his suspicions to Sandross, which included news of the C-273 being seated. Sandross wanted it and he ordered Gaston to get it."

Nathan again followed the thread. "But Gaston didn't want GRID to have it, so he claimed it came unseated from the rocks and couldn't be found. Sandross, figuring if you had one and it'd been lost, you'd replace it with another. So he sent Gaston to get it."

Kate nodded. "That's when he pulled the attack on your tent."

"He knew we were there, and he made sure he was seen leaving with his own black box, wearing the red scarf."

"He had to do more than that to see to it, Nathan. We were in the middle of a sandstorm. What kid is going to be out looking around in a sandstorm?"

"Gaston bribed the kid."

"I'd bet on it. Then he took the fake back to Sandross. I'd love to see what kind of replica he gave them."

Nathan shrugged. "That would put their suspicions at ease and get him back in their good graces."

"It'd also keep him alive and inside GRID, where he could report what they're doing." Kate dropped her voice another notch. "And he also reported the location of your men, Nathan." A good feeling washed over her. "Gaston hasn't turned traitor."

"No." The remark was genuine; it showed in his tone and expression. "I'm glad. It really gets to me when one of our own turns on us."

They took refuge from the sun under a stretched canvas, ate MRE emergency rations and cooled their heels, waiting for the order to move.

One of the men Kate didn't know sighed. "What's taking them so long?"

Riley answered. "Hey, this takes a while, you know? People have to be found and diplomatic channels have to be worked. You can't just snap your fingers and this stuff gets done."

Kate smiled behind her hand. Riley performed those duties ordinarily, and if he sounded irritated it was because he clearly was. It was a common rivalry between guys in the field facing the action, and guys manning the stations, running through political minefields. Frankly, Kate never understood the rivalry. Neither group could do squat without the other.

The order finally came in shortly after sunset.

"Douglas?" Nathan shouted over to where he sat talking with his team. "Let's get this show on the road."

"Yes, sir, Commander."

Kate put on her headgear, heard the summons from Maggie at Home Base, and quickly adjusted her lip mike. "Go ahead, Base."

"Intel says Iran will know you're inside their borders within ten minutes of arrival. The colonel informed the honchos, and the secretary has conferred with his consultants."

What exactly did that mean? "And? Has the pump been primed or what?" Kate wished she'd gotten Amanda or Darcy or even Colonel Drake online, but all were tied up with other facets of this same mission.

"They've done the risk assessment, Bluefish. Iran could blow the chopper out of the sky, or confiscate it and try you and the team as spies. You'd be executed."

"I know all that." Her nerves sizzled. "What else?"

"They could also let you evacuate the prisoners. Iran doesn't want American prisoners any more than America wants Iran to have them."

"Iran also doesn't want to screw up its source for weapons." Kate had enough of this. She had a grip on the potential scenarios. She wanted the bottom line. "What are the odds?"

"Strategists are rating the odds fifty-fifty that Iran will play stupid and ignore the rescue mission."

"Great." Getting hot under the collar, Kate raised her voice. "That's like saying, 'maybe they will or maybe they won't.' We don't need strategists for that kind of answer. It doesn't tell me a damn thing I didn't already know."

"I wasn't finished."

"Well, by all means go ahead then." The men would be

dead and buried before Maggie got to the bottom line, even after being asked to skip to it.

"The secretary bettered the odds. He activated a satellite tracker in one of the men. We don't know who, but we suspect Gaston."

That would be a reasonable assumption, considering Gaston initially reported the location of the missing men. "Okay, that'll help." Apparently the pilot already had the coordinates since the order to move out had come through Nathan's chain of command. "We're going in."

"The chopper will be putting down about two miles east of the target's current GPS coordinates."

"Roger. Two miles east of target." Repeating the message so Nathan got it, she gave him the nod.

He issued a flurry of orders, getting Douglas and the team on board the chopper and Riley and the others in position, manning their command post operations.

Kate climbed into the chopper, sat near the door and checked her fanny pack. Wire, caps, fuses, remote detonators, bullets… No C-4. "Douglas?"

He passed her two minibricks. "Direct order to put it in your hands."

She released a steadying breath. "Thanks." The idea of going in without any had her stomach doing flips.

Douglas blinked and his smile faded. "Thanks for hauling my ass out of the horror chamber."

"You knew I'd come." Tilting her head, she looked up at him. "What woman in her right mind could ignore such a charming summons?"

Curious, his team was all ears. "What'd he send you, Captain?" one asked.

"Something irresistible to women, Carlisle." She tugged

her cap down to shade the twinkle in her eye. "Completely irresistible."

Nathan coughed in his hand to hide a smile.

The team did a verbal crawl all over Douglas, trying to find out exactly what women found irresistible. Kate looked at Nathan and waggled her eyebrows. He treated her to a wink.

A bear of a guy Kate didn't know shouted to be heard over the clamor of the others. "Hey, Douglas. MacAlister here needs a double dose of whatever you got, bud. Help the loser out."

"Loser?" a third said. "Hell, have you seen Beth? She's a knockout."

"She's also dated half the guys in the unit."

"Damn right," MacAlister said. "None of you *losers* could hang on to her."

Kate again sought and found Nathan's gaze. For the moment, the premission tension was under control.

When the chopper off-loaded and they were on the ground, Kate tapped Douglas. "I'm not going to remember names."

"One through five." He shrugged. "What's to remember?" His eyes gleamed with insider knowledge he wanted to flaunt a little. "I assume you'll be able to recall the commander's?"

A slow smile curled her lips. "I'll manage."

Douglas grunted. "It's my own damn fault. I should've followed up after our last mission."

"Sweetie, if you had, you'd hate me by now," she said honestly. "This is better."

"Yeah, I guess you're right." He nodded toward Nathan no longer flirting or wistful for what could've been between them, but sincere about what was between her and Nathan. "You're good for him."

"Yes, I think I am." And her tone proved it surprised no one more than Kate herself.

"I'm glad." Douglas looked down at the ground as if afraid she'd see too much in his eyes. "We all are."

"Because he's less bitchy?" she speculated.

"Oh, no." Douglas grunted. "He's had a burr up his ass since he heard you on the radio, last mission." Douglas glanced back her and let her see his gratitude. "But he isn't sad anymore. We're, um, we're all happy about that."

They genuinely cared about Nathan.

"Kate?" Nathan's stern tone surprised her and she turned to look at him as he walked up to her and Douglas. His face looked flushed. "Security update."

She stepped over to him and, when Douglas returned to the team, Nathan continued. "Two miles east. The bastards are lining my men up in a stadium."

Oh, God. She'd seen the tactic used in this region of the world before. It immediately preceded executions. "If they're all together, we can't move in as a team without being detected." She started to precheck her gear. "I'm going alone."

"No, you're not."

She stilled, her hand on her fanny pack. "Nathan, this is my job."

"I know that. And I know you're good at it. But I'm going with you."

"Fine." No sense arguing with him. He'd just pull rank on her. "Let's move."

Kate pulled on her backpack, hooked the straps on her shoulders, checked her gun inside her top between her breasts, her rifle and scope, her knife, fanny pack and canteen, then adjusted her headgear and mike. Then, watching Nathan pull his precheck, she contacted Maggie.

"Home Base, do you copy?"

"Go ahead, Bluefish."

"Going in. I'm taking—" Her first thought was to say "Guppy" to punish Nathan for acting as if she needed a protector. But because he had been so adorable about it, she decided to forgive him and not razz him in front of his men, who were also monitoring—likely right along with half of the Iranian forces. "Shark is backup."

"Roger that."

"Maintain radio silence until further notice."

"Home Base silent and standing by."

Nathan glanced down at the GPS locator and thermal heat sensor in his hand, double-checking their target's location.

"We good?"

"We're good. Go."

Kate took off in a slow sprint across the moonless desert. Nathan ran beside her. Douglas and his team gave them a thirty-second lead and then followed, hanging back and taking up posts along the route.

In a few short minutes the glow of lights silhouetted a stadium. A soccer field, according to Darcy's earlier report. The perimeter had been reinforced with concrete walls ten feet high and topped with razor wire.

The ground under Kate's feet vibrated. She motioned to Nathan to get down, then dropped to her stomach in the sand. Beside her, he motioned right with a tilt of his head.

Kate pulled her dart gun, sensing the guard before she saw him. Downwind, the smell of his sweat reached her first. She got a visual through her scope, then aimed the silent dart gun and fired.

A slight thump sounded. He'd hit the ground.

She waited to see if anyone else noticed and reacted. Ten seconds… Twenty… A full minute… Seeing and hearing only sleepy sounds of a quiet night and gentle wind, she hiked a shoulder and verified with Nathan.

He scanned the vicinity with the heat sensor, and gave her a thumbs-up. She pointed two fingers forward, then they rose quickly and pressed on.

Thirty yards out, noises filled the night air. Shouts, cheers and jeers all carried from inside the stadium over the concrete wall. It sounded like a damn ballgame instead of the beginning phases of a mass execution. Kate stopped and whispered to Douglas through her mike. "One. Position?"

"On the mark," he whispered back.

"Stay here," she told Nathan before disappearing into the night.

Using stealth tactics, she slowly made her way around the stadium, pausing to assess and set charges that would act as cover for Nathan's men. With each progressive step forward, the tension in her coiled tighter. Nowhere along the nearly three-quarters of ground she'd covered had she seen the first GRID guard. Maybe they figured they were safe, being on Iranian soil. Maybe they figured they were safe inside the stadium. She could only guess, but she'd have felt a damn sight better about their absence if the noise inside weren't getting louder and more frenzied. The energy emanating from inside the place felt almost frenetic. It set her teeth on edge.

Near the wall, the guards' shouts were clear enough to decipher. U.S. bashing, blaming Nathan's men for everything done and undone, whipping up anger and outrage. They didn't just want executions; the bloodthirsty bastards wanted brutal slayings.

Get a grip on your emotions, Kate. You're dealing with GRID. That's Kunz and Marcus Sandross. You know they're twisted; their penchants and sick sadistic love of torture. Just focus on the rescue. Ignore the static and get to the men.

The last of four broad doors leading into the stadium, like the previous three, was shut and locked tight from the inside. As she had with the other three, Kate set a charge to blow it off the hinges, rigged a remote detonator, then backed off to sprint into the cover of the shadows, heading back toward Nathan's position.

Inside, what had been cheering and chanting turned to screaming. GRID, thank God, and not Nathan's men. Not yet. Men were going to die and they acted as if it meant no more than a night's entertainment.

A voice boomed out over a loudspeaker. A voice she believed belonged to a man she had hoped had died in the cave explosion. Marcus Sandross. Kunz's second-in-command. The only man Gaston ever had met who loved to kill as much as Kunz.

She made the last leg of the stadium loop, and met up with Nathan. "I need your help."

He smiled and, unable to imagine why in the world he would, considering circumstances, she realized what she'd said. It stunned her. Kate, the loner who always went in alone and would refuse assistance if offered it unless it threatened life, had asked him to help her. His smile proved he considered himself honored.

"Sure," he whispered. "What do you want me to do?"

She scissor-wiggled her fingers and pointed to the stadium, signaling they would start there.

When they got into place just beyond the fall of the lights about five feet to the left of the stadium door, she drove a stake into the ground, bent wire around a metal post on it, then shoved the reel of wire into Nathan's hands and motioned for him to stretch it back to—she held up her index finger—signaling Douglas's position.

Five feet from the left side of the door, she paralleled him, drove in a second stake and stretched wire from it, walking with Nathan.

When they neared Douglas, she warned him, "Incoming, One."

"Roger."

A minute later, her heart pumping hard, a sweat sheen glistening on her face, she dropped to the dirt beside Douglas to handle preparations on the wires on this end.

Nathan kicked up a little cloud of dust next to her, waiting until she was done for a quick briefing.

"Four doors—one on each side. No guards on the outer perimeter. I'm going to blow the doors simultaneously, then light up a gauntlet for our guys to run. Fire down both sides will give them the best cover." She looked from Nathan to Douglas. "You and your team be waiting and help them back to the chopper. From the sounds of those bastards, some of them aren't going to be mobile."

She wiped at her forehead. "I need help up front, Nathan. I've set the charges, but the guys need cover coming out. The time they're between the stadium door and when they enter the gauntlet, they're totally vulnerable." GRID would pick them off like ducks in a row.

He nodded. "If you blow all the doors, how will my men know where to go?"

"Evade-and-escape training," she said. "They'll look for the fire. The GRID operatives won't know to run to it and not away from the fire, though they'll be busy enough shooting at our guys to stop them from leaving." She took a long drink of water from her canteen. "We've got to get them into the gauntlet."

"I get it, but not all of my men have evade-and-escape training. Some of them are raw recruits."

"Nathan," she said in a low, level tone. "Trust your men. You didn't train them to find the latrine, either, but they managed. They'll follow the men who have been trained."

"You're right." He let out a deep breath. "You're right."

They ran through the gauntlet toward the stadium and Kate set and checked the charges. The damn detonator on the left side wouldn't set. She took it out and totally re-worked it. No way, could she risk it failing. Not with these stakes.

Nathan stooped at her side. "Done?"

"Almost."

The sound of a gun hammer being pulled at her back sent chills screaming up and down her spine.

"Hands up."

Chapter 22

"Do it now, Captain Kane."

Even without turning around, Kate knew that voice. "Moss."

"I'm surprised you remembered." He grunted to his partner. "She remembered me. Isn't that special?"

Kate bumped the release on her knife sheath, raising her hands, and slowly stood, then turned toward him. A man stood at his left. She took a long, hard look at him. Broad, bullish build. Bad acne scars and a hooked nose. Brown hair slicked back in a ponytail. Yet another face not on the S.A.S.S. watch list and one she didn't personally recognize from research or experience.

"Nice of you to join our party. With fireworks, no less."

"Thought you'd enjoy it, Moss." She stole a glance at Nathan. He signaled with blinks to attack on three.

Afraid Douglas would intercede, she issued him a direct order. "One, hold fast," and tilted her head, signaling Nathan she'd take Moss.

Nathan signaled. Two.

Kate rolled her shoulder. "Can I let my arm down?"

"Why not?" Moss said. "But reach for that knife and you're a dead woman."

She didn't. Three. She side-armed Moss in the throat, then followed up with a boot to his groin.

Nathan simultaneously lunged at his opponent and she heard the sounds of scuffling: fists to flesh, grunts and tussling, the crunch of bone. Moss pivoted and raised his gun. Kate rushed him, diverting his aim, but he was stronger, had a deeper reach. She drove in, slamming the heel of her hand to his nose.

His blood spurted. "You crazy bitch. You think you can beat me?" He landed a solid right to her jaw and knocked her sprawling. "You can't beat me."

"My mother could beat you, Moss." She laughed, goading him, hitting him hardest where he hated it most: in the ego. "You're barely holding my attention."

"Right. But you're on your ass, not me."

She scissor-cut his legs, knocking them out from under him, and threw her weight behind a slammed kick to his kneecap.

He let out a keening howl and charged her.

She whipped out her knife and felt her elbow give. Pain shot up her arm to her shoulder. She snagged the blade with her left hand, ducked an inside jab and slashed at Moss's throat.

He grabbed it, cursing her, his breath gurgling, and charged her again.

Kate forced herself to wait, to stay cool and wait for the

perfect timing. The moment came. She raised her foot and slammed it into his groin.

His breath swooshed out, splattering blood with it. He bent double and just stood there, teetering on his feet, before he dropped suddenly as if he'd folded over.

Breathing hard and heavy, Kate spun around. Nathan stood a few feet away, silent and still, watching her. His opponent lay crumpled on the ground.

"You okay?" Nathan rubbed at his jaw. "Bastard had a hard right."

She nodded she was fine. "You?"

He nodded back.

The frenzy inside the stadium grew louder still, echoing in her ears, chilling her blood. Kate motioned to Nathan to get positioned outside the gauntlet, then she moved beyond the perimeter toward the other side. He stood, AK-47 raised and waiting.

She held the remotes, ready to detonate.

"One," she summoned Douglas. "Position countdown."

"Go," he said, starting the sound off that would relay through the tactical team.

"On point," Kate whispered. "We're going to light up their world like the Fourth of July." She activated the remotes.

The explosions sounded in rapid succession, blasting the doors to bits. The gauntlet fired up, stretching two parallel walls of fire flaming fifteen feet from the ground to the sky.

Inside the stadium, confusion and chaos erupted. Kate held her breath. What if the men didn't come? What if Nathan had been right and the raw recruits didn't follow?

"First man out," a man shouted. "First man out."

"This way!" Nathan yelled at him. "Simpson, Crash, here!"

Kate heard the exchange and then saw the men running

for the gauntlet. GRID guards chased them, carrying swords. Where were their guns? she wondered. Maybe Iran wouldn't let them carry guns. Could she be so lucky?

A stream of Nathan's men charged out of the stadium. "Here they come, One. Be ready."

Nathan fired the first shot, dropping a GRID operative in his tracks. Another guard was about to behead a man when another man from the unit tackled him from behind.

The hand-to-hand combat grew fierce and Kate had a hell of time sighting in on the guards to help out, but the men were nearly to the gauntlet. Thirty seconds more. They needed thirty seconds more.

She lifted another remote and activated it. The explosion ripped through the stadium, bellowing smoke.

Nathan laid down a dozen shots in rapid succession, clearing a path for them. Kate positioned herself and did the same, then they kept firing nonstop, putting a slight break between the men and the guards.

"Need help up there?" Douglas asked, sounding worried.

The men started disappearing into the gauntlet, shielded by the fire. "Stay put. Gauntlet's heavy." She took down a guard, spun left and took out another. "We're two minutes out. Repeat. Gauntlet's heavy. We're two minutes out." She shoved the mike out of her way and kept fighting.

When a lapse in men entering the gauntlet occurred, she tugged the mike back into place. "Shark, are they all in?"

"Roger. Last one just stepped inside. Guards are no longer in pursuit."

They'd retreated into the stadium. And that was news she'd hoped for but hadn't dared to expect. Picking up the last remote, she took deep pleasure in depressing the activator switch.

The explosion blasted her ears and blew concrete dust to where she stood. A secondary explosion fired, throwing flames and debris far up into the velvety night sky. A third charge fired and blew out the walls.

The stadium had been obliterated.

Running a quick check, she verified that the men had cleared the gauntlet. "One, you got 'em?"

"Affirmative, ma'am. We're escorting them in."

Kate smiled, turned to Nathan and felt such joy that they'd gotten his men to the chopper, she threw her arms around his waist and hugged him hard. "We did it, Nathan. They're going to be okay."

"Yeah. They're going to be fine." He dropped a kiss to her crown. "Let's go now."

"Just a second." She pulled back and sniffed. Then depressed a little black button on the last remote.

A whistling light streaked through the sky, shooting sparks of red, white and blue.

"Fireworks?" Nathan wrapped an arm around her shoulder.

"Mmm." Firmly noncommittal, Kate chuckled. "Actually, I left a little present for Kunz and Sandross."

"Uh-huh." Nathan steered her back toward the chopper. "That present has smoke in the sky as far as I can see."

"Just wait a second."

Explosions ticked off faster than a lighted pack of firecrackers. One over the other, with another, before and after several others.

"What the hell is that?"

"My present." Kate hiked her chin and didn't look back. "I suspected Kunz had weapons stored under the stadium. He loves underground hiding places, and it was just so convenient."

"So you're blowing them up?"

"Yep." They were in Iran. It wasn't as if she'd have another chance tomorrow.

"Do you think he was there?"

"At first, I hoped. But no, he wasn't there." She sighed. Her elbow throbbed and her arm felt as though it was going to fall off.

"We'd better run, Nathan. We've got to get out of here." He picked up his speed, matching hers. "Iran isn't going to appreciate that crater. We put this part of GRID out of operation, and they're probably not going to like it that much, either, and right now, Iran is our greater threat." From this point until they crossed the border, they were more vulnerable than on the entire mission.

"One," Nathan said into the mike, running beside her. "Is egress ready?"

"The men are boarding now, sir."

"Hustle."

"Yes, sir."

Minutes later Kate and Nathan climbed onto the chopper. When it lifted off and the guys saw them, the men broke into applause. Kate was deeply moved. They respected Nathan. And after tonight, they respected her.

She wasn't an outsider anymore.

Kate savored the moment of grace; appreciating it for the rare and precious gift it was, letting the laughter and excited chatter flow over and through her.

"Commander!" A member of the flight crew rushed back from the front of the plane. "We've got a problem, sir."

Nathan spun around to face him.

"We've picked up an Iranian escort. Right wingtip."

The men went silent.

Kate's stomach sank. She adjusted her lip mike. "Bluefish to Home Base."

"I read you," Maggie responded.

"We've got the unit. No additional hostages. Currently attempting egress. An Iranian chopper just dropped into formation, right wingtip. Escort position. Repeat. Escort position. Not hostile."

"Stand by."

A moment later Colonel Drake spoke to Kate. "Captain, you have encroached into Iranian airspace. Revert to backup GPS system, verify your position and evacuate Iranian airspace immediately."

"Yes, ma'am. I'm sorry, ma'am," Kate said. "Equipment malfunction." She paused a second, noted the worried looks of all the men focused on her. "Backup systems are now active. Error acknowledged and accepted. Please extend my apologies to the Iranian government, and let them know I appreciate their indulgence."

It was bullshit all around. The pilots knew it, Nathan and his men knew it, Home Base knew it, and the Iranians knew it. But the Iranians were shoveling their own branded version of it, too. They didn't want American hostages inside their borders that America would certainly attempt to rescue. They didn't want the GRID executions to take place and create an international incident. They just wanted American forces to know they were aware the U.S. had been there and Iran wanted them out. And all that sat just fine with Kate. She'd take the hit, gladly, and be damn grateful for it.

The chopper tracked with them all the way to the border. Silence reigned on the chopper, all eyes on the Iranian aircraft.

When it peeled off and circled back, Kate finally breathed easier. The men did, too.

Douglas came over to Kate and Nathan. "Kramer just reported a positive ID on one the GRID members in the stadium."

"Anyone we know?" Kate asked.

"Yeah." Douglas frowned. "Thomas Kunz."

"Another one?" Nathan asked. Then, dropping his voice, he added, "Or *the* one?"

"Begging your pardon, Commander, but who the hell can tell?"

Boy, had Douglas pegged it. Kate squeezed her eyes shut and inwardly groaned. "Odds are that it wasn't him."

"You can't know that, Kate." Nathan warned her against jumping to conclusions.

"It's a reasonable deduction," she countered. "He knew we were close. If he was in the area, you can bet your ass he departed long before I entered the cave the first time."

"How can you be sure?"

"Experience." She swiveled her gaze to Douglas. "Thomas Kunz is devious and brutal and, I'm sorry to say, absolutely brilliant. But he's also a coward."

"A coward?" Douglas's eyebrows shot halfway up his forehead. "Jesus, Captain, he's the meanest bastard in the world. Every man who knows he exists dreads going up against him."

"Every woman, too," she agreed. "But he hides out in his fortresses and leaves his fighting and blood-spilling to his minion mercenaries."

"She's right about that." Nathan agreed. "Does Kramer know if this Kunz was there when the stadium exploded?"

"I don't know about Kramer, but when MacAlister entered the gauntlet, someone shouted his name. Thinking it was one of our guys, he looked back and the stadium exploded."

"Kunz called him," Kate suggested. "Standing front and center, right?"

"Yeah." Douglas looked surprised, and then the reason for Kunz calling out to MacAlister dawned on him. "Damn it, he wanted us to see him. He wanted us to know he was dead."

"Exactly." She looked at Nathan. "Another clone."

"Why do these people die for him?" Douglas asked.

"Different culture," Nathan said. "Different beliefs."

Kate was less diplomatic. "Money and virgins." She lifted a hand. "All through recorded history, this region has suffered more war than peace, and many families are poor. Just-this-side-of-starving poor. The family receives a fortune and the martyr gets paradise, which includes fifty virgins."

"But GRID members are all nationalities."

"True, but the majority of them we've gone up against here have been from this region."

"Commander," Riley said. "Captain says to prepare for landing."

Kate sat and Nathan took the place beside her. She scanned the benches at the men. They were bruised and banged up, some sooty, some still with greasepaint smeared on their faces, but many of them were smiling, and from the banter and cheerful conversations going on all around her, they realized how lucky they were to be alive.

Nathan clasped her arm. "Thanks, Kate."

She smiled at him. "It's been a good day, Nathan."

They'd survived.

Chapter 23

It was a good afternoon, too.

Back at the outpost, in honor of her assistance in rescuing them, the men gave her dibs on the shower. While they stood lined up outside, waiting for their turns, not one of them so much as murmured a wish that she'd hurry.

Though they did seem hell-bent on chatting with her the entire time she stood in the stall. Not that she minded. She could talk about explosives and arsenals for a week non-stop.

Figuring they'd been patient long enough, she hit the crank and grabbed a towel. She started to just wrap it around her and head out, but remembered that Nathan had taken serious exception to that. Now, he'd likely be even worse. She took the extra time to tug on clean fatigues and then stepped outside, carrying her boots.

"What? No towel stroll today?" Douglas, of course.

The dozen men in line let out a collective boo.

Kate laughed. "Maybe next time."

Nathan rounded the tent corner just in time to hear that remark. "I'd bet against it."

The men sobered, went silent.

Kate ignored Nathan's stern expression and wrinkled her nose at him. "What would you bet?"

The guys were listening. "Your rank."

She smiled. "I'm not under your command, Major. Would you really petition headquarters to take my rank?"

"Come on, Commander." Kramer jumped to her defense. "That's a little harsh. She was just…"

Nathan silenced him with a scathing glare. "I know exactly what she's doing." He turned to the men. "She's in love with me, and she wants me to let you all know it."

She stretched her eyes wide. "Excuse me?"

"She also wants you to know that I'm in love with her."

"Actually, I didn't want either." She stared up at Nathan, certain he'd lost his mind. "What in hell are you doing?"

He clasped her hand and pulled her to him. "Staking my claim."

He kissed her hard, then released her, before turning and walking off toward the command tent, leaving Kate standing there feeling like…well, torn. Part of her wanted to pop his ass, and another part wanted to kiss him again.

"Arrogant, cuss, isn't he?" she asked the guys.

They responded with a lot of amused smirks and noncommittal babble. "Wimps," she said, knowing they were anything but.

Walking his way, she shouted after him. "Forester!"

He stopped.

She walked on, then paused about ten feet from him and crooked her finger. "Come here."

He hesitated, frowned, blushed—totally charming, that—grumbled and muttered, but he came over. And when he did, she curled her arms around his neck and whispered, "Fair is fair." Then she jumped up into his arms and wrapped her legs around his hips.

"Damn it, Kate," he muttered against her mouth.

He had to hold her or drop her. And if she went down, she wasn't going alone.

The guys behind her laughed hard and loud. She broke their kiss, looked into Nathan's eyes, and saw a twinkle of pure joy.

"You're undermining my authority with my men."

"No, I'm not." She kissed the tip of his nose. "I'm not one of your men—and don't bullshit me, Forester. You wanted them to know about us."

He sighed hard and heavy. "You're going to give me hell for the next fifty years, aren't you?"

"Yeah." She rubbed their noses. "I think I am."

Riley came out of the command post tent. "Captain Kane?" His owl eyes stretched wide.

Nathan lowered her to the ground. "Yes, Riley?"

"It's…it's a phone call, ma'am," he said, still sputtering. "Secure line. A Captain Maggie Holt."

"Thanks." She walked into the tent and took the call. Nathan looked damned happy with himself.

She hoped he was at least as happy as she felt. "Bluefish, here." Even though the line was supposedly secure, Kate wasn't taking any chances. GRID was too powerful.

"It's Home Base."

"Right. What's up?" She had already filed the mission summary report on the rescue, and overt units had taken over the cave excavation. She was essentially done.

"You've been ordered back to Providence."

S.A.S.S.'s new headquarters in Florida. "Now?"

"Right now."

"What's going on?" Worry filled Kate.

"It's Intel."

Darcy. Darcy Clark. One of the best S.A.S.S. operatives in the history of the unit, but because of a freak accident, a woman who had no choice but to remain isolated most of the time. "What's wrong?"

"Nothing." Maggie sounded tense, like a spring wound too tight. "The colonel is sending her out on a mission."

Shock stormed through Kate. "She's what?" *It has to be that damn red hair dye.* It'd frazzled Colonel Drake's brain. She knew Darcy couldn't withstand the sensory input of being around people.

"I knew you'd be pissed," Maggie said. "I tried to make Amanda call you, but she said, 'No way.' So I got stuck—"

"Oh, stuff it, and tell me what this is about."

Seemingly not offended, she answered. "GRID, of course."

Kate resisted an urge to jump through the phone and jerk out the woman's vocal cords. "What about GRID? Why Intel?"

"I can't tell you—even on a secure line." She blew out a sharp breath. "Don't kill the messenger, okay?"

She had a point. Worry for Darcy had her ill-tempered. Normally she'd put a little more effort into being civil. After all, it wasn't Maggie's fault that she was new. They had all been new to S.A.S.S. at one time or another.

Yeah, and the senior operatives had been impatient as hell with them, too, Kate recalled. It had forced her to wise up faster and work harder.

"When do I leave?"

"Transport is arranged. Actually, in about thirty minutes. Chopper pilot will give you the details."

"Travel civilian or military?"

"Military. Noncombat."

"Okay, then."

"I'll pick you up on this end."

The end without Nathan. Her spirit sank. "Thanks." She put down the receiver, then looked over at Nathan.

"You're leaving."

It wasn't a question, but she nodded anyway. "In half an hour."

"My orders came through, too. They're moving the unit. Tonight."

"Where to?"

He smiled his regrets.

"Sorry." She shrugged, realizing she shouldn't have asked. "So what happens now, with us?"

He walked around the desk and clasped her by the shoulders. "It'll work out."

"How?" They were in different parts of the world. Even their permanent stations were across the country from each other. Nathan in Washington, her in Florida. With their colliding careers keeping them on the move, how would it work out?

"Trust me."

"Nathan, trust doesn't have a damn thing to do with this." She backed up. "This is reality. This is fact. Ours can't be even just a long-distance relationship. It's a remote long-distance relationship."

"It is whatever it is, Kate. That doesn't change a thing." He looked at her hard. "Unless you didn't mean... Is that it? Were you just playing a flirting game with me, and now that the mission is over, we're over, too?"

"Nathan Forester, I can't believe you said that. Are you crazy?"

"Maybe." He pulled her into his arms and hugged her tightly. "I won't lose you, Kate."

"No, you'll put me in the position of losing myself."

"What are you talking about?"

"Maybe not today, but soon, you'll want me to give up my job."

"No, I promise." He flatly denied it. "That's one thing I'd never ask you to do." He stepped back. "You just saved the lives of sixty men. *My* men. I know the value of what you do, and I swear to you, I'd never ask you to give it up."

The backs of her eyes burned. "I don't want to lose you, either, Nathan. It took me my whole damn life just to find you."

"Not possible." He dragged at his lip with his teeth. "I'll be at Providence in three weeks. We'll work it all out then."

"Okay." It was wise. They were exhausted, their emotions supercharged. Waiting to make important decisions would be the best thing all around.

Riley cleared his throat from behind them. "Ma'am. Your chopper's here. Douglas already on-loaded your gear."

"They're early." She sniffed. "Thanks, Riley."

Nathan smiled. "I'll walk with you." He curled an arm around her waist.

Outside, the men stood in two lines, leading to the chopper pad. They'd formed an honor guard for her to walk through?

Overwhelmed, Kate felt tears spring to her eyes, burn and slide down her cheeks. "Damn it, guys. This isn't fair."

A few chuckled, but the others stood stern-faced and at attention, holding on to discipline, while she and Nathan walked through. Near the chopper she turned. "Stay safe."

They broke ranks and gathered around. "Hey, Captain. Can we call if we need a bailout?"

She smiled. They'd taken her in and claimed her as one of them. "Absolutely, Carlisle!"

Nathan dropped a quick kiss on her lips.

Kate smiled at him. "Three weeks." When he nodded, she turned, then stopped and swung back around to face him. "Don't make me hunt you down, Forester."

Douglas grunted, ribbing him. "Yeah, that's one woman's heart you don't want to break. She knows seven hundred and fifty ways to kill you!"

Nathan laughed.

Kate hiked a cryptic brow. "He's right, you know. Not that I would, but I could."

Nathan sobered.

Kate laughed. "I'll miss you, Nathan." He was so easy to razz. "You know I will."

She climbed into the chopper and took her seat.

On the ground outside, Nathan held up three fingers and winked.

Chapter 24

The last leg of the long flight home was on a commercial charter flight. Kate had slept a great deal of the way and arrived at the Okaloosa Regional Airport feeling grungy and grouchy.

Apparently it was under major expansion construction. The airport shared runway space with Eglin Air Force Base, which was about twenty-five miles to the southeast of Providence and its closest military facility.

Kate had missed the S.A.S.S. unit's move from Washington, D.C., thanks to the mission, but she agreed with General Shaw and Secretary Reynolds that putting some distance between S.A.S.S. and the political heavyweights in Washington was a good idea. If out of sight, maybe S.A.S.S. would be out of mind and avoid interference that could jeopardize effectively dealing with GRID. Everyone in the business knew there were more leaks in Congress than in a sieve. Leaks, in addition to doubles on the inside, S.A.S.S. didn't need.

Personally, she'd like living in a rooted community again. In D.C., everyone was from somewhere else, brought there because of the job. She'd been curious about the new digs, of course, but every time she had asked Maggie about them, she'd avoided answering. Only now did that concern Kate. And only now did she wonder if that avoidance had been deliberate.

She departed the plane and hiked a good quarter mile into the terminal under white tarps stretched over metal-pipe frames. When she left the secure area, she saw Maggie waiting.

"Hi."

"Hello, Kate." Maggie fell into step. "Welcome home." She motioned to the right. "Baggage claim is this way."

Maggie filled her in on area attractions—the reigning king and queen were the sugar-white sandy beaches and emerald green water—and then told Kate that Amanda had rented her an apartment to hold her over until she decided whether or not to buy a house.

Kate appreciated it. She had a home to go to rather than the visiting officer's quarters. Nice.

Maggie walked down the narrow hallway, alight with neon signs. "I got your household goods delivered, and bought perishable groceries. I wasn't sure exactly what you needed, but I got two containers of chocolate ice cream. Amanda said Blue Bell's Chocolate Fudge Brownie is your favorite, and I figured if you had that, you'd be human until you could get whatever else is missing."

Kate was stunned. She'd been bitchy to Maggie and yet the woman had gone a long way out of her way to make things easy for Kate. "That was very thoughtful. I'll reimburse you, of course." She couldn't reimburse the kindness, but she would certainly remember it.

"No problem." Maggie smiled. "Glad to do it."

They got Kate's bags and soon dumped them in the car. "Home, right?"

"If you can spare the time, I'd like to see the new office."

Maggie looked away.

"What?"

"I was afraid you would say that." She looked over at her. "It's a good hour from here."

"It's a workday, you're in uniform, it's—" she glanced at the digital clock on the Honda's dashboard "—one in the afternoon. What's the problem?"

"Nothing." Maggie let out a resigned sigh. "No problem at all."

It was a pleasant ride. Tall pines, twisted by former hurricanes, lined the road north. It was all divided highway, easy traveling. Kate relaxed and enjoyed it.

"You did a great job over there, Kate," Maggie said, signaling to pass a slow-moving truck. "The detainees have been reintegrated into their lives, and four doubles are now in jail, with more on the way. Dr. Foster is at the facility giving them treatments to reveal the truth about themselves, and to see what they know."

Joan had been through this before. Hell, she'd programmed six months' worth of doubles while Kunz held her hostage. "She knows exactly what to do."

"Yes, bless her heart, she does."

Maggie drove right past the sign that read Providence Air Force Base.

"You missed your turn."

"No, I'm sorry to say, I didn't. That's the Base. We're not stationed on the base."

Kate frowned. "Then where are we stationed?"

"Unfortunately, the pissing contest between Colonels Drake and Gray rages on."

Drake had gotten the command of S.A.S.S. and Gray had wanted it. They were sworn enemies. But that was old news.

"Since Gray's the commander at Providence, he assigns us our office space. And he's holding a whopper of a grudge."

"Oh, great." Kate cringed. This wasn't looking so good. He'd probably stuffed them into a condemned building somewhere.

"It's not as bad as it would have been. Amanda's Mark, Captain Cross—"

"I know him."

"He's worked wonders out there."

"'Out there'?" Kate didn't like the sound of that.

Maggie sent her a sympathetic look. "You'll see."

They drove for another twenty miles. Maggie finally hooked a right onto what could generously be called a dirt road. Not a thing in sight except for tire treads in the dirt, potholes and trees and underbrush along both sides of the path.

Her stomach sank deeper. "Is there anything out here?"

Maggie grimaced and hunched a shoulder. "Us."

Soon they came to an area enclosed by a six-foot wire fence. Every eight feet, there was a sign: Use Of Deadly Force Authorized.

"What is that all about?" Kate asked. This wasn't Roswell, for pity's sake.

"It's a dormant bombing range."

"Gray stuck us out on a bombing range?" Kate shouted; she couldn't help herself.

"A dormant range," Maggie clarified. "But, yeah. More or less."

"Well, which is it, Maggie?" Kate frowned. "It's a simple question."

"It's not so simple." She turned and went through the gate, then hit a remote on her visor to close it behind her.

A mile in, a second wire fence blocked their path. This one was topped with razor wire. "What in heaven's name are they protecting?" Kate asked.

"An artillery battery." The same remote opened and closed this gate.

"Is it dormant, too?"

"No."

"Great. Just great." Kate looked out the windshield, focusing on nothing. She wished Nathan were here to listen to her bitch. He was a really great listener, and if he were here, she'd been in a far better mood.

Maggie stopped near a dilapidated shack. "Well, this is "

Kate just stared, her jaw hanging open. "You've got to be kidding me."

"It's not as bad as it looks, Kate."

Yeah, right. She wasn't blind. "The damn thing's falling apart."

"It has its fair share of leaks, all right."

Why wasn't she irritated? How could Maggie take this crap from Gray and not be bitter or angry? "Do we have water?"

"There's a well to the right, near the inner fence. It's potable."

"Well, then. We're all set." Kate grumbled. Living in

field conditions every day at work wasn't her idea of a
healthy work environment. "What about our equipment?"
The place was awfully small. It was going to be impossi-
bly tight working conditions. Darcy must be going nuts!
"How's Darcy handling this?"

"Handling what?"

Kate looked at Maggie as if she'd lost her mind. "The
tight quarters. For pity's sake, Maggie, you do know she
can't deal with a lot of sensory input, right?"

"Of course." Maggie shrugged. "Darcy loves it here.
She says it's good for her."

How had that happened? "Being crowded doesn't
bother her?"

"Mark took care of that. He took care of everything."
Maggie smiled. "You'll see." She cranked open the door
and slid out of the car.

Kate got out and followed Maggie to the shack. Above
the door someone had hand-carved a sign on a two-by-
four: Regret.

"What's the significance of this?" Regret that they'd
moved the unit from D.C. most likely. "I have to say, on
this round in the pissing contest, points definitely go to
Colonel Gray."

"Colonel Drake was totally frosted," Maggie confided.
"At least, she was at first. But she was better after she saw
the sign, and better still when Mark showed her what else
he had done."

"Who did the sign?"

"Mark." Maggie grinned. "He said if Colonel Gray
thought sticking us out here was going to get to any of us,
he'd regret it."

Typical Mark. Making lemonade. He'd done it his
whole life.

She and Nathan had, too. Damn it, she missed him. Was he going to think of him all the time for the next three weeks?

More likely, for the next fifty years. "I'm sure looking for something to make me feel better about this place. So far, it's ranking right down there between pond scum and bottom-of-the-pit scrapings."

"Keep the faith." Maggie stepped inside.

Kate followed. It wasn't any better. The outer shell of the shack. Dirt floor. Rays of light beaming across the floor through the cracks in the wall that the termites hadn't eaten through, and the holes in the roof. That was it. "Where is everyone?"

"This way." Maggie walked to the right shack wall and pressed a board more gray and aged than the others.

A split door slid open. "An elevator?"

Maggie nodded, cut her a sly look. "Come on."

"We work underground?"

"The whole unit is a vault. Surrounded by earth, Kate. Isn't that cool?"

Kate responded by rote. "Probably about 70 degrees. Once you get below six feet, the temperature is fairly constant."

Maggie rolled her eyes back in her head. "There's only one level down." A chime sounded and the door opened.

Kate stepped out and nearly dropped from shock. Private offices lined the walls. An amazingly well-equipped operations center occupied the east end, and broad doors beyond marked it as Darcy's private domain. She could open or close the doors at will, giving herself all the isolation—and company—she wanted. Broad screens covered the common walls. On them were photographs of the FBI's most wanted, Homeland Security's high alerts and S.A.S.S.'s watch list.

Kate kept looking, kept seeing new things she'd missed. "We have a full kitchen?"

Maggie giggled. "Yes, and a place to crash, and a living room—complete with a gas fireplace, if you can believe it."

"I can't." She saw Colonel Drake's office door, situated to the right of the elevator. "I *know* Colonel Gray didn't do all this. How'd we get it?"

"Mark Cross."

Mark. Engaged to Amanda, Kate's surrogate family, an awesome military lawyer, covert operative and a damn good man. He'd made a fortune creating the "Dirty Side Down" computer games that were all the rage—not that he mentioned it. Kate admired only one man as much. Nathan

Her heart lurched a little. What was he doing now? Did he miss her? Would he really be here in three weeks?

"There's a catch."

Wasn't there always? Kate looked at Maggie. "What?"

"Gray can't know any of this is here."

"Excuse me?" Hadn't he authorized the funding for it? He was the Providence commander, so this was definitely his domain.

"He'll jerk us out of here and toss us in the swamp, and call it an office, Kate. Gray has to think we're working out of a hell house." She motioned to the shack above them.

"It's empty. That's not apt to convince him we're working here, is it?"

"We've got a trailer parked behind it. Gray knows the shack is depilated. He hoped Colonel Drake would go running to General Shaw to bitch, but she wouldn't give him the satisfaction. He thinks we're all jammed in the trailer trying to work." Maggie frowned. "That seems to be sufficient misery to satisfy him."

"A real charmer, isn't he?" Gray had a bad case of little/big-man syndrome. That Colonel Drake won S.A.S.S. over him ticked him off enough that he put in his papers to retire. Unfortunately, he couldn't do it until next fall. So between now and then he was playing the "retired on active duty" jerk, getting his kicks out of making Colonel Drake miserable. The rest of the S.A.S.S. unit was just along for the ride.

"He's a lovely human being." Maggie spread her lips in a fake smile that showed every tooth in her mouth.

"So when we know he's coming, we hit the trailer, right?"

"Right." Maggie walked on into the main hall. "There's an alarm."

If Mark designed it, it was irreverent. "Will I know it when I hear it?"

"Oh, yeah." Maggie nodded to confirm her claim. "Think bodily function sounds—and be grateful this one carries no scent."

A huge fart. Kate gave Maggie a wicked grin. "Got it."

Colonel Drake stepped out of her office. "Kate, glad you're back."

"Thanks." If she hadn't left Nathan behind at the outpost, she'd be glad to be back, too. She set down her gear. So far, regret was proving interesting.

For some reason, Colonel Drake looked back into her office. "Come on out."

A man's voice carried into the hallway. "You sure she isn't armed?"

Kate thought she recognized the voice, though she couldn't tag from where. Yet it struck her as both chilling and familiar, and that made her uneasy.

Colonel Drake hiked an eyebrow, silently putting the question to Kate.

Curious, she shook her head that she wasn't armed—but she had the instinctive warning that, if she was smart, she would be. Definitely wary, she darted a glance at Maggie, who stood stone-faced.

Colonel Drake stepped aside. The man walked out of her office and stopped beside her. "Hello, Kate."

She was looking into the smiling face of Marcus Sandross.

Kate couldn't move. She looked at Maggie—still stone-faced—then at Colonel Drake, who looked back at her as if she'd lost her mind.

He'd duped them!

Wild-eyed, Kate attacked, going for his throat, his eyes.

"Whoa! Whoa!" Colonel Drake interceded, pulling Kate off him. "He's on our side!"

Her chest heaving, she stopped throwing lethal jabs and backed off, reaching for her bag to get her gun. "He is *not* on our side. He was killing people left and right inside the compound!"

Sandross's face bleached white. He clamped his mouth shut and said nothing.

Kate got her gun in hand and drew down on Sandross. "Don't move, you son of a bitch."

Colonel Drake looked from Kate to Sandross, then back to Kate. "What the hell are you talking about?"

"He's replaced Paul Reese as Thomas Kunz's second-in-command, Colonel." She hiked her chin toward him, her chest heaving. "This piece of scum had a hell of a reputation inside GRID. He killed people—for nothing. He freaking executed them, Colonel." She turned a glare on Sandross. "That's not the way our side operates."

Coming from behind her, Amanda moved to her side. "Give me the gun, Kate."

"No, damn it."

"Kate," she insisted. "Give me the gun."

Kate hesitated, but saw in Amanda's eyes that if he needed killing, she'd gladly do the honors. Knowing she was more objective at the moment, Kate passed her the gun.

Bold, now that the gun was out of her hands, Sandross stepped toward her. "You're lying."

Kate went after him again. By this time, Mark and even Darcy had come into the hallway to see what the commotion was about.

Maggie, Mark and Amanda pulled Kate off Sandross and held her to keep her from going after him again.

When things settled down to a quiet roar, Colonel Drake turned to her. "Kate, did you see these executions?"

"No, ma'am, I did not."

"See?" Sandross grunted. "She's lying through her teeth."

"Sandross," Colonel Drake turned on him. "I strongly suggest you refrain from personal comments for the duration of this conversation, or I will not move to protect you. And I further suggest that you refrain indefinitely from making slanderous remarks you cannot prove. Otherwise, I'm going to write your ass up and play slice-and-dice with your career. Are we clear on this?"

"Yes, Colonel." He pinched his lips and clamped his jaw, then slid Kate an icy glare.

"Kate?" The colonel turned to her. "If you didn't see these executions, then what's your source?"

"CIA, ma'am. Firsthand report."

"Gaston?" Sandross guffawed. "You're going to take the word of a bastard traitor over mine?"

"He is not a traitor, you lying son of a bitch." Kate went

after him again—and this time Mark, Amanda, and Maggie folded their arms and watched her unleash.

After she'd gotten in a few good licks, Mark pulled her off Sandross. "That's enough, Kate." He jerked her to his side. "That's enough."

She released a shuddered breath, pulled back and forced down the red haze that had blinded her, burying it deep inside. Through the remaining mist, she pointed a finger at Sandross, giving him fair warning. "Say another word against Gaston or call me a liar again, and I'll shoot you right here. That's a promise."

"I did *not* hear that!" Colonel Drake shouted, her temper and red-spiked hair standing on end. "Say not another word!"

Kate hadn't seen Sally Drake furious often, but she was ticked to the gills now.

"Mark," the colonel barked. "Do we have a holding cell in this facility?"

"Yes, ma'am, we do."

"Put him in it." She pointed to Sandross. "You're being held for questioning. Complain once, and I'll immediately call in the OSI and CIA. You know the consequences."

They all did. Guilty until proven innocent. Military court. Three times stiffer penalties than in a civilian court. He'd be dead before he again saw daylight.

Mark and Amanda led Sandross down the hallway, past Darcy's office, to the holding cell. Maybe Colonel Drake would let the wretch rot there.

She turned to Kate. "You got this information from Gaston, right?"

"Yes, I did." Kate chose her words carefully. "Colonel, I thought for a time, too, that Gaston was a traitor, but he wasn't. He was doing his job, and going to extraordinary lengths to protect Major Forester's unit and me. He's no traitor, ma'am. I'd stake my life on that."

"You did, Kate. And it hasn't gone unnoticed by me, Secretary Reynolds or the CIA." Disappointment creased her brow, deepened in the lines in her face. "Why would Sandross turn on us?"

"Money." Kate shrugged. "It's always money with GRID."

"The great seducer," Maggie added.

Darcy swept back her hair. "Kate is right about this, Colonel. I have substantiating evidence from Gaston, proving it." She passed a stack of photos to the colonel.

Colonel Drake reviewed them one by one. "Gruesome and brutal," she mumbled, then looked up at Kate with remnants of the horror she'd seen still in her eyes. "What kind of monster is this guy?"

"One who loves to kill."

With a heartfelt sigh, she passed the photos back to Darcy. "Get the OSI and CIA on a teleconference ASAP."

They had to figure out how to best play this overtly. S.A.S.S. couldn't bust Sandross; it didn't exist. One of the overt agencies would have to step in. Kate didn't care which one. So long as Sandross ended up busted or dead and stayed that way—which had to be a consideration when dealing with Thomas Kunz—she was fine with it.

"Don't worry, Kate," Colonel Drake assured her. "Effective now, he's permanently out of commission. Obviously he didn't know you'd be back so early. He was checking out our new Base. Bastard."

He'd be neutralized, eliminated. What other choice did the honchos have? If they cut him loose, he'd make a beeline for GRID. If Kunz took him in, he'd expose everything he knew that was classified, and that would kill a lot of good men and women. Americans and others. They had to neutralize him. And Kate didn't waste a second of her time regretting it.

"Come on." Maggie clasped Kate's arm. "Let me show you your new office."

They walked down the open expanse to the second office on the right. Her name was on the door. Kate smiled. It was the first time since she'd been in covert ops that she'd seen her name on anything tangible. She looked inside. Plush gray carpet, soft blue walls, a gorgeous waterfall painting she loved opposite her desk. "Ooh, nice." She looked on, and her gaze halted on an oak desk she'd once told Mark she'd wanted but couldn't afford. "Dang him."

"He already said for you not to bother. He's *not* sending it back."

Kate smiled. "Vintage Mark." Something atop her desk caught her eye. It looked like a photo frame. She had no photos on her desk—or anywhere else. "Whose is that?"

"Yours." Maggie smiled, her eyes twinkling mischief.

Kate rounded the desk and looked into the tender eyes of Nathan Forester. He'd signed it, and she tilted her head to read what he'd written. "My love always, Nathan." Tears sprang to her eyes.

"I told you, Mark," Amanda said, lingering at the doorway. "No man has that look in his eyes unless he's looking at a woman he loves—even if he's only seeing her image in his mind."

"What are you saying?" Mark looked at his fiancée.

"Honey, it's so simple." Amanda grinned from ear to ear. "Kate's in love."

Kate read the emotions flitting across his face. He didn't believe it. It wasn't possible that she'd let anyone get close enough to love. "It happened to you."

"It did." Worry and hope filled his voice. "So are you saying, it happened to you, too?"

Her ears burned hot. "Get out of here, guys." She reached for the door to swing it closed. "Go pester some other love-drunk idiot."

Maggie rocked side to side on her toes. "He pouched it to us and said to keep you alive and in line until he could get here."

Mark grunted. "If I'd known Sandross was crooked, I'd have told Forester to get his ass over here and handle you himself. You cracked my damn jaw back there, Kate."

"I'm sorry." She gave Mark the halfhearted apology, but her mind was on the photograph. She'd so envied the intimacy implied in Nathan's eyes toward Emily's photograph. He'd known Kate needed her own, and had given it to her. God, what a special man.

"He sent you something else, Kate." About this Maggie didn't sound so sure. "I wasn't sure what to do with it, so I put it in the top drawer of your desk."

"Okay, that's it. I love you all. I'm glad to be home. Hell of a job on the new facility, Mark. Damn thoughtful of you to get me a place and food and to come and get me," Kate ran through the list. "Now get out."

Amanda chuckled. "So diplomatic, Kate."

"Today!" she insisted, eager to see what was in the desk drawer, but not so eager to share it with them until she knew exactly what it was. Hell, it could be a Dear Joan letter, dumping Kate. Maggie hadn't said it was good. Only that it was in the drawer and she hadn't known what to do with it. And she hadn't looked too happy about it, either.

Maggie shut the door, leaving Kate alone in her office. She stared at the desk drawer. Her hands were trembling, her stomach had knots and her chest was so tight she was half afraid a full breath would crack her ribs. "Okay, Kate. Just do it. Just open the damn drawer and see if he's dumped you on your ass or if he—"

Her hand froze midair. She couldn't move. She loved him. He loved and accepted her. What if it was lust? What if he, who had been so sure he loved her, realized he didn't?

Well, would it be the end of the world? Hell, Kate. You've lived without love your entire life.

True. She could make her way alone just fine. She was a strong woman. Capable. Complete. She'd never needed a man, and she didn't need one now.

But she wanted him.

Oh, how she wanted him.

Then open the damn drawer.

She clasped the knob, squeezed her eyes shut, and pulled.

Screwing up her courage, she opened her eyes and burst into laughter.

Tucked in the drawer was a plastic bag of sand.

* * * * *

*Don't miss Darcy Clark's exciting story
in TOTAL RECALL,
in stores now as part of the
Signature Select Collection
SMOKESCREEN!
And watch for Captain Maggie Holt's
story DOUBLE DARE, coming to
Silhouette Bombshell in December 2005!*

Chapter 1

Everything was going perfectly that night until the door that was supposed to be locked crashed open and the man with the gun stepped through.

Kate Foster turned in her seat at the NASA Command Center computer terminal and stared at him, her mind still caught up in the web of data she'd started entering to communicate with the HW-1 satellite.

Vernon, at the far end of the CC, was the first to speak. "Sir, authorized personnel only in this area."

It took Kate a moment to realize that the cubical partitions blocked her assistant's view of the short-muzzled automatic weapon held hip level by the intruder.

Then Cambridge screamed, and Tommy, standing beside her, whispered, "Oh, shit." And Kate's brain snapped into gear.

Her left hand slipped beneath the desktop and found the

smooth plastic panic button even as the fingertips of her other hand hit three keys in succession on the board in front of her. The monitor screen flashed once then went black.

Her heart hammering in her chest, Kate stood and turned to face the intruder as two other people, a man and a woman also in camouflage, also armed, stepped through the door behind him. The guns…Kate could only assume they were Uzis; she'd seen them, or similar weapons, in movie after movie. They were black and ugly and far more terrifying in real life.

"What do you want?" she asked, struggling to come up with a reason for their being in her lab.

"Which one of you is Dr. Foster?" the leader growled in a thick accent. His features and coloring could have been Middle Eastern or South American. For a moment his dark eyes rested on Kate then slid around the room to her silent team members, searching their faces.

"I am Kate Foster." Somehow she kept her voice calm. "Listen, there's absolutely nothing here of value to you. No money. No drugs. If it's weapons you're after, we have access to nothing like that. This is a research laboratory."

"Shut up." The man waved the muzzle of his gun menacingly, inches from her face. "Go!" he barked at the woman who'd followed him into the room.

She stepped around and behind Kate then started hitting keys on the keyboard. "Nothing. Goddammit, Zed, the bitch locked it down!"

"We're just running tests on a satellite," Kate tried to explain.

"It's a peacetime scientific experiment," Frank Hess added, moving up to flank Kate on the opposite side from Tommy. "No onboard arms of any kind."

Hess, her senior scientist on Project Heat Wave, had

worked with her on other NASA operations. A brilliant man, but he had a temper. When she glanced sideways at him, his face was flushed with anger, as if he considered the intrusion a personal affront.

Not now, Frank, she prayed silently. *Keep your cool for once.*

But the man called Zed ignored the middle-aged, balding physicist. "Sit down, Dr. Kate," he growled, "and turn on your computer."

Before she could ask why or move, Hess stepped between her and the Uzi-toting leader. "You leave Dr. Foster alone!"

"Frank!" Kate warned.

Zed swung his gun arm wide, striking Hess a vicious blow across the side of his face, knocking him out of his way. Kate swallowed a scream. "Dr. Foster? If you will?" Zed motioned toward her chair, his mock politeness contrasting with the violence of his attack on Hess seconds earlier. He gave her a tilted smile that made her stomach clench. "Let us now talk to your satellite."

She glanced quickly toward Hess, then clicked on the power and quickly entered her password. The computer started its booting up process. She tried to think of ways to stall for time. How long had it been since she'd pushed the silent alarm? How many more minutes before security responded?

Her palms itched, felt hot and damp with sweat. A wave of nausea flowed over her, like an oil slick over calm water, blurring her thoughts. If she cleared the Power System Command-Inhibit Flags, the first part of Zed's instructions, HW-1 would be vulnerable to virtually any command from any source. The next encrypted commands would capture the Command Data Base, virtually handing Zed the satellite on a platinum platter.

The initiation screen came up, a sky-blue background with the NASA logo. Kate hesitated, her fingertips hovering over the keyboard.

"Go on, contact the satellite," Zed instructed.

Kate looked around the room at her team.

Cambridge Mackenzie stood stiffly between cubicles, her dark skin glowing with perspiration. Their eyes met for an instant. Cam shook her head slowly. *Don't do it.*

"I need to know what you intend to do with this equipment before I bring it online," Kate said, working at keeping her voice steady.

"Power this thing up now or—" The woman swung her arm up, the butt of her weapon over Kate's head.

"No!" Zed roared. "She's too important." He glared at Kate. "I do not have time to play your games. Do as I say or there will be consequences."

The man beside Zed looked at his watch. A long, jagged scar ran from the outer corner of one eye and across his cheek to his chin. He wore a wool skullcap and she couldn't tell what color hair he had, or if he had any at all. "Two minutes gone."

"She's stalling!" The woman slapped the side of her weapon against her palm, her impatience building. "Zed, Five minutes max, remember?"

So, Kate thought, they're racing Security's response. *They know about the alarm.*

But why were they here at all? It made no sense.

Zed took a piece of ordinary-looking paper from his shirt pocket and handed it to her. "Here are your instructions."

Kate unfolded the sheet and scanned the sophisticated lines of script, the language programmers used to talk to their computers whether in the next room or launched in a space probe circling the sun.

Frank was reading over her shoulder. "Oh, God," he breathed.

She looked up at Zed. "You're changing the FARM!" The Frame Acceptance Reporting Mechanism enabled scientists on the ground to communicate with and command the satellite. "You're hijacking my satellite. Why?"

"You cannot guess?" He laughed at her confusion.

"Three minutes," the man with the scar stated without emotion.

"Do it!" the woman screamed. "Now!"

Kate glanced at Frank. He was frowning, looking as confused as she was.

Zed lowered the muzzle of the Uzi to Kate's chest and poked the cold steel circle into the valley between her breasts. "Now, Doctor."

She inhaled a shaky breath, felt the chill of death hover near, but slowly shook her head. "No. I won't do it."

One tropical reality TV show

**Eight players competing
for a million dollars**

And one unexpected guest...

The Contestant
Silhouette Bombshell #52
by Stephanie Doyle

A murder has changed all the rules of this
competition. And more could die unless
Talia Mooney can beat the killer at his own game.

Available July 2005 at your favorite retail outlet.

COMING NEXT MONTH

#49 ONCE A THIEF by Michele Hauf
International cat burglar Rachel Blu had finally escaped the
diabolical man who'd taught her all she knew about thieving.
Now all she wanted was to live an honest life—but fate had
other plans. When a priceless ruby was stolen, she was
blamed. Locating the missing jewel would set things right.
Could Rachel grab the gem before the police nabbed her?

#50 HOT PURSUIT by Kathryn Jensen
NASA engineer Kate Foster never thought her job would
involve chasing terrorists—until armed intruders invaded
her laboratory and hijacked a sophisticated satellite capable
of being used as a deadly weapon. Now it was up to Kate,
international intelligence experts and counterterrorist expert
Daniel Rooker to find the satellite before the terrorists used
the weapon for their own gain....

#51 COURTING DANGER by Carol Stephenson
Legal Weapons
When lawyer Kate Rochelle was summoned to Palm Beach
to represent a family friend on trial for murder, she hadn't
expected to flee gunfire, escape explosions or unearth thirty-
year-old clues about her grandparents' mysterious deaths. But
someone wanted the past to *stay* in the past—even if they had
to kill Kate to keep it there.

#52 THE CONTESTANT by Stephanie Doyle
Talia Mooney's father was in serious danger from loan sharks,
and the only way to earn the money fast was for Talia to win
a reality-TV survival show. But when a killer was reported
missing in the area, she realized that someone in the game
wasn't who they claimed to be. And when a cameraman
turned up dead, Talia found it was up to her to protect the
group from one of their own....